The Gathering Storm
A Novel

To help you remember that you read this book, you may put your initials in a box below. Please do not write on the book pages. Thank you.

Tombigbee Regional Library Sys
338 Commerce
West Point, MS 39773

This is a work of fiction. The characters, incidents, and dialogues are products of the author's imagination and are not to be construed as real. Any resemblance to actual events or persons, living or dead, is entirely coincidental.

Scripture quotations are from the Holy Bible, New International Version®. Copyright © 1973, 1978, 1984 by International Bible Society. Used by permission of Zondervan Publishing House. All rights reserved.

The Gathering Storm—A Novel
by Barbara Warren

Copyright © 2006 by Barbara Warren

Cover design by Jessie C. Jacobs

ALL RIGHTS RESERVED.
No part of this publication may be reproduced, in any form or by any means—electronic, mechanical, photocopying, recording or otherwise—without prior written permission.

Published by *Jireh*
Suisun City, CA 94585-1911

ISBN 1-893995-27-5/978-1-893995-27-7

Library of Congress Cataloging-in-Publication Data

Warren, Barbara, 1934-
   The gathering storm : a novel / Barbara Warren.
      p. cm.
   ISBN-13: 978-1-893995-27-7 (pbk.)
   ISBN-10: 1-893995-27-5 (pbk.)
   1. Fathers and daughters--Fiction. I. Title.
   PS3623.A8644G37 2006
   813'.6--dc22
                                          2006025100

This is a work of fiction. The characters, incidents, and dialogues are products of the author's imagination and are not to be construed as real. Any resemblance to actual events or persons, living or dead, is entirely coincidental.

Scripture quotations are from the Holy Bible, New International Version®. Copyright © 1973, 1978, 1984 by International Bible Society. Used by permission of Zondervan Publishing House. All rights reserved.

The Gathering Storm—A Novel
by Barbara Warren

Copyright © 2006 by Barbara Warren

Cover design by Jessie C. Jacobs

ALL RIGHTS RESERVED.
No part of this publication may be reproduced, in any form or by any means—electronic, mechanical, photocopying, recording or otherwise—without prior written permission.

Published by *Jireh*
Suisun City, CA 94585-1911

ISBN 1-893995-27-5/978-1-893995-27-7

Library of Congress Cataloging-in-Publication Data

Warren, Barbara, 1934-
   The gathering storm : a novel / Barbara Warren.
     p. cm.
   ISBN-13: 978-1-893995-27-7 (pbk.)
   ISBN-10: 1-893995-27-5 (pbk.)
   1. Fathers and daughters--Fiction. I. Title.
   PS3623.A8644G37 2006
   813'.6--dc22
                                        2006025100

The Gathering Storm
A Novel

To help you remember that you read this book, you may put your initials in a box below. Please do not write on the book pages. Thank you.

Tombigbee Regional Library Sys
338 Commerce
West Point, MS 39773

In memory of
Goldie Mary Ennis, my mother, my number one fan,
my best friend

Acknowledgment

A hearty thank you to Nita Waxelman, Linda Sartin, Charlotte Carter, Allen Merritt, Dona Fellows, and the late Stella Johnston, members of the Mid-South Writer's Group for their excellent critiques and for their support and encouragement. Cheryl Hodde for being there for me all of these years. My life has been much richer because of you. Donna Bowman for her prayers on my behalf, and for her belief in me. Janice Holman, my editor at Jireh Publishing for taking a chance on me, and for being so great to work with. Each of you had a part in this book and I am blessed for knowing you. God bless.

1

As soon as Stephanie Walker saw the blue Cadillac parked in her driveway, her foot automatically hit the brake. No one she knew could afford anything that flashy, so her visitor had to be either a messenger from Publisher's Clearing House Sweepstakes or Marty. Since she hadn't returned her entry, it was a sure bet her charming, undependable, not quite honest father had turned up like the proverbial bad penny.

The last she'd heard, Marty and his wife, country singer Monica Harrington, were on a tour of the southwest. This would have made a visit to her home in Independence, Missouri, very much out of his way, so what was he doing here? She mentally checked her bank account. If he wanted a loan, he was out of luck.

For a moment she was tempted to drive on by, but common sense prevailed. What did it matter? After years of trying to win the approval of a father who flitted in and out of her life at widely spaced intervals, she realized she didn't care anymore. He was here, but he wouldn't stay, and that was fine with her.

She parked her aging Ford and watched as he approached, his green eyes gleaming, his mane of red hair sporting streaks of silver. Funny, she'd never thought of Marty getting older. He'd always seemed like a modern-day Peter Pan, endlessly stuck in a state of perpetual adolescence. She had inherited his height, the red hair, and the green eyes, but the charm he exuded so effortlessly when he chose had eluded her.

A flick of anger touched her heart and moved on, surprising her at this lack of emotion. Apparently since her mother's funeral, she had finally accepted the truth. Marty loved Marty. There wasn't anything left over for anyone else. Some things never change, no matter how much you want them to.

He greeted her with all of the enthusiasm of a master of ceremonies at a beauty pageant. "Stephanie! It's wonderful to see you again."

"Hello, Marty. What a surprise."

"A pleasant one, I hope."

That would depend on how much this visit would cost her, financially and emotionally. A casual onlooker seeing them together might think that this was a moment of father and daughter closeness. That casual onlooker would definitely be wrong. Marty didn't understand closeness. A natural actor, he had the knack of being whatever you wanted him to be at the moment, but the moment never lasted. Now he was the epitome of a loving father, and even though Stephanie knew he was only pretending, his performance seemed too real to be questioned.

He stopped in front of her, wearing a confident smile. "How's my favorite daughter?"

It was an effort, but pride kept her voice steady. "I'm fine, Marty. How are you?"

"Badly in need of a hug." He pulled her close, resting his cheek against her hair. The jacket he wore smelled of leather and too many smoky lounges—a scent she always associated with her father. Stephanie forced her body to relax, resisting the urge to pull away.

Never mind that it had been three years ago, the day of her mother's funeral, that she had last seen or heard from him. Today he was a <u>Father</u>. Capitalize that. Underline it. Daddy had come home. Well, Daddy's little girl had grown up, and her capacity for pretending had developed a bad case of rigor mortis.

He dropped his arms, looking wounded at her lack of response. "Aren't you glad to see me?"

"Of course I am. You should have brought Monica with you."

His grin acknowledged her hit. "She was devastated she couldn't make it."

"Yeah, I'll bet she was." Even Stephanie had to smile at the vision of the Queen of Country Music showing up on her doorstep. In the seventeen years they'd been together, Monica had successfully ignored the fact that Marty had a daughter. Just like she'd rejected his last name.

When Stephanie was in a mood to be reasonable, she admitted the name thing made sense. After all, they'd been married for only the last three years, and Monica Harrington was already well-known in the music business. On the other hand, if a woman chased a man until she got him to leave his wife and daughter for her, she might as well take his name too as part of the package.

Marty followed her into the two-story house Stephanie had inherited from her mother. The sage green slipcovers on the couch and chair blended with the darker green of the walls.

A Thomas Kinkade print that had cost her a month's salary brightened the space over the antique card table, and her mother's piano filled one corner of the living room.

He smiled in appreciation. "Nice. You have Bess's flair for decorating."

"Fair enough. I can't sing a note."

"Neither can I. I just write 'em. I don't sing 'em."

He stopped in front of the print, looking at the lighted windows in the cottage, the beds of flowers, painted in glowing colors. "You like Kinkade?"

"Yes, don't you?"

"A little sweet for my tastes. This is escapism."

"There's nothing wrong with escapism. It can beat reality some of the time." Like when you lost your mother to cancer and your father hit the trail for the bright lights and loud music, apparently forgetting he left a grieving daughter behind. She indicated the packages she clutched. "I'll put these away."

Upstairs, Stephanie tossed her bundles onto the bed and

placed the box containing Aunt Margaret's diamond necklace in her jewelry cabinet, where it should be safe. The three-foot-tall cabinet was one of the few nice gifts she'd received from Marty and had an inner drawer that could be opened only if you knew where to find the secret latch.

She hadn't wanted to borrow the necklace—she wasn't the diamond type, but Julie, her boss at the Total Woman Boutique, had planned a spring bash, and all of her employees were expected to show up to take care of any bothersome details. Aunt Margaret, always ready to prod her niece down the aisle to the tune of the wedding march, thought the necklace would add a touch of window dressing.

Aunt Margaret needed a new focus in life instead of the present one of finding a husband for her niece whether she wanted one or not. Stephanie hadn't seen anything in the bitter battlefield of her parents' marriage worth wrecking her bank balance to buy a wedding gown. So far she had successfully avoided the love trap, and she intended to keep it that way.

When she went back downstairs, Marty had poured himself a tall glass of cold grape juice. "This the strongest you have?"

"Right. That's as strong as it gets around here."

"Grape juice is fine. I just wondered about your lifestyle. We've been out of touch." He raised the glass in a mock salute.

"Are you saying it's my fault we've been out of touch? You knew where to find me."

He ignored her comment. "I thought you'd have outgrown your mother's influence by now. She's been gone for two years."

"Make that three years next month." He couldn't remember

the date of his wife's *death*? They'd been married for twenty-three years, even if he'd chosen to spend seventeen of those years with his live-in lover instead of with his wife and daughter.

She rinsed the empty glass, leaving it on the drain board, and led the way back to the living room, wondering why he was here. Not just to see her, surely. If this visit followed his normal pattern, he wanted something.

Marty trailed after her, stopping to pick up a picture of her mother from off the piano. He stared at it, smiling. "She was a lovely woman, my Bess." His voice caressed her name.

More acting? He'd been mostly an absentee father, bent on pursuing his dream of becoming a famous songwriter, until when Stephanie was seven, he'd met Monica Harrington. Once they became a team, their careers exploded. Marty hit the celebrity trail, leaving his wife and daughter behind. Call her a skeptic, but she had a hard time feeling sentimental.

He didn't seem to notice her silence. "Bess was a fine woman, but we were too different. If she'd traveled with me, it might have been better. I got lonesome on the road." He replaced the picture, glancing at Stephanie as if waiting for her reaction.

She let the moment pass, knowing she had nothing to gain by arguing with him. Marty had a silver tongue that could take either side or the middle of any subject, sometimes all three at once. The man could talk an owl out of a tree, but she'd learned the hard way to take everything he said with a hearty dose of skepticism.

He was right about one thing. Her parents had each been so different from the other that she often wondered how they had gotten together in the first place. Bess Walker had been a devout Christian, who hated the easy-living, easy-loving life Marty had chosen. She never skipped a Sunday-morning worship service if she could help it. Her faith in God had been as strong and enduring as the Ozark Mountains she loved, while, as far as Stephanie could tell, the only thing Marty really believed in was himself.

Her mother had planned everything according to God's will, and in Bess's opinion, the Almighty intended for people to get married, make a home, and stay put. Bess never missed a church service no matter how rotten she felt and how bad the weather. Stephanie was the only child in her Sunday-school class at the Mountain Oak Baptist Church with a perfect attendance record. Even the preacher's kids stayed home sick sometimes. Bess Walker's little girl never did. Stephanie still attended church occasionally out of respect for her mother's memory, but she had decided religion was mostly an illusion. If God was in control, He was certainly making a mess of things.

Marty placed his fingers on the piano keys and picked out a few chords.

She waited, knowing this scene would be played out according to *his* timetable.

He stopped playing and moved on to the bookcase, checking out the titles. "I know you blamed me for the divorce, but it wasn't my fault we broke up. I wanted to stay with Bess, but she smothered me until I couldn't write songs. I needed to follow the action."

This casual dismissal of the woman who had loved Marty so much she never got over losing him stung Stephanie into replying. "You followed the action all right. It must be nice to just walk away from your family and start a brand-new life."

He looked uncomfortable, which surprised her. She couldn't remember Marty caring what anyone else thought. He glanced away, then back again. "Let's not fight, Stephanie, but if you're going to dwell on the past, why not look at both sides?"

She clamped her lips tightly together, biting back words that were best left unsaid. What good would it do to let him see the hurt she lived with where he was concerned? She couldn't resist just one jab. "All right, Marty, but let's not forget I lived that life too, and I didn't get to make the decisions."

He prowled around the room, picking up an ornament here, looking at a picture there, until she couldn't stand it any longer.

"You didn't drop by just to visit. What do you want?"

He replaced the snow globe he'd lifted from a shelf, and his eyes locked with hers. "I want you to come to the lodge."

Her mouth dropped open. She couldn't believe he'd actually said that. "I can't go to Harrington Lodge. You've told me they don't want me there."

"*I* want you. That's all that matters. You're an outsider with a fresh point of view. You might see things I'd miss."

She pursed her lips, thinking fast. Marty was good at having an agenda that benefited him. So what was behind this request? She let her cynicism show. "You've never wanted me before. Why now?"

"I want someone to watch my back. I won't ask you to forgive me, but I really do need you, Stephanie. If you'll come, I'll see you don't regret it."

Was this more of his dramatics? His expression was serious, his eyes watchful. Stephanie closed her teeth on her lower lip, considering. It wasn't like him to beg. She suspected he was in trouble and, as usual, wanted someone to bail him out. "That sounds like you've gotten involved in something dangerous."

For a moment she thought he intended to give her an honest answer, but if so, he changed his mind. "Just come. Keep your eyes open and tell me what you see and hear. I need the opinion of someone I can trust."

"What makes you think you can trust me?"

He picked up a Dreamsickles figurine, a gift from Aunt Margaret, turning it over in his hands as if the chubby, grinning cherub could give him the answers to whatever bothered him. "I can trust you because Bess raised you. Your mother was the most honest, dependable person I ever met, and you're a lot like her. Come to the lodge, Stephanie. I need you."

There it was again. He needed her. He'd never used that line before, and she couldn't buy it now. Even if she wanted to, which she didn't, she couldn't visit Harrington Lodge without an invitation. She'd never met Monica or her son Lance and had no desire to do so, but if she ever did, it would be because they initiated the meeting, not because she had barged in where she wasn't wanted.

"Are you in some sort of trouble?"

He hesitated. "No, probably not. It's just. . .people don't change, not their character and personality anyway."

Well, wasn't this a moment of truth? "I know, Marty. I've waited a long time for you to change. Now I realize you never will. I don't know what this is all about, but surely you see I can't go to the lodge."

"You won't reconsider?"

Drop in on the Harrington family uninvited? She didn't have that kind of nerve. "I'm sorry, but no."

He shrugged. "All right, Stephanie. It was worth a try, but I won't press you. Could I use your bathroom? I have a long drive home."

So, all that talk about needing her, wanting her, was just part of the act. Otherwise why give up so easily? She pressed her lips together, blinking back tears. He wouldn't see her cry. Not this time.

The old schoolroom clock on the wall ticked the minutes away. He'd been gone too long for a casual trip to the bathroom, but before she could go looking for him, he bounced down the stairs and his hands caressed her shoulders. "I'm proud of you, Stephanie. My little girl has grown up."

"I've been grown for several years, Marty. You just haven't bothered to look."

He gripped her chin, forcing her to look at him. "I realize you don't trust me, and you have a reason to feel that way. I know I've hurt you, and I'm sorry for that, but I can't change the past. I can do something about the future, though, if you'll just give me a chance."

She didn't answer, partly because she didn't believe him and partly because she wanted so badly to believe.

He dropped a kiss on her forehead. "I'll be seeing you, a lot sooner than you planned." A wink, a gentle hug, and he left, closing the door behind him.

It took a minute for the full import of his words to hit her. She ran to open the front door. "Marty? You come back here!"

He backed out of the drive, waving and grinning, and drove away.

She dashed for the stairs, the sinking feeling in the pit of her stomach telling her what she would find. Of course he would remember the secret drawer, and being Marty, he would check to see what it held. From the bedroom door she could see the drawer standing open and the note propped against the cabinet. "Come to the lodge, Stephanie. I'll be waiting. Room 324."

Aunt Margaret's necklace was gone.

* * *

Multipronged lightning blazed above the Ozark hills, creating a glare similar to a war zone. Stephanie fought the wheel, almost driving off the road before her eyes adjusted to the darkness again. She hated driving at night, and the weather turned this trip into a nightmare. A cannon blast of thunder rolled overhead. Wind rocked the car. She leaned forward, peering at the windshield, barely able to see through the driving curtain of rain. Only an idiot would be out in weather like this. She should have called Aunt Margaret the minute she realized the necklace was missing and let her handle it.

She knew why she hadn't, though. She was still protecting Marty from the consequences for his behavior. Aunt Margaret would have had him arrested with no more compunction than she would have shown a stray bug crawling across her immaculate floor. Stephanie didn't want to see Marty in jail. She just wanted to deck him.

Rain slashed the windshield, cutting visibility to near zero. Lightning again scorched the sky and lights from an oncoming vehicle caught her full in the face. A white van straddling the yellow line and coming much too fast skidded around the curve in her direction. She swerved to the right as far as she dared, conscious of the dark line of timber banking the right-of-way. The van slid by with only inches to spare.

"Did you just buy the road?" she yelled, stress exploding in a vocal barrage.

She gripped the wheel with hands gone slick with perspiration. Driving in this downpour was a number-one nightmare, which was another thing against Marty. It was his fault she was risking her life on this dangerous highway. She knew she wasn't being completely honest about her reason for being there. No, she really didn't want Marty to be arrested, but she also burned for a confrontation that had been a long time coming.

Stephanie lifted one hand from the steering wheel and rubbed the back of her neck, admitting the anger coursing through her had nothing to do with today's events. For most of her life, she'd lived with resentment caused by her father's neglect. Now she was ready to fight back in a blazing inferno that threatened to consume her. It was dangerous to get this angry. The roaring storm rocking her car only intensified the storm raging inside her. Payback time had finally arrived. A whole flock of chickens was about to descend on Marty's home roost.

At the foot of the Roaring River Hill, the road took a sharp turn to the right, then back to the left and across a bridge. Rain-slicked cars and campers glistened in the glare of the park lights. Rainbow trout season had opened the first of March, and the Roaring River state park would be busy from now until the close of the season in the fall.

Harrington Lodge was located somewhere past the small town of Eagle Rock, Missouri, and just this side of the Arkansas line. If she missed the entrance, she would soon be lost in this swerving, swooping nightmare of wet-black highway and lightning-torched skies.

In spite of her efforts to be alert, she almost drove past the stone pillars where the driveway met the road. Partially hidden by a thicket of dogwood trees and white pines, the rambling three-story compound of Ozark limestone and oak lumber looked like a millionaire's hideaway. Cars, ranging from luxury automobiles to battered pickup trucks with gun racks in the back window, filled the well-lit parking lot. Lights glowed in cabins scattered among the trees. From years of reading about this place, she knew the Harrington family also offered rooms in the lodge proper. The food was supposed to be gourmet quality.

Stephanie had worked out her strategy, such as it was, on the five-hour drive down from Independence. Get the necklace, give Marty a hot-tongued lecture on the evils of stealing, and get out. If she could, she'd book a room at the lodge without telling her father, and tomorrow she'd slip over into Arkansas and spend some time in the Eureka Springs flea markets and antique shops before driving home. She loved Eureka, with its steep hills and

Painted Ladies—the old-fashioned, brightly painted houses—and maybe she'd have time to see the Great Passion Play and the huge, white statue of the Christ of the Ozarks.

Julie had grudgingly agreed to give her time off, insisting it be considered part of her vacation. Therefore, Stephanie intended to enjoy herself as much as possible. She put up with Julie's slacking off and loud-mouthed abusive remarks because she needed her job as assistant manager of the boutique, not because she cared for her boss.

She parked across the lodge entrance and climbed the broad wooden steps to the wide front porch lined with comfortable-looking rocking chairs. In the lobby, guests crowded around a blazing fire in the massive fieldstone fireplace. A large, gold-framed painting of a bald eagle soaring over mist-shrouded hills hung above the mantel.

Stephanie strode toward the reception area, looking straight ahead. She wanted to get this confrontation over as quickly as possible. Find him, say it, get the necklace, and get out.

The girl at the desk was a blonde by way of the bottle. Her frizzed, overpermed hair looked like an unmade bed. She gave Stephanie a long, straight look out of surprisingly shrewd eyes. "May I help you?"

"Which elevator do I take to Marty Walker's room?"

"Is he expecting you?"

"Yes he is." Of course he was. That's why he had taken the necklace, to get his own way. He was about to get more than he'd bargained for. The heat index of her temper had zoomed from simmering to a point a few degrees below that of boiling lava.

She was ready to erupt, and if he got scorched in the blast, so much the better.

The girl hesitated. "We don't normally give out information about family members."

"In that case, call and tell him Stephanie is here."

She looked uncertain, but then she shrugged. "Well, I'll let Marty sort it out. He's in the family quarters. Use that elevator over there."

"Thank you."

"Quite all right." The receptionist still had a considering expression on her face, as if trying to decide whether to call for help.

Stephanie whirled to head for the elevator and, lips tight, eyes blazing, caught a glimpse of herself in the oak-framed mirror across from the desk. She looked like trouble on the hoof.

She took a deep breath and turned around, forcing a smile. The girl at the desk didn't smile back.

2

Brad Wilson, lodge employee, forest expert, and all-around general odd-jobs man, watched as the redhead strode across the hotel lobby. Catching a glimpse of her tightened lips and blazing green eyes, he knew that someone was about to get straightened out, and he was glad it wasn't him.

He turned away to answer a guest's question and looked back just in time to see Stephanie take the elevator up to the family quarters. Bonnie, at the desk, motioned, and he walked across to see what she wanted.

"You have a problem?"

"Did you see that woman who was just here?"

Brad nodded. "The redhead?" He'd have noticed her even if she hadn't been cruising for trouble. Tall, long-legged, nice figure, and that mop of fiery curls, who wouldn't have noticed? "What about her?"

"She was mad enough to whip her weight in wildcats."

"I noticed that too."

"She's headed for Marty's suite."

"Oh yeah?" Things just got a whole lot clearer. He'd guess that particular ray of sunshine was one of Marty's groupies, and something had really put her in a snit.

Bonnie eyed him. "You gonna do something about it?"

Did he care if the invader created a scene by yelling at Marty? Not really, but then, again, Lance had been good to him when he had really needed a friend, and he liked Monica. He might as well earn his money.

He nodded. "I'll check it out."

* * *

Deep, plush carpet muffled Stephanie's footsteps. She knocked on Marty's door, but no one answered. A swift scurry of movement told her someone waited behind that closed slab of walnut. She knocked louder.

"Marty! Let me in." The knob turned in her hand, and she gave a swift, hard push and stepped inside. "Marty?"

From the other room came the soft sound of a door closing. She charged into the bedroom, banging her leg on the sharp edge of the king-sized bed. A startled yelp escaped her lips. She rounded the corner and slid to a stop, almost falling over the body lying in a pool of blood. One hand seemed to be reaching out in a mute cry for help. His once-white terrycloth robe, now stained a vivid red, bunched up around his thighs.

Stephanie couldn't have moved if a tornado had been bearing down on the room. Her throat closed on a scream that emerged sounding more like a whimper. *Marty! Oh, no. Please God, not Marty.*

She dropped to her knees, fumbling for a pulse. Blood seeped from multiple wounds on his back, hands, and arms, clinging to her fingers as she rolled him over, face up. His wrist was still warm, and for one frantic instant she hoped some frail thread of life survived, but his eyes had already started to glaze.

She had come too late. Her father was dead.

Stephanie sat back on her heels and reached out to caress his forehead. *Oh, Marty! What have they done to you?* The anger that had driven her dissipated, leaving an incredible sadness in its wake. A rush of grief clogged her throat, erupting in great sobs. Tears rolled unheeded down her face. All her childhood love for this man flooded her heart. For that moment anyway, she forgave him for the pain he had caused her.

A sound from the other room seemed to echo in the still air. She froze. Someone was in there. The murderer? Had she blocked his escape? She got to her feet, moving slowly, trying not to make any noise.

"What's going on here?" A man's voice demanded.

Stephanie whirled, the scream dying in her throat. One hand pressed against her chest as her heart shifted into overdrive. A dark-haired man a little over six feet tall, lean and wiry as a racehorse, stood before her.

He stepped around so he could see the body and sucked in his breath, the sound like a small explosion in the quiet room. His blue eyes were as hard as hailstones and just as cold when he turned to look at her.

"What happened here? I was down in the lobby when you stormed through. I thought I'd better check it out, but I never expected anything like this."

She stared at him, barely taking in what he said. "He's dead," she stammered. "Marty's dead."

"Yeah, I can see that." He strode over to the telephone, picked up the receiver, and started punching buttons. "Lance? You'd better come to Marty's suite. He's dead, and I found a woman with him." He listened for a moment while the telephone made squawking noises so loud Stephanie could hear them without being able to distinguish words. He replaced the receiver and gave her his full attention. "He'll be here in a few minutes. Until then we wait."

"No. I'm calling an ambulance." Even though she knew it was too late, it still seemed the proper thing to do.

He yanked the telephone out of her reach. "We'll make the necessary calls. Right now you just sit down and be quiet."

Stephanie wanted to fight back, but one look at his rigid features told her it would be a waste of time. Her knees gave way, too weak to hold her, and she sank down on the bed, struggling to deal with this nightmare. She fished a tissue out of her pocket, trying to blot the tears that wouldn't stop falling. Marty! The rank smell of blood filled her nostrils, and she choked back a sob. The image of his brutalized body flooded her mind. Who could have done that to him?

She looked up at the man who watched her as if he expected her to break and run. "What were you doing in my father's room?"

Brad nodded, looking disgusted. "You're not the first woman to try to claim she's related to Marty. Save it, okay?"

Claim? He said *claim?* She started to correct him when the door opened and after a moment Lance Harrington, Marty's stepson, entered the bedroom. Stephanie had seen pictures of Monica's son, but they hadn't done him justice. A big man, with the build of a football player and close-cropped hair the color of molasses taffy, he glanced at her, his brown eyes curious.

"Who are you?"

She got to her feet, still dazed. "Stephanie. . . I'm Stephanie."

"This is the family quarters. What are you doing here?"

"She stormed through the lobby, asking for Marty," Brad said. "Take a look over there."

Lance stepped around the bed to stare down at the crumpled body. "Oh, man!" He shifted his attention to Stephanie. "Who did this?"

She shook her head in denial of his unspoken question. "He was dead when I got here. I found him like that."

He just looked at her, not saying anything. She glanced down at her hands, at the rusty red smears staining her fingers. Tears seeped again at the sight of the dark stain. Marty's blood. This was her fault. If only she'd come with him he might still be alive. Surely she could have prevented this atrocity.

Lance bent over the body, taking in the sight but not touching anything. Brad stepped back out of the way, his blue eyes alert, as if searching for clues. Stephanie again sat down on the edge of the bed, suddenly conscious of her own vulnerability. She was the stranger here, a perfect scapegoat. Brad had shown up much too soon to her way of thinking, and she didn't trust either of the two men. Would they try to blame her for Marty's death?

Looking frustrated, Lance ran one hand through his hair. "How am I going to tell Mom? She'll take it hard. And we have a house full of guests downstairs. They'll hit the panic button when they hear there's been a murder. What do we do now?"

"Like I'm the expert?" Brad asked, his voice silky soft.

"That's not what I meant, and you know it. Don't get your back up and start looking for imaginary problems. We have enough real ones to deal with."

Brad took a deep breath, his chest rising and falling with the effort. "Right. I'm a little on edge. Since you asked my opinion, I'd call the police, although we're already a little behind on that."

"I suppose so, but if he had to end up dead, why did it have to happen here? This is going to be a real mess."

Well, that was one way of looking at it, Stephanie guessed. Evidently grief took a back-seat to the inconvenience of having someone turn up dead in Lance's fancy lodge. If they were shedding any tears for Marty, she'd certainly missed it. They seemed to have forgotten her, but she noticed Brad standing between her and the doorway, cutting off her escape.

The suite door opened and closed. The whisper of footsteps crossing the sitting room brought all conversation to a halt. Stephanie swerved around to check the newcomer. A small, blonde woman dressed in jeans and a white silk shirt stood in the doorway. Monica Harrington! She felt a sudden throb of dismay. What else could go wrong? This was not the way she wanted to meet the woman who had taken her father.

Monica looked puzzled. "What are you all doin' in here? Where's Marty?"

"Uh . . ." Lance sounded like someone had just punched him in the stomach.

Monica narrowed her eyes at him, a skeptical expression crossing her face. "That's exactly the way you used to look when you were a boy, hidin' something from me. What's wrong?"

Lance took her arm. "You shouldn't be here, Mom. Let me take you to your suite."

Monica pulled away, looking puzzled. "I'm not goin' anywhere until I find out why you people are in Marty's bedroom. He wouldn't like you bein' here, and you know it. Where is he?"

Stephanie started to stand up then changed her mind. Things were moving too fast for her. She had often wondered what she would do if the two of them ever met, but nothing could have prepared her for this nightmare.

Recognition dawned in Monica's eyes. "You're Stephanie. I didn't know you were here. When did you come?"

"You know her?" Lance asked.

"Well, I've never met her, but I know who she is. She's Marty's daughter." Monica spoke with a soft drawl, not deep south, just borderline southern with its occasional dropped 'g'. Stephanie recognized it as a classic Missouri Ozark way of speaking. Her grandmother used to have the same sort of accent.

"I see." Lance still sounded suspicious.

Monica's eyes held a question, and Stephanie answered it. "Someone killed Marty." Her voice broke, and she dabbed at the sudden tears. No matter how often she said the words, she couldn't believe it.

Monica's lips parted, her eyes went wide with shock. "Killed. . .?"

Brad looked uncomfortable, like he wished he could be anyplace but here. He motioned toward the body, which lay hidden from view. "I came in and found her kneeling over him."

Monica walked around to where she could see. "Marty!" The cry rang in the room like a death knell. "Oh, no. *No!*" She started for him, but Lance held her back.

"Don't, Mom. Don't mess up the evidence."

They stood, frozen in place until Monica slumped down on the bed, burying her face in her hands.

Stephanie looked away from the grieving woman, blinking back her own tears. She'd been so angry at Marty, and now the pain from losing him was like a shard of glass in her heart. He may not have been much of a father, but he was all she had. She glanced at the three people, wondering where they'd been when a vicious killer had stabbed Marty Walker to death.

Monica straightened, her hands clasped in her lap. Her teeth clamped so hard on her lower lip, a crimson drop of blood gleamed against the soft rose of her lipstick. Tears rolled down her cheeks, and Brad clumsily patted her shoulder, but she didn't seem aware of him. An occasional sob wracked her slender body.

Lance made the call to the police. When he replaced the receiver, he ignored the others, speaking directly to his mother. "I talked to Rob. He'll be here right away."

"Rob?" Stephanie asked.

"Rob Daugherty," Monica said, mechanically. "The sheriff. He's an old friend of ours."

Great. Just her luck to draw a sheriff who was buddies with

the Harrington clan. With Lance and Brad openly suspecting the out-of-town daughter, he'd probably arrest her on the spot.

Brad hovered over Monica. "Why don't you go to your suite? This is no place for you."

"No, my place is with my husband." Her voice trembled, but her expression was determined.

Lance rested his hand on her shoulder. "The police are on their way, Mom. We need to clear the room so they can work. Why don't you wait in your suite until Rob's ready to talk to you, okay? We'll let you know when he comes."

Monica clamped her lips together, looking like she wanted to refuse, before drawing a shuddering breath and getting to her feet. "All right. I'll take Stephanie with me. This is no place for her, either. You tell Rob where to find us."

Stephanie shook her head. "No! I'm staying here."

Brad loomed over her. He shook his head. "Sorry, but it's important to secure the crime scene. I'm asking you to wait in the other room."

She got to her feet, glaring at him. "So I have to leave, and you get to stay? What are you? Some kind of expert?"

"I used to be a lawyer."

"Used to be?"

He placed his hand on the small of her back, urging her forward. "You'll get a chance to tell your story when the sheriff gets here. The crime scene's been contaminated enough as it is. You wait with Monica."

He opened the door for them, and Stephanie gasped in surprise. This was Monica's suite? The murderer had come through here? Where was Marty's wife while he was being slashed to death? Maybe she shouldn't be so suspicious in the face of her stepmother's obvious grief, but someone had killed her father.

The door closed behind them, and she heard the click of the latch, shutting her out. Monica sank down on the chaise, color seeping back into her cheeks. She drew a long, shuddering breath, ignoring Stephanie for the moment, her expression heavy with grief.

Stephanie sat on the edge of a plush chair, still smarting at being ejected from the other room. This suite, a sweetly scented bower in shades of rose and lavender laced with burgundy, consisting of a sitting room, bedroom, and bath, was exactly what she expected from a pampered butterfly like Monica Harrington.

She watched Monica, trying not to get caught in the process. She'd seen her pictures, of course, smiling out from countless magazine covers, and had most of her tapes and CDs, especially the songs Marty had written for her, but the "other woman" was prettier than she had expected.

Monica Harrington's face was as softly contoured as a girl's, although Monica must have been pushing fifty. Her pale blonde hair was knotted loosely at the back of her head, with wispy tendrils framing her face. Large gold hoops swung from her earlobes, and a gold chain with dangling beads of semiprecious stones circled her neck.

Stephanie, windblown, rain damped, and wearing a bloodstained corduroy jacket, felt frowzy in comparison. Sickened at the smell of blood and the memory of Marty's body, she peeled off her jacket and dropped it on the floor, pushing it under her chair, out of sight.

Monica's voice broke through her thoughts. "Were you there when he died? What happened?"

"I don't know. I heard a door close, and when I ran through to the other room, I found him like that." She closed her eyes, reliving the moment. His hands . . . his arms. He'd died fighting to save himself.

The wail of sirens sliced the night air. The tramp of heavy feet and the murmur of voices sounded in the next room. Monica's eyelashes lay like shadows on her cheeks.

Twin tears escaped to roll downward, glimmering in the softly shaded light.

Suddenly Stephanie remembered the necklace. How could she claim a valuable piece of jewelry without explaining how it happened to be at the lodge? That necklace would make a glittering rope to hang her.

Monica opened her eyes. "I don't want to be rude, but why did you come? After all these years, why now?"

"I needed to talk to Marty." Way to go Stephanie, like telephones hadn't been invented. Probably no one would believe what she said, but she wished she'd been able to do better than that.

Monica's face went blank, wiped free of all expression. "I suppose you were curious about us."

"That's not why I came," Stephanie protested.

"We should have invited you, but somehow . . . ."

"I'll go away as soon as I talk to the sheriff."

"If you're allowed to go."

Someone knocked, and the door swung open to reveal Brad. "Rob's here."

The sheriff stood almost as tall as Brad and twice as wide. His face was a full moon, and his stomach nearly hid the ornate silver-and-turquoise low-riding belt buckle. Judging from the western shirt and jeans he wore, they'd caught him on his night off. His thick, gray hair curled crisply back from his forehead.

He spoke to Monica, "You doing all right?"

"Fine."

He transferred his attention to Stephanie. "So you're Marty's daughter?"

She nodded. Would anything she said be used against her? She'd never had any dealings with the police before, not even a traffic ticket.

He worried a toothpick between his teeth. "Hear you found him."

"Yes, I did." Stephanie caught herself listening carefully to the sound of her voice. Did she sound nervous? Too defiant? She gripped her hands together in an effort to stop their trembling.

The sheriff removed the toothpick from his mouth and eyed it as if he wondered where it had come from. "Want to tell me what happened?"

"I knocked on the door, and I could hear someone moving around inside, but no one answered. I just opened the door and walked in and found him like that."

"That right?" He tossed the toothpick into an ivory porcelain dish shaped like a scallop shell. "You didn't see anyone?"

"No, but I did hear someone leaving by the other door."

He pounced on that bit of information.

Monica spread her hands in a helpless gesture. "The door's never locked. Certainly someone could have come through here, but they took a chance on being seen."

The expression on his face as he watched her wasn't any warmer than when he had looked at Stephanie. "Unless they had a reason to be on this floor."

"Are you accusin' a member of my family of murderin' my husband?" Monica coated every word with ice. "If that is what you are thinkin', I would suggest you collect a little proof first."

The sheriff scribbled a few entries in a small notebook he carried in his shirt pocket. "I've got to consider all the possibilities. You ought to know that." He stood up and tugged at the waistband of his pants, settling his stomach more comfortably. Stephanie squirmed inside as he shifted his attention to her. "You staying here?"

She nodded with uncertainty. "I'd planned to spend the night if I could get a room."

"How come you drove all the way from Independence just for an overnight? No one seems to have known you were coming."

"Marty was at my house, and he asked me to come back with him. I said no, but after he left, I changed my mind."

Of course she could always tell the truth—that her father, whom she had seen maybe a dozen times in the past seventeen years, had taken a valuable piece of jewelry and she had chased after him from Independence in a violent rainstorm, swearing to rip him into confetti. Ten minutes after she hit the lodge she was found kneeling over his dead body. She didn't need a lawyer to tell her how interested the sheriff would be in that story."

He nodded. "I see. I'd appreciate it if you stayed." It didn't sound like a request.

Monica pulled herself off the lounge. A soft sheen of perspiration moistened her forehead. "She'll be here. You can talk to her in the morning." Her voice cracked, and she sounded about two seconds away from a screaming fit. "Isn't this enough for tonight, Rob?"

Stephanie fought a sudden urge to protest. She didn't want to stay. For years she had tried to hate this woman, certain that if it hadn't been for her, Marty would have come back to Independence. Monica didn't want her here, either. She was just making the best of a bad situation. Give her credit for that.

The sheriff nodded. "Guess I'm through with you both for right now. We'll be working most of the night, Monica, so you'll need to find someplace else to sleep. Don't take anything out of this room without clearing it with me." He left, closing the door behind him. The two women stared at each other, listening to the sounds of men's voices coming from the other room.

"He thinks I killed Marty," Stephanie blurted.

"He's also checking out my rooms." Monica sounded royally ticked. "Apparently you're not the only suspect. I suppose if you're innocent you don't have anything to worry about. It looks like we'll finally have a chance to get acquainted." Monica led the way to a suite down the hall, flicking on lights and pointing out the bathroom and the supply of toiletries stocked there. If you'll give me your keys I'll have someone bring up your luggage." Monica's voice trembled, and she kept blinking back tears.

Stephanie was relieved when Monica finally said goodnight and left.

A lodge employee brought up Stephanie's bag, eyeing her with an eager curiosity. Everyone downstairs would soon have a detailed description of Marty's daughter, but Stephanie didn't care about that now. She longed for the faith that had bolstered her mother when she was dying of cancer. Bess Walker had never once doubted that her God was there, giving the strength and peace she needed so badly. Stephanie could use some of that strength and peace right now. But God, if He was out there, didn't care about her. She was on her own.

Later when the lodge was quiet and the rain whispered against the eaves, she turned her face to the softness of her pillow and wept for Marty, for good times lost, and for all the things that had never been.

***

Brad sat in front of the fireplace in his cabin, drinking coffee and thinking about what had happened tonight. Marty was dead, and they were facing a murder investigation. He'd been in the room, probably had blood on him. Circumstantial evidence at best, but he knew only too well that circumstantial evidence could send a man to prison.

Caesar, his chocolate-colored Lab, must have sensed his uneasiness, because he thrust his head under Brad's hand. Brad rubbed the dog's silky ears, thinking it was no wonder people claimed a dog was a man's best friend. Sometimes he felt that Caesar was his only friend. He knew he could count on Lance, but the list of people he trusted was very short. Betrayal did that to you.

Why did *he* have to be the one who had followed Stephanie Walker across that lobby and up to Marty's room? What he found there brought it all back—the blood, the knife wounds . . . and that woman. Marty's daughter. Something about her intrigued him. She was a fighter, not like Marty, who was out for what he could get any way he could get it and not above trying a stint at extortion.

For a few moments tonight, he'd been glad that Marty was dead. A Christian shouldn't feel that way. Brad knew what the Bible said about forgiveness, but he'd discovered that it was easier to talk about than to actually put into practice. It would have been easier to forgive Marty for his trespasses if the guy hadn't been such a self-centered jerk. Take the way he treated Monica. Any man would be glad to have a woman like Monica Harrington for a wife. But then Marty Walker wasn't just any man.

In the eyes of the world, Marty had been successful, charming, and witty. Brad wanted to gag, just thinking of it. He forced his thoughts away from Marty. Think about Stephanie, the daughter. Another woman Marty Walker had used and abused. She had sat there in her blood-stained jacket, freckles livid against the pallor of her skin, fighting tears, and he'd been forced to steel himself against the sudden surge of compassion .

Funny, he'd never looked at another woman after Kelly died. He just couldn't work up any interest, and he wasn't trying to now. But he couldn't help feeling sorry for Marty's daughter. Rob Daugherty might be a country cop, but he knew his business. If

Stephanie had something to hide, she might be in trouble.

He picked up his Bible, turning to the thirty-second psalm, reading the familiar words: "You are my hiding place; you will protect me from trouble and surround me with songs of deliverance" (Psalm 32:7).

The Bible he held in his hands mocked him. "How long, O Lord?" He'd cried those words over and over, and they'd come back to haunt him.

How long was he going to refuse to follow God's calling? He had a personal acquaintance with that hiding place. There had been a time when he had clung to God, pleading for deliverance. Well, deliverance had come, and now it was payback time, and he had nothing left to give.

3

Stephanie woke to a strange room and feeling disoriented. It took a minute to remember why she was here. The storm had blown itself out, leaving a fresh March morning. Birds sang outside the window, and a stray sunbeam finger-walked across the bed. She felt limp, drained by the shock of Marty's death. Her eyes were swollen from crying, and her head felt stuffy, plus she had a laundry list of problems.

The necklace was gone, and she had no idea where to look for it, and Barry County's good-old-boy sheriff would probably show up today with a warrant for her arrest. If anything else could go wrong, it probably would. For lack of something better to do, she dressed and wandered downstairs for breakfast.

Marty's suite, three doors down from hers, was sealed with yellow crime tape. She turned her eyes away, thinking death had touched her too many times, first her mother and now Marty. Bess Walker had died slowly and with almost visible agony. Marty's death had been fast and vicious. Someone must have hated him real bad.

Monica waved from a table set close to the curving bay window and separated from the public dining area by a wide planter of ferns. Her smile seemed forced. "Good morning, Stephanie. I hope you slept well."

"As well as could be expected, I suppose." She wasn't sure whether she should join them or not.

Monica wore her blonde hair pulled back into a simple chignon. A navy-blue dress with a wide, white collar accentuated the pallor of her face. Her eyes were red rimmed, but she seemed calm enough. Three other people shared her table. A tall, thin man with a toothbrush mustache seated next to Monica reminded Stephanie of that movie star her mother had liked. David Niven. Silver touched his dark hair at the temples. He looked . . . aristocratic. That was the only word she could think of to describe him. Monica introduced him as her cousin, Clyde Andrews. Clyde got to his feet to pull out a chair for Stephanie.

The dark-haired woman, barely topping five two, with eyes the soft blue-green of a robin's egg and skin the texture of a magnolia petal, was Loralee Stevens. She made Stephanie awkwardly conscious of her own height and the dusting of freckles across her nose. Small women affected her that way.

The fourth member at the table, a young girl perhaps ten years old, concentrated on her breakfast. "My granddaughter, Kate," Monica said.

Kate looked up at Stephanie, her expression questioning, but she didn't say anything. The child was a miniature copy of Lance Harrington, with the same taffy-colored hair, hers worn in a ponytail, the same sherry-brown eyes. She wasn't a conventionally pretty child, but the planes of her face hinted of beauty to come. Her somber expression showed she was aware of Marty's death.

Stephanie felt a stab of resentment. This child had probably been closer to Marty than his own daughter. While she watched, Kate sniffed and wiped away a tear with the back of her hand, and Stephanie felt ashamed of herself. Whatever her personal feelings, this young girl was not to blame for Marty and Monica's behavior.

"Clyde lives on down the ridge from us." Monica volunteered the information, as if aware of Stephanie's curiosity.

"On down the ridge?" Loralee's laugh held a touch of malice. "You sound like a native."

"I am a native." Monica's blue eyes held a touch of frost. "I was born and raised about seven miles from here, and I've learned it doesn't pay to forget your roots."

Stephanie glanced from one to the other, sensing tension between the two women. Clyde Andrews casually went about his breakfast, unconcerned. He had the self-assured, almost arrogant manner of someone who feels his social position is topdrawer. He buttered a piece of toast, then glanced up. "So you're Marty's daughter. This is a surprise."

Not a good one, apparently, judging from the tone of his voice. His cool, gray eyes made Stephanie feel like checking to see if she had dirt on her face. Obviously Mr. Andrews wasn't impressed with her.

The brunette moved a plate of fresh cinnamon rolls over

within reach. "It's good to meet you, Stephanie. I'm Lance's cousin by marriage."

Clyde chewed on a small bite of ham and washed it down with coffee before speaking, his words clipped and precise. "Is this a short visit, or do you plan to stay for a while?"

Stephanie shrugged. Like her plans had anything to do with it. She was here courtesy of the sheriff. "I suppose I'll have to stay until they find out who killed my father."

"Oh?" He took another sip of coffee. "And if they never find the murderer?"

"Then I'll leave when they say I can."

To her relief, Clyde shifted his attention to Monica. "I wish you had called me last night. You should not have had to go through that alone."

"I wasn't exactly alone." Monica's voice held a flick of irritation. She bit into a lush, ripe strawberry. "I didn't know we had so many policemen."

Stephanie's treacherous subconscience, which had blocked out the full horror of what she had seen, now flooded her mind with pictures, like a gory, slow-moving television reel. She saw again the slick pool of blood and the deep cuts on Marty's hands and forearms where he had tried to protect himself. Would she ever forget? Did she want to? No, not as long as Marty's killer walked free.

She forced her thoughts back to the present. "I noticed Marty's room is sealed."

Monica lifted her coffee cup and then set it down untouched. "Rob and his crew were here all night. They're supposed to be finished with it sometime this morning." She shuddered. "They made me go in to see if anything was missing. There's so much blood."

"Rob should be ashamed of himself for forcing you to do that," Clyde protested. "I can't believe he could be so callous."

"We'll go through more than that before we're finished," Monica said with a touch of impatience, as if rejecting his concern. "It's a long way from being over. He wants to talk to us again this mornin'."

"Talk to who?" Loralee said sharply. "What about?"

Stephanie eyed her curiously. She hadn't said one word after introducing herself. Was she always this quiet? She seemed agitated enough now. And what was her position at the lodge? Cousin by marriage? Where was Lance's wife?

Monica shrugged. "I have no idea what or who Rob will want, but here he comes. You can ask him."

Kate slid from her chair and kissed her grandmother's cheek. "Bye, Nana. I have to go to school now."

Monica returned the caress. "Goodbye, darlin'. Have a good day."

The child left, and Stephanie watched as Rob threaded his way through the other diners to their table. Her stomach fluttered in a very disconcerting manner. Nerves. Even though she was innocent, she dreaded talking to him again. What if he took something she said the wrong way?

The sheriff pulled out a chair and sat down, looking tired. He shoved Kate's dishes to one side. "I'm taking over the library to interview people. If that's all right with you," he added as an apparent afterthought.

Monica twisted the corner off a flaky croissant. "And if it isn't?"

"Then I guess I can haul the whole bunch of you down to the jail and talk to you there."

Clyde frowned. "I believe you're taking too much on yourself. When we put you in office it wasn't so you could turn on self-respecting, law-abiding citizens. Your job is to find the criminal who did this."

"That's what I'm fixing to do." Rob accepted a cup of coffee from a young waitress and waved away the menu. "Bring me a slice of ham, biscuits and gravy, and two eggs over easy."

"That's on the house, Nancy," Monica said.

Rob held up his hand. "No, it's not. I'm on duty investigating a crime. This isn't a social visit."

Monica raised her eyebrows. "You think I'd try to bribe you with a plate of ham and eggs?"

Rob grinned for the first time. "No, I guess not, but I'm still paying for what I eat."

Stephanie pushed her plate back and started to get up, but the sheriff pointed a finger at her. "You stay put. I want to talk to you."

She sank back down, a fire starting to build in her stomach. "Just me?"

"No. I'll get to the rest later, but you're first." The waitress slid a full plate in front of him and topped off his coffee.

Stephanie folded her arms and leaned back in her chair. Was he saying she was the number-one suspect because she was the stranger here? She glowered at him from beneath lowered brows.

He glanced at her over a fork full of eggs. "What? You didn't expect to be questioned?"

"I didn't expect to be a scapegoat."

"If you're not guilty, then you shouldn't mind talking to me."

"I told you everything last night," she said stubbornly. "What else can you hope to learn?"

"Well now, I won't know that until I hear what you have to say, will I?" A half grin quirked one corner of his mouth. "Relax. We're just going to talk."

She refused to relent. "Talking to you can be harmful to my peace of mind."

Clyde dabbed at his mouth with a napkin. "If that's what you have on your schedule, I'll be leaving then, since Rob obviously intends to carry out this charade. Unless of course you need me to stay, Monica."

"Charade? That your name for a police investigation?" Rob asked. "You're in and out of this place like you own it. Who's to say you weren't here last night?"

Clyde flushed, brick red. "You can't possibly accuse *me* of killing someone like *Marty*! The Andrews name means something in this area, and I have no intention of submitting to a police inquiry like a common criminal."

Rob chewed on a bite of ham. "I have a few intentions myself. I intend to solve this case whatever it takes and no matter whose toes I step on. Call your lawyer if you think you need one, but understand this." His words became slower, evenly spaced. "You leave here before I say you can and I'll have you brought in, and you won't like the way I do it."

Clyde's lips thinned until they were barely visible behind his mustache. "You go too far, this will be your last term. I'll personally see to that."

"Maybe so," Rob said. "I don't know if you can do that or not, and I guess if you could, the job wouldn't be worth having anyway. But as long as I'm sheriff, I'm playing by the rules, and the fact that I've known you people all my life doesn't change a thing. This is a murder investigation."

"If we didn't know it before, I guess we do now," Monica said. "More coffee?"

"Yeah, I'll take a refill." Rob gulped his breakfast as if in a hurry to get to the questioning.

Monica motioned to Nancy, the waitress, who hurried to their table with the coffee pot. Clyde refused a refill, but Stephanie noticed he didn't make any effort to leave. She was surprised at the state of animosity between the two men.

Rob ignored the disgruntled looks coming his way and transferred his attention to Loralee. "I'll want to talk to you next."

Loralee widened her eyes, her expression going spun-sugar sweet, as if she couldn't possibly believe he could be serious. "What could I tell you? I didn't even know he'd been murdered until I woke up this morning."

He cocked an eyebrow, looking skeptical. "You didn't hear the police come last night?"

Stephanie eyed Loralee, thinking sourly that "little old me" routine was definitely overdone. Where had Little Miss Precious been last night? The police had been fairly quiet, but as Monica said, there'd been a lot of them, and they'd made noise, enough to wake anyone sleeping on that floor.

"I had taken a sleeping pill." Loralee placed one hand on the sheriff's arm and smiled. "Rob, you *know* me. You can't possibly think I'd kill anyone."

Her voice was honeyed soft, and Monica shot her an inquiring glance, looking startled. Loralee caught her eye and flushed.

Rob pushed back his chair and stood up. "I'd hate to think you did, but you can't always tell who'll kill and who won't. You ready, Stephanie? Let's get started."

Stephanie followed him to the elevator, dread swirling in the pit of her stomach. Did she need a lawyer? Nothing in her sheltered life had prepared her to be questioned by the police. Her mother would be spinning in her grave, and she didn't want to think of what Aunt Margaret would say. Surrounded by people who had no reason to like her and every reason to want Marty's murder pinned on her, she had never felt so lost and alone.

Rob held open the door to the library, and she entered a pleasant room with wide double windows. Sunlight streamed through, brushing the shelves of books with gold. A crystal vase on a narrow table held red tulips. He motioned her to a chair, settling himself behind the desk.

Another policeman sat at a small table, ready to take notes, and Stephanie eyed him nervously. Rob picked up a pen and rolled it between his fingers. "We're going to be running a tape recorder. That all right with you?"

She nodded, afraid to say anything.

He waited, and she muttered, "Yes."

"Okay, let's go over your story again. What time did you leave Independence yesterday?

"About four-thirty, I suppose. I didn't look at the clock."

"And you arrived here when?"

"Eight-thirty or so. I'm sorry I can't be more accurate than that." If she'd known she was going to be questioned by the police she would have had a detailed report ready.

Rob squinted down at the pen in his fingers as if trying to read the lettering. "Bonnie McIntire said the minute she saw you she knew you were going to kill someone."

Stephanie's mouth dropped open. "*Who* is Bonnie McIntire?"

Rob grinned. "Girl at the desk. Excitable sort. Her whole family's like that. After the dust clears, you'll find they knew all along what was going to happen."

"Do you believe her?"

"Thought I'd wait and see what you had to say."

"I was tired and stressed after driving in a rainstorm, but that doesn't give her a reason to make an accusation like that."

The girl at the desk? The one who had eyed her as if she expected Stephanie to whip out a Saturday night special or something? Probably several people were ready to testify about the way she had rampaged through the lobby, looking ready to explode. Stephanie sighed. It was beginning to look like she'd have to dip into her savings to hire a lawyer. How much did they charge an hour? Probably Brad, the ex-lawyer would know. How does a person get to be an ex-lawyer anyway?

The sheriff took her back over her whole story, asking about her relationship with the Harringtons, with Marty. Finally he said, "We need to take some samples. You can do it now, or we can do it at the jail. Which will it be?"

"What kind of samples?"

"Fingernail scrapings, hair samples, blood sample, fingerprints."

She shook her head in disbelief. "I do not believe this. You really do think I killed him, don't you?"

"I don't know what I think yet."

"Are you taking samples from everyone? Or just me?"

"Everyone I consider a suspect." He motioned to the other officer. "Tommy here will take over now. Just be patient. It won't take long."

Tommy carefully took the necessary samples, placing each in a plastic bag and labeling it before going on to the next. Finally he took her fingerprints, rolling each finger carefully over a fingerprint card. Right hand first, then left. At the bottom of the card he had her place the four fingers of her right hand flat, not rolled this time, then the left. In the center were the two spaces for her thumbs

Stephanie looked at the strange smudges, which were supposed to convey information. They all looked alike to her. "I know all fingerprints are supposed to be different, but how can you tell my prints from the others?" She couldn't tell the prints of one hand from the other.

Tommy had a nice smile. "You'll notice these lines aren't all curved or straight. They stop and start, form islands. There are ridge endings, dots, short ridges, lots of things that have to match. Don't worry, we won't get yours mixed up with someone else's."

"There can't be that many variations can there?" She wanted to be sure about this.

"You'd be surprised. I had my doubts too at first, but I can swear no one will mistake yours for anyone else's. You don't have to worry about that."

Stephanie stared at the lines and whorls each uniquely hers. Maybe not, but she had plenty of other things to worry about. Her fingerprints would be in the room. Not only had she handled things, she'd gotten Marty's blood on her hands and clothes. Brad had found her with the body. Would the sheriff look past this circumstantial evidence? Or would he protect those long-time friends and pin the murder on the out-of-town daughter?

She could feel the noose tightening around her neck.

4

An hour later when Stephanie left her room she met Loralee in the hall and made a motion for her to stop. "Could I ask you a couple of questions?"

Loralee paused, her expression wary. "What about?"

"About Marty. Is there someplace we can be private? The sheriff's using the library."

After just enough hesitation to be noticeable, Loralee led the way down the hall. Since they had walked past the family rooms, Stephanie wasn't prepared when Loralee threw open the door of a large suite. Done in ivory and gold with accents of coolest jade, the opulence was startling.

Glittering crystal lamps with gold satin shades matched the bedspread and the velvet lounge and vanity bench. Pale-gold brocade shimmered on the walls, and pleated ivory silk covered the ceiling. Overhead, a crystal-and-gold chandelier caught dancing rainbows from the sunlight. A subtle fragrance of gardenia permeated the air.

Loralee looked around the room and took a deep breath.

"This is Tara's suite."

"Tara?" Stephanie asked. "Who's Tara?"

"Lance's wife."

"Oh. I haven't met her yet."

"She isn't here." Loralee picked up a photograph in a silver frame from the cherrywood vanity and stared at it. "She disappeared three years ago." The words were flat and unemotional, but they seemed to hang in the air.

Chilly fingers crept up Stephanie's spine. "Disappeared? What do you mean?"

"Lance believes she ran away with another man, but I don't think she did. She wouldn't have gone without telling me. At the very least, she would have written to me. We're first cousins and very close." She handed the photograph to Stephanie.

The smiling face of Lance Harrington's wife stared from the ornate frame. Her luxurious black hair and blue eyes were like Loralee's. In fact, the two women looked enough alike to be sisters instead of cousins. They had the same raven hair, the same petal-soft complexion and delicate features, but Loralee wore only a slight dusting of face powder and just the merest skim of lipstick. Her hair was skinned back from her face, while Tara's curled and waved in what looked like careless abandon and was probably planned right down to the last ringlet.

Tara's face was thinner than Loralee's, and her makeup had a polished perfection that came only from hours of practice. Stephanie could tell by looking that Tara wouldn't have been caught in her cousin's denim dress and clunky shoes. The pendant Tara wore, a dark red oval surrounded by intertwined strands of gold set with diamonds, confirmed Stephanie's first impression: this was a high-fashion junkie.

The difference went deeper than just a similar appearance and a cosmetic job. Tara had a wild, untamed air and a way of preening as if she were in love with the camera. Her smile was too knowing, too seductive. Stephanie handed the picture back, thinking if this luxurious suite was any indication of her personality, Tara seemed an odd choice as a wife for rugged Lance Harrington.

Loralee set the photograph back on the dresser. Her hands moved restlessly among the array of toiletries; her eyes in the mirror were watchful. "Why did you kill Marty?"

Stephanie froze. "I *didn't* kill him. Why would you say that?"

"It's what everyone thinks. He's lived among us for years. You show up, and just like that, he's dead."

Stephanie shook her head in denial. "That won't wash. I hadn't seen him for three years. It seems more likely someone who lived here would come nearer having a motive."

Loralee flipped a switch, turning the chandelier into a blaze of light. She sank down on the gold-and-ivory chaise lounge, waving Stephanie to a footstool with an imperious gesture.

"That lets me out, then. I've been back here only about six months."

"You've been gone? I thought you'd always lived here." This was disappointing. She'd hoped Loralee would know about the inner conflicts of the people living at the lodge. Maybe shed light on some event that might have led to Marty's death.

"I left after Tara disappeared. I couldn't stay here. Everywhere I looked there were reminders of her."

"Why did you return then?"

Loralee let her shoulders lift and fall. "Monica tracked me down and begged me to move back. I'm supposed to help her talk Lance into building a theater in Branson and take over the PR responsibilities, although so far I've mostly filled in working for Lance in the office since his secretary quit."

"So you're going to live here again?" Stephanie thought about what it would be like to live in the lodge and discovered she would hate it. She liked more privacy and something less ostentatious. She was used to the simple life.

Loralee sucked in her lower lip, looking thoughtful. "I'll have to stay for a while. I came back only because Monica didn't give me a choice." There was a hint of resentment in her voice. "Now I'm mixed up in a murder investigation."

"We all are."

"Yes, but I'm innocent."

"We're all innocent . . . except one," Stephanie said.

"One's enough."

"So you don't have any idea who killed him?" Might as well ask. She had to start somewhere.

Loralee smirked. "Maybe Monica got tired of putting up with his cheating."

Stephanie tried that out in her mind. "She's put up with him for years. Why go berserk now?"

"I was just joking, but she did get wild when he took up with Tara."

Stephanie felt sick at the implication of her words. Would

Marty have had an affair with his stepson's wife? She stared at Loralee, willing her to be wrong. However, she knew that with her father anything was possible.

"Did Lance know?"

"Of course he knew. She never made any secret of her affairs. Why should she? People like Tara aren't bound by the rules the rest of us live by."

Loralee pulled the ribbon from her hair, letting it fall in a black satin cloud around her shoulders. Her eyes sparkled with malice. "Lance even fought with Marty over Tara, but he couldn't stop them. No one could."

"What about Monica?"

"Oh, Monica." Loralee shrugged, as if what Marty's wife wanted wasn't important. "Monica would forgive him anything as long as he kept writing songs for her."

Was this the way the couple the music industry billed as America's Country Sweethearts had ended? Nothing left but the music they shared? Had the woman who broke up her parents' marriage not been able to hold him either?

The bustle of the lodge didn't reach them here. The silence should have been peaceful, but instead Stephanie had a strange notion that the room waited for something to happen or some familiar form to materialize. The hair on her arms furred. Something about this situation made her definitely uncomfortable.

Loralee changed the subject. "Since I've come back, I take care of this suite myself. I won't let anyone else touch Tara's things. Sometimes I sleep here, pretending I'm Tara. I even dress in her clothes. Lance doesn't like it, but he can't stop me. He knows how I feel about these rooms."

Stephanie got to her feet, needing to get out of here, get away from the stifling luxury so in contrast to the rugged comfort of the lodge. She didn't need this. "I want to talk to Monica. Are you ready to leave?"

Loralee shook her head. "You go on, I'll stay here for a while."

Stephanie closed the door behind her, breathing deeply of the unscented air of the hallway. So Tara had been gone for three years? Did her disappearance have anything to do with Marty's death? She needed to learn more about Lance Harrington's wife.

She found Monica in the library, going through a stack of papers. Evidently Rob had left, but no doubt he would be back. Stephanie liked this room. The well-filled bookshelves lining the walls beckoned, but she turned her back on them. Later she could yield to her passion for reading. Now she had other things to do. Like finding out who might have hated Marty enough to slash him to death.

Monica looked up from her work. "Stephanie, I should have asked you before. Would you like to go to Eureka with us to make funeral arrangements?"

Stephanie flinched. Pick out a casket for Marty? She'd done that for her mother. She couldn't do it again.

"No, that's all right," she muttered. "I'd really rather stay here."

Monica didn't push it. "I don't blame you. I'd skip it myself if I could. There'll probably be reporters at the funeral home. Marty was one of the best songwriters in the business."

"I know. That's something good to remember, isn't it?" She

desperately needed something to hold on to.

"Yes, it is." Monica stacked the papers she had been working on in a neat pile. "You know, Stephanie, outsiders couldn't understand Marty the way we do. He needed his freedom, but in his own way, he loved us."

Stephanie wanted to set the record straight. "I'm sorry you have to put up with me under these circumstances. The sheriff won't let me leave just yet, but perhaps it would be easier for you if I took a cabin."

"Nonsense. You should have come for a visit years ago."

"I understood that I wasn't welcome."

Monica's eyes widened, a flush stained her cheeks. "Of course you were welcome. Marty said you wouldn't come cause you resented my takin' your mother's place."

"Marty said that? Was there some reason he didn't want us to meet?"

"Probably." Monica picked up a cobalt blue paperweight splashed with white snowflakes, stared at it absently, then put it down a few inches from its original place. "I guess he didn't want to share us."

Stephanie nodded. That made sense in a strange way. Marty had regarded people as possessions. "Why didn't you come to my mother's funeral?" She hadn't planned to ask the question—it just slipped out.

Monica flinched as if she had been hit. "Since your mother's family never accepted me, I thought it might be best if I stayed home. I'm not makin' excuses, Stephanie. I always knew I didn't have a right to Marty, but I tried to convince myself love was reason enough to destroy a marriage. I've paid for my sins. More than you know."

Paid? What did Monica Harrington know about paying? What about the wife and daughter she had hurt with her behavior? Stephanie searched for something to say, but the words wouldn't come. Finally she turned and walked away, closing the door behind her.

* * *

As soon as Clyde and Monica left, Stephanie hurried down the hall to Marty's suite, intending to search for the necklace. The yellow police tape had been removed, and the staff would soon be ready to start cleaning. She made sure no one was watching before she pushed open the door.

Every nerve she had screamed at her to get out of here, but she knew this would probably be her only chance to do a thorough search.

Marty's sitting room was more masculine than Monica's ultrafeminine retreat. The drapes, a geometric design of beige, burgundy, and forest green, repeated the colors of the big, square cushions on the couch. A luxurious room, but nothing here seemed to relate to her father; no piano, no sheet music lying around, and only a couple of the original wildlife prints he collected.

One item surprised her—a Bible, looking fairly new, lay on the glass-topped coffee table. She flipped open the cover to read the inscription: "To Marty from Monica. May He lead you in the paths of righteousness."

That was certainly wishful thinking. She could remember only too clearly her father's biting comments about her mother's Bible reading. Not wanting to go too far down that road, she turned her attention to the rest of the room.

Marks on the carpet showed where the furniture had been moved. Sheriff Daugherty and his men had been thorough in their search for clues. What could she hope to find? She entered the bedroom, which repeated the same color scheme, noticing things that hadn't registered last night. A signed print of a white-tailed deer hung above the bed. She recognized it as one Marty had bought at a Kansas City gallery. He spent a lot of money on those prints. More than he had ever spent on his wife and daughter.

Red-brown smudges marred the wall. A large piece had been cut out of the carpet, and the bedspread was missing. Smudges of black fingerprinting powder were scattered everywhere. Stephanie swallowed hard, fighting nausea. She checked the drawers in the huge walnut dresser, but of course the sheriff's men had gone through them first. She'd heard the women who cleaned the lodge talking. The police had vacuumed the carpet, sweeping up hair, fibers, even dirt tracked in by people who had been in the room. She wondered what they would find.

Stephanie riffled through the clothing in Marty's closet. An old jacket hung at the back behind everything else. She pulled it from the hanger and buried her face in the worn softness. A slim envelope, closed with a paper clip, slid out of an inside pocket, fluttering to the floor. She picked it up, slightly curious. The contents couldn't be too important or the police wouldn't have left it.

She pulled the jacket around her, sliding her arms through the sleeves, trying to find comfort for her loss. Anger surged through her like an electrical current, surprising her with its intensity. Marty would never have become the father she wanted. It was too late in their relationship for that, but his murder had slammed the door on whatever they could have established. He had fought a losing battle for his life. She would take up the fight, never stopping until the person who had killed him was brought to justice.

She caught a glimpse of herself in the full-length mirror. The welting on the jacket's left facing didn't hang right. Her probing fingers detected stiffness in one area. A closer inspection revealed a tiny slit in the leather. She worked at it carefully until a small key slid out into her hand. Surely it had some special significance for Marty. Otherwise why hide it? If she gave the key to the sheriff and he started openly asking questions, whatever it fit might disappear. Or she could quietly search the lodge on her own. She slid the key into her pocket, determined to learn the story behind it.

The memory of what had happened in this room hit her like a runaway truck. She could almost see Marty's body, smell the blood. Bit by bit she drew out every recollection, examining them to see if she had forgotten anything important. *Her jacket*! It wasn't in her room. Where had she left it? She stood completely still, thinking back to when she had removed it in Monica's suite.

Finally accepting that the necklace wasn't in Marty's suite, she gave up the search. There wasn't anything there that the key fit, either. It looked like she could mark Marty's room off her list.

She had so little of her father, surely no one would care if she took the jacket. She slung it over her arm and left the room, taking the envelope with her.

On the way back to her suite, she dropped by Monica's sitting room to collect the corduroy jacket she had been wearing when Marty died. She found it, stiff with dried blood, under the chair where she had been sitting. Since the suite was empty, she did a quick check through the rooms, looking for anything the key might fit, but nothing caught her attention.

Upon reaching her suite, she hung both jackets in her closet. The key she slipped on a silver chain to hang around her neck, where it would be concealed by her sweater until she found the lock it fit. Until then it would be her secret. She paused in the act of fastening the clasp. The key had been Marty's secret. Did it have anything to do with his death?

* * *

Brad held the screen door open to allow Caesar to come out for their daily walk. When they reached the rocky lakeshore, he was surprised to see Mac Davison, a waiter at the lodge and one of Marty's barhopping buddies, holding a fishing rod and looking bored. A frequenter of smoke-filled rooms and dim lights, Mac seemed out of place in an outdoor setting.

"Morning. Catching anything?"

"Didn't plan to. Fishin's not my bag."

"Then why go through the motions?"

Mac shrugged. "Rob's at the lodge again. Thought I'd stay out of the way."

So he was just pretending to fish? Probably wanted to stay close but look busy for Rob's benefit. Brad sat down on a rock and watched as Caesar ran along the shore, checking out interesting smells. "What does Rob think about our recent crime?"

Mac made an awkward cast. "Don't know and didn't ask. For my money, I'm bettin' on the daughter, which would sure be a waste. That's one outstanding babe."

Brad was aware of a ripple of irritation. Stephanie *was* pretty, and there *was* a possibility she had killed her father, but he hoped not. He pushed the thought aside, uncomfortable with it. For some reason that he didn't want to examine, he resented Mac's talking about Stephanie Walker in such a familiar way.

"I thought you had your sights set on Loralee."

Mac reeled in his line and dropped the rod on the ground. "I'm not interested in Clyde's leftovers."

Brad stared at him, caught unaware. "You're kidding. Clyde and Loralee?"

Mac looked like he wished he hadn't said anything.

"Come on, give."

"Oh, well, not on his part. You know Clyde. Loralee wouldn't be fancy enough for him. She wanted him for a while, but then she left and nothing ever came of it."

"That's funny. I never suspected."

"I don't guess anyone did but me." Mac rested his elbows on his knees, leaning forward. "She had a big fight with Tara over him. I heard part of it."

"When was that?"

"The day Tara walked out. First time I ever saw Loralee

stand up for herself, but she sure cut loose that day."

"I'm surprised Marty didn't make a play for her. Or maybe he did and I didn't know about it," Brad said.

Mac picked up a pebble and tossed it into the water. "Who do *you* think stiffed Marty?"

"I have no idea. I suppose half the county had a reason. The guy scammed everyone he could."

"Yeah. But give him credit. He didn't play tricks with his music."

"Sorry, I'm not a fan of his. I never could figure out why anyone with a wife like Monica would fool around."

Mac picked up his fishing rod and got to his feet. "I hear you didn't have any love for Marty."

He walked away, and Brad watched him go. So the talking had started. How long until Rob began getting ideas.

5

Brad watched as Stephanie worked her way toward the family table in the lodge dining room, where he and Loralee were having breakfast. Stephanie pulled out a chair and sat down, glancing at him as if not sure how to react to his presence. As a matter of fact, he wasn't sure how to react, either. Something about her made him nervous. Like she was a threat to the peaceful existence he had created for himself.

A certain tightness in her expression hinted that she might not have forgiven him for his attitude in Marty's room. He'd been shook, to put it mildly, prone to blurt out what had seemed reasonable at the time. Now that he'd thought it over, he wasn't so sure.

Rob and his men had gone over that suite inch by inch and hadn't found a murder weapon. Brad had gotten there shortly after Stephanie had romped through the lobby, and he'd been the one to practically push her out of the room. He was willing to swear she didn't have a knife on her.

He smiled at her. "Morning. Nice day."

She allowed him a cool nod. "I guess so."

"About the other night, . . .," he began, but the look in her eyes stopped him.

"Yes?"

He started over. "Look. I'm sorry I got carried away, okay?"

"You mean when you practically accused me of murder?"

Yep. Definitely hadn't forgiven him. "I guess I jumped the gun a bit."

"So you've decided I'm innocent?"

He thought about that. "No. I'm not sure I'd go that far."

"Then exactly what are you saying?"

"I'm saying I don't know who killed him. But I've had time to think about it, and I'm having trouble figuring how you could have done it."

She raised her eyebrows, one hand beating a faint tattoo on the tabletop. "That's big of you. What are you basing your decision on?"

"You didn't have time, for one thing. And not enough blood on you. Rob said you couldn't cut up a man like that and not be covered with it."

Loralee made a choking sound of protest. "I'm eating."

"Sorry. And I'm sure you didn't have a knife on you."

Stephanie nodded. "I've been doing some thinking too, and it has occurred to me you might know more about the murder than you're letting on."

Brad thumped his coffee cup on the table. Here he was, trying to be nice, and look what it got him. "Like what?"

"You got there right behind me. Maybe you killed him,

slipped out of the apartment, and then hurried back around and sneaked up behind me, pretending to have just arrived."

"That's crazy." It could have worked, though. Even he could see that. Bonnie in the lobby would vouch for him, but it was a short jump to thinking he could have taken care of Marty before he went downstairs. He glowered at Stephanie. He'd known the minute he saw this woman she was trouble.

Stephanie accepted a menu from Mac and opened it, looking as calm as if she hadn't just accused Brad of murder. "I think the sheriff would find it a fascinating theory, don't you?"

Judging from the wary glances Mac kept shooting in his direction, *Brad* certainly found it fascinating enough. He waited until she'd given her order and Mac had left.

"Okay. Maybe I had that coming. Instead of wasting a lot of time suspecting each other, why don't we join forces and find out who really killed Marty."

Loralee snorted. "Are you talking about becoming detectives?"

"Why not?" Brad asked. "Wilson and Walker. Sounds very professional."

Stephanie hesitated. "You mean we start with the assumption we're both innocent?"

"Well. . . ." He caught the look in her eye. "Okay. Put it this way. We don't suspect each other unless we have strong evidence to the contrary."

Mac brought Stephanie's plate of muffins and fresh fruit, and Stephanie picked up a strawberry and bit into it before nodding. "All right, I guess."

"So, are we friends?" he asked, relieved to be on a better footing with her.

She shook her head. "No."

"No?"

"I don't make friends that easily. Friendly maybe?"

He sighed. "That'll work for now."

Stephanie changed the subject. "I've been trying to picture Marty at the lodge. He never liked the country."

"He didn't like the lodge either." Brad ate a bite of sausage. "Marty liked dim lights and hot music."

"Yet he spent time here. Or I suppose he did."

He caught the wistful note in her voice. If he knew Marty, and unfortunately he did, the guy probably hadn't put in a lot of effort at being a father.

Loralee poured syrup over her waffles. Maple fragrance drifted across the table, mingling with the sharp, lush scent of the cantaloupe on Stephanie's plate. "Actually, he spent very little time at the lodge when I lived here," she said. "Mostly they traveled, living in their bus. A lot of people didn't understand Marty. Brad included."

"I understood plenty about him." Brad finished his coffee and glanced at his watch. "I hate to hurry off, but I'm late for work. We'll talk more about this detecting business, Stephanie. Maybe we can come up with something."

He pulled his denim jacket from the chair and left. The morning was fresh and cool, the rows of seedlings bright with new growth, but it was hard to check for diseases in young pines when in spite of himself his thoughts kept straying back to

Marty's red-haired daughter.

* * *

Stephanie munched absently on a sliver of melon, waiting for Loralee to say something. The silence stretched out, and she buttered half of a bran muffin studded with chunks of dried cherries. The combination of muffin, butter, and tart cherries made her taste buds tingle. Store-bought Danish would never taste the same after this.

"Loralee, you said Marty and Tara were very good friends."

Loralee's lips twitched in a knowing smile. "I guess that's one way to put it."

"Were you good friends with Marty too?"

The smile disappeared. "Not the way you mean."

"Marty liked women."

"You never met Tara. Not many women could compete with her. She was like a flame, warming everyone around her."

"I see. What do you think happened to her?"

Loralee's mouth tightened. "I think she's dead. Otherwise she would have stayed in touch with me."

"But you left. How would she have known where to find you?"

Loralee pushed her chair back and stood up to leave. "Don't take Brad's joke about being detectives too seriously. Rob's conducting a criminal investigation. You'd do well to stay out of it."

"My father has been murdered. You can't expect me to forget what happened."

"Nothing can bring Marty back now, but you can hurt innocent bystanders."

"If they're helping to hide a murderer, then they're not all that innocent."

"A lot of the people here at the lodge suspect you might have had something to do with it." Loralee turned on her heel and strode out of the dining room.

Stephanie pushed her plate aside, not hungry anymore. Her clumsy attempt at asking questions hadn't helped much. Evidently there was more to being a detective than she had thought. She shoved her chair back and got up, feeling a sudden need for fresh air.

A narrow, winding path curved away from the manicured lawn. Stephanie set a brisk pace trying to find the way down to the bit of lake she could see gleaming in the sun. A bulky figure cut across her path—Sheriff Rob Daugherty, complete with uniform and badge and a pearl-gray Stetson hat. If she had seen him sooner, she would have avoided him.

He waited for her. "Taking a walk?"

"Is there a law against it?" She did not want to talk to this man again.

He fell in beside her. "Not that I know of."

"I thought you had already questioned everyone."

"Oh, I'm just poking around, turning over rocks. You never know what you'll find. You ready to tell me why you hightailed it down here? Not that I think you've been anything but completely honest."

She ignored the sarcasm. "I understand Lance Harrington's wife disappeared three years ago."

Rob broke off a sassafras twig and stuck it in his mouth.

"She's gone anyway. Wasn't any evidence of foul play. She just upped and left."

"Do you think her disappearance is connected in any way with my father's death?" She didn't know why, but she had a feeling the two were linked.

"I don't see how it could have been. We're looking at it, of course. Thing is, Tara and Marty were a lot alike. They both thought life revolved around them, and they never cared how much damage they did to anyone else."

She thought about this. "You're saying both Marty and Tara were high maintenance?"

"Very high maintenance. Everyone else existed to burnish the image."

"Why would Tara walk away from her family?"

"Who says she did? We don't know where she is, but since she's not here, we know she didn't kill Marty, and that's the only name I've eliminated so far."

"Did you ask Lance where he was when my father was killed? Evidently he was one of the last persons to talk to him, and he doesn't seem to have liked Marty very much."

Rob shrugged. "Maybe not, but you can't arrest a man just because he didn't like the victim. Not too many people did like Marty."

She spoke without thinking. "Did Marty really love Tara?"

"Who told you that?"

"Loralee."

"I see." He nodded. "Loralee. Reminds me of you in a way." He pushed the gate open, motioning for her to go ahead.

Stephanie bristled at the comparison.

"Both of you trying to live up to someone. Loralee always wanted to be like Tara. She never could. Not in a million years."

"Are you another one who fell for Tara's charms? She must have gone after every man in the county."

"No." He sucked nosily on the sassafras. "I never liked her much. Loralee is worth a hundred like Tara, but she could never see it." She was aware of him watching her out of the corner of his eyes. "Take you. I'll bet you always tried to live up to what Marty wanted. You never saw he wasn't worth all that devotion."

Stephanie flushed and turned away. This country sheriff read her all too easily. He was also much smarter than she had originally thought. "You don't understand." She was appalled at how much she sounded like Loralee.

"Sure I do," he said. "I've read the books. The mind does funny things. You probably thought you were to blame for your father going away. Felt guilty, tried to be extra good because of the trouble you believed you'd caused."

"You have it all figured out, haven't you? I didn't know psychology was part of your training."

"You'd be surprised," he said unperturbed. "Even country sheriffs have to know a few things. We may not have as many crimes as the city cops do, but we manage to hold our own."

He threw away the chewed twig. "Don't plan on leaving the lodge. I'd hate to have the Independence police bring you back."

"If you're so suspicious why don't you arrest me?"

"I would if I could figure out how you could have gotten rid of the murder weapon. That's about the only thing in your favor so far."

He tipped his hat and walked back toward the lodge. Stephanie watched as he disappeared around a stand of red cedar. She wished she had never heard of Aunt Margaret's diamond necklace. If Sheriff Rob Daugherty found out her real reason for being here, he would arrest her in an Arkansas second.

* * *

She turned to find Brad leaning against the slender trunk of a dogwood tree, watching. "Sheriff Rob giving you a hard time?"

"Nothing I can't handle. You knew Marty. Who would have a reason to kill him?"

"Practically anyone. Marty was a leech, always causing trouble, sticking his nose in where he wasn't wanted." He scowled, his thick, dark eyebrows nearly meeting in the middle. "Whoever killed Marty might not hesitate to go after his daughter too. Have you thought of that?"

"Why would anyone want to hurt me?" She shivered. Someone walking over her grave? She wasn't superstitious. She had read, though, that murder could become addictive.

"You can't guess how a killer will act." A slanting ray of sunlight lingered on his shoulders. "Did you hear how Marty was killed? Someone using a long, thin blade got him about fourteen times."

"A long, thin blade?" She remembered a craft show in Independence, an ivory-handled dagger of Toledo steel. Fourteen times? That accounted for all the blood.

"What are you thinking? I can almost see the wheels turning."

"Marty had a dagger with an ivory handle he used as a letter opener. He bought it in Independence."

"That's right, he did. Hauled it around every time they traveled. I wonder if it's in his room."

She didn't answer, and he shrugged his shoulders. "Well, Rob will find it. Don't go too far into the woods. Someone had a grudge to settle with Marty. They might transfer those feelings to you." He disappeared behind a thicket of red cedar.

She almost ran back to the lodge.

* * *

Rob was sitting in one of the Adirondack chairs on the front porch when Brad got back to his cabin. Brad stopped, feigning surprise. "You here to see me?"

Rob shook his head. "No reason to get your back up. I just want to ask some questions."

"And if I choose not to answer?"

"Up to you." Rob's calm expression didn't change. "I'll get my answers one way or another. Why not do it the easy way?"

"Am I a suspect?"

"If I said no, would you believe me?"

Brad laughed bitterly. "No. I would expect to be high on your list."

"You're on it, along with everyone else, but you're not all that high yet. How about inviting me in?"

Brad hesitated, wanting to say no, but nothing could be gained by refusing to talk to him, and to give the sheriff his due, Rob Daugherty was fair for a cop. What could it hurt to go along with him?

He pushed the door open. "Come on in. Might as well get it over with."

Rob sat down on the couch in front of the fireplace. "Nice place you've got here."

"I like it." Brad brought mugs of coffee. "Sugar, cream?"

"No, black's fine." Rob took a drink, then set the mug down on the table. "All right, let's go over your story again. I'm not trying to trip you up, but sometimes people forget little things that are important. What did you see when you entered Marty's suite?"

"I heard a woman crying, and I went into the bedroom, and Stephanie was kneeling beside him."

"Did you see a knife? A weapon of any kind?"

Brad shook his head. "No. I've been thinking about that. I'm fairly certain the weapon wasn't in that room."

"Well, it sure had been."

"I don't see how Stephanie could have used it and got it out of there without being caught."

Rob shot him a quizzical look. "I'd think you'd want her to be guilty. Take the heat off you."

Brad didn't answer. The truth was he didn't know why he felt this urge to protect Stephanie. He just knew that every time he looked at her he found himself wishing there were dragons to tilt at so he could ride to the rescue. Real knight in shining armor stuff, and an impulse that would probably get him in trouble.

Rob shrugged. "Thing is, we searched the rooms and came up empty. So someone who was there smuggled out the murder weapon."

"You're saying it had to be one of us?"

"You four and whoever Stephanie heard leaving."

"Yeah, I'd forgotten there was someone else. Why are you so sure the field is that narrow?"

"I'm not sure about anything, but there's the time element, and not many people had access to the family's quarters. Of course, there might not have been anyone else. Maybe it was one of you circling back."

"You've been talking to Stephanie."

"Why? Is that her theory too?"

"She brought it up this morning, pointing to me."

Rob got up. "Smart woman, Stephanie. You think of anything new, give me a call."

Brad watched him leave. Rob was smart too. He wasn't out of the woods on this one. Neither was Stephanie. They had discovered the body. Like it or not, he had to get
involved. And God help him if he made the wrong move.

6

The family hadn't come down to dinner when Stephanie reached the dining room. She didn't want to sit at their table alone, so she chose a spot some distance away. The waiter, a good-looking blond guy, his hair pulled back in a ponytail, brought a menu. His nametag said "Mac."

Stephanie read over the menu. "Any suggestions?"

He shrugged and plopped a glass of water in front of her. "It's all good."

Stephanie glanced at him, surprised at the tone of his voice. He eyed her over his order pad, his expression faintly hostile. She turned her attention back to the menu, making her choices. He left without comment, but she felt faintly uneasy at his attitude.

He brought her dinner—tarragon chicken, roasted potatoes with red pepper sauce, and buttered asparagus, and white-chocolate cheesecake for dessert.

"Look, I didn't see much of my father. Was he a friend of yours?"

He looked surprised. "I play a little guitar and plunk around on the piano. We used to jam once in a while. Thing is, Marty pushed it a little, but not where his music was concerned. He kept that separate. You know?"

She knew. Music was the only part of Marty's life he didn't play games with. She kept her voice neutral. "I'd like to talk to you about him sometime."

He hesitated. "Marty had his faults, and a lot of people didn't like him, but I don't go for murder."

"I don't like it myself. You knew Marty better than I did. Why would anyone hate him so much?"

He hesitated and she pleaded. "Tell me, please. I'm just tying to understand."

He looked toward the Harrington table where the family had gathered. "I don't know anything about it."

She watched him leave, thinking that coming here had been a bad mistake. She wanted to get in her car and drive home to her peaceful house, her boring life, and never see Harrington Lodge again.

Brad came through the front door and looked around before making for her table. He pulled out a chair and sat down. "I've been thinking."

"That's a start. What were you thinking about?"

He pointed a finger at her. "Anyone ever mention you've got a smart mouth?"

She grinned reluctantly. "Quite often. Sorry."

"Thank you. Now as I was saying, I've been thinking."

She waited, figuring he would get to the point in his own

time. He looked good tonight, plenty of dark hair, cut short and combed crisply back from his forehead. Blue sweatshirt a couple of shades darker than his eyes. Nice smile. She realized he was talking.

"Like I said, I think we need to try to solve this murder case."

"Right. As if we could." Talking was easy, but actually discovering facts was a lot more difficult. She was beginning to wonder how the police ever solved anything.

He held up a hand to still her protests. "No, but listen. Let's try the process of elimination. You were on your way up to Marty's room. I was in the lobby in front of a dozen guests."

"Will that Bonnie what's-her-name vouch for you?"

"McIntire. Yes she will. Now, who's next?"

"Monica said she was in the library, but that doesn't prove she really was." Someone had slipped out of Marty's bedroom through the adjoining door to his wife's suite. Stephanie had her doubts about Monica's innocence.

"All right, Monica in the library." Brad held up one finger. "Who's next?"

"You called Lance, but he could have gone down the stairs to the office."

"Lance in office." Brad held up a second finger. "Loralee's suite is on that floor. Well, everyone is on that floor except me. And Clyde is in and out so much no one would notice him."

"Why does he spend so much time here?"

"He's starstruck. Tara was the same. She was in heaven if she got to ride the Harrington Express."

"She had a daughter. How could she be gone like that?"

"Huh!" It sounded like a snort. "When Tara wasn't chasing after Monica and Marty, she was off taking acting lessons or performing in some little theater drama. She was too busy trying to be a star to spend much time here."

Stephanie couldn't understand that mindset. How could a mother put her desires ahead of her child's welfare?

Brad dismissed both Tara and Clyde. "Where were we?"

"Nowhere. We don't really know where anyone was."

He shook his head. "No, and that's the frustrating part. I don't guess we're very good at detecting."

"Probably not," she said. "I hope the sheriff is having more luck."

"One thing—how did the murderer get out without being seen? I came up the stairs, and I didn't meet anyone. The elevator was still on the third floor."

Stephanie thought about it. "Maybe they didn't go down until after we were all in Marty's room."

"Or they took the back stairs. I'll ask around in the kitchen. See if they saw anything. I bet Rob's already thought of that, though."

Stephanie laughed. "Are you kidding? I imagine Rob's already thought of anything *we* can come up with. He's nobody's fool."

"Yeah. You're probably right." Brad agreed. "I still think it's important we do what we can to help, though."

Mac stopped at their table. "One of the guests is having tire trouble."

Brad looked wary. "What kind of trouble?"

"A flat. Needs someone to change it."

"Then go do it."

"Can't, I'm on duty. Lance said to tell you."

Brad sighed. "All right, I'll go. Talk to you later, Stephanie. We need to spend some time working on this."

Stephanie lingered, hoping Brad would come back. Maybe if they kicked things around long enough they could come up with something useful, but then again, maybe he was just pretending to help find the killer to cover his own guilt.

* * *

Brad fixed the tire and sent the guest on his way. Instead of going back to the lodge he wandered down to his cabin. Lance had scheduled him to work on the boat dock. Some of the boards were showing signs of rot and needed to be replaced. He had time to do it before dark.

He gathered the necessary tools and drove down to the lake. Since he'd already measured and cut the boards, all he had to do was remove the rotted ones and fit in the new. He turned around to pick up another board and was surprised to see Clyde standing there. The sound of the hammering must have drowned out his approach.

"Good evening." Clyde wore jeans and a navy-blue sweatshirt under a denim jacket, standard wear for this part of the country, but on him they seemed out of place.

No matter what he wore, Clyde always looked spit-shined.

Brad nodded and picked up a handful of nails, placing a few in his mouth to hold them ready for use. He spoke around them.

"What're you up to?"

"Just taking a walk." Clyde inspected the repair work. "Good job."

"Thanks." So what had brought the heir to the Andrews name down here to mingle with the hired help? He knew Clyde well enough to doubt he was just looking for company.

Clyde kicked aimlessly at a loose board. "You've spent time talking to that daughter of Marty's. Why did she come to the lodge?"

Brad took a nail out of his mouth, positioned it, and drove it home with a few well-aimed blows. "I have no idea."

"The general opinion around town is that someone meant to stop him from causing trouble. Perhaps she knows what he was up to, and that's why she came."

"You mean blackmail? She doesn't seem to be the type."

Clyde picked up a piece of scrap lumber, looked at it, and tossed it away. "Monica says Marty had changed. I can't say I've noticed it, but do you think he might have been ready to expose someone?"

"Without getting paid?" Brad shook his head. "I'd come nearer believing he punched the wrong button on someone who had a lot to lose."

"Has Rob asked you for a statement of your movements that night?" Clyde asked.

"Sure. I was under the impression he asked everyone. Where were you?"

Clyde's lips thinned beneath his neat mustache. "I was at home, of course. Why do you ask?"

"Just wondering." Since Clyde was here almost every available moment, why would he have stayed away on the one night they had a crime?

A speedboat passed, and the resulting waves lapped the shore. Clyde watched the boat, his expression thoughtful. "It never occurred to me before, but someone could have arrived by water and made their way up to Marty's room without going through the lobby."

Brad sat back on his heels and watched the boat as it circled and started back. He supposed it could have happened. They'd have had to come in through the back where the kitchen was or a side door. At this stage of the investigation, he was ready to accept anything that might point them in any direction at all.

"She could have had an accomplice." Clyde said.

"Who?"

"Stephanie. That daughter. She's the obvious suspect."

"There's no proof Stephanie did anything. I entered that room just minutes behind her. She didn't have time to kill Marty and hide the knife."

"Are you sure you didn't know her before?"

"Very sure, but I'm beginning to wonder why you're so anxious to pin this murder on her."

Clyde looked affronted. "I'm not trying to pin anything on anyone. I just have some interesting theories I'll pass on to Rob."

He walked away, and Brad pursed his lips, wondering what that was all about. Why was Clyde involving himself in a murder investigation? He couldn't think of anything more out of character.

Brad sat down on the dock and dangled his legs above the

water. A slight breeze ruffled his hair, and he lifted his face to the sky. Only someone who had been shut away where the sun didn't shine could appreciate a day like this. His thoughts turned to their current problem. Why would Clyde want to see Stephanie blamed for killing Marty, and what could he do to stop him?

* * *

Monica was already at the breakfast table the next morning, a newspaper spread out before her. Stephanie pulled out a chair and sat down. A new waiter, one she hadn't seen before, arrived to take her order. Monica waited until the waiter left before speaking. "All the arrangements are taken care of."

At Stephanie's startled look, she said, "What's the matter? You knew I was making the funeral arrangements." There was a flick of anger in her voice. "The scene at the funeral home yesterday was pure bedlam. Reporters everywhere."

"Because it was Marty?"

"Because he was murdered. It was horrible."

"I can imagine." Nothing in her quiet, ordered life had equipped her to deal with this type of publicity. She had assumed they would be left to bury their dead in peace. She should have known better.

"I realize you didn't come prepared for this." Monica moved her plate out of the way and rested her arms on the table. "You might want to drive into Eureka Springs and
shop for clothing, or I'd be happy to loan you something of mine. That would probably be best. You won't want to deal with the

reporters."

"Not if I can avoid them." She wouldn't have time to have anything sent from home, and the only clothes she had with her were too casual for a funeral. Wearing Monica's clothing didn't appeal to her, but neither did a confrontation with the media.

"When is the funeral?"

"Tomorrow. Private services at the chapel here at the lodge. He'll be buried in our family cemetery."

"No! I don't want him to be buried here. He belongs in Independence."

"No, he doesn't!" Monica set down her cup so hard it sounded like she had cracked the saucer. "I suppose you want him buried beside your mother. Well, he wasn't her husband anymore. He was my husband, and he will be buried here."

Her fingers tore at a fresh croissant, reducing it to shreds. The soft curves of her lips tightened and hardened. Stephanie wanted to protest, but she did understand. Marty had been Monica's husband, and Monica had a right to make plans. Stephanie's parents hadn't shared a life for years. Why insist they share a burial place.

"All right. He'll be buried here."

Monica wasn't mollified. "That woman did everything she could to bind Marty to her. She refused to give him a divorce, even though he begged for one."

"I won't listen to this! My mother never stood in Marty's way. He could have had a divorce anytime he wanted. All he had to do was ask."

"That's not true!" Monica leaped to her feet, her face red and distorted with anger. "All those years of waiting, just because a selfish woman wouldn't let go of what she had already lost." She turned so fast she knocked over her chair.

Stephanie watched in dismay as Monica rushed from the room, leaving her to face the startled gaze of their fellow diners. She knew they hadn't married until after her mother died, but it had never occurred to her to wonder why they waited so long. Bess Walker had been a proud woman with strong Christian principles. Never having approved of divorce, she had probably dug in her heels and refused to budge. Stephanie, when she had bothered to think about it, had just assumed that Marty didn't want to marry again. Apparently she didn't know as much about her parents' lives as she had believed. The thought troubled her.

7

Stephanie pulled on the black, silk sheath and smoothed it over her hips, examining the result in the mirror. Not bad, but not good either. The matching coat stretched tight across the back and wouldn't button in the front, but it would have to do. The hemline struck her higher than she usually wore her skirts, but she was slender, where Monica was softly rounded, so it fit well enough.

If she hadn't been such a coward, she could have gone into Eureka Springs and bought something to wear instead of borrowing from her hostess, but she couldn't bring herself to face the pack of reporters camped outside the gate.

The peach-colored enamel clock on the corner table ticked a warning. Time to go. Everyone would be watching to see how the daughter suspected of killing her father would behave. Her mother's training would help her now. The words she had heard so many times rang through her mind. "Chin up, shoulders back, eyes front." Dignified to the end. "This one's for you, Marty," she whispered. "I won't let you down." She closed the bedroom door and walked down the hall to the elevator.

The others were gathered in the lobby. Monica wore a black suit that nipped in at the waist and curved smoothly across her hips. A small, black hat tilted over her forehead, and her golden hair gleamed under a black veil, the perfect picture of a grieving widow. Stephanie felt ashamed of her cynicism when she saw her stepmother's strained expression and swollen, red eyelids.

Clyde, dressed in somber gray with a black-and-gray geometric print tie, took Monica's hand and gently drew it through the crook of his elbow. "All right now?"

Monica nodded, but her smile trembled around the edges.

The press waited at the chapel. Monica strode past them as if they didn't exist. Stephanie didn't have her aplomb. They yelled and pushed close, reminding her of a pack of hungry jackals she had seen once in a nature film.

"Miss Walker? Over here." One determined man shoved a microphone at Stephanie. "How do you feel about your father's death?"

Brad's hand closed around hers. "No comment." She looked up at him, and he said, "Don't let them get to you. This is their job, but you don't have to help them. Just keep moving."

She gripped his hand, grateful for his support. Dressed in a dark blue suit with a burgundy-and-navy tie, his expression appropriately solemn, he looked just as good as he did in jeans and a sweatshirt.

"I guess they serve a purpose."

He grinned. "So do vultures."

She realized he was still holding her hand. He drew it through his elbow, binding them together and she was intensely aware of his presence, but she didn't pull away.

A man in police uniform held the door open for the family, keeping the reporters outside. She recognized some of the people inside the chapel as guests at Harrington Lodge. Sheriff Rob Daugherty, seated toward the back, nodded when she passed. He wasn't in uniform today, and the navy-blue of his suit swelled across his stomach.

A blanket of red roses from Monica covered the oak casket. Stephanie's own sheaf of lily-of-the-valley nestled inside the lid, gleaming like pearls in the dim light. The air was heavy with the perfume associated with large floral arrangements and funeral parlors. The fragrance of death.

The mortician had done a good job. The body in the casket bore little resemblance to the broken, bloody ruin that had been Stephanie's last memory of Marty, but nothing could ever erase that image, which she would carry in her mind forever.

* * *

Brad watched Stephanie as she looked around the chapel. This had to be rough for her. No family, no friends to share her grief. She looked so alone, his heart constricted in sympathy. What was there about her that caught his attention? Sure she was good to look at. So were a lot of women who had never attracted him.

She sat with her shoulders straight, her head high, expression composed. She had to know that people were curious about her, but she gave an outward show of self-control. Her hand had trembled in his, though, so he knew she wasn't as calm as she appeared.

She turned to look at him, and he smiled, pleased to see an answering spark in her eyes. He wished they had met under other circumstances.

* * *

The crush of people was overwhelming. Stephanie took a slow, deep breath, feeling smothered. The chapel was full, with a crowd standing outside. How many were friends of Marty's, and how many were just curious about a celebrity death by violence?

Loralee sat on the other side of Brad. Monica and Clyde were close together, and Lance held Kate's hand. A lilting soprano sang "The Lord's Prayer."

A young man with smooth, brown hair read the obituary. His voice, as cultured as oiled silk, droned: "He leaves behind his wife, Monica; a stepson, Lance Harrington of the home; a stepgranddaughter, Kate Harrington of the home; and two daughters, Stephanie of Independence, Missouri, and Heather of Hot Springs, Arkansas."

Stephanie, stunned by what she had heard, jerked her head around to stare incredulously at him. Whoever wrote the obituary had the wrong information. She'd see that that got straightened out. Marty had no other daughters.

The minister, a handsome gray-haired man, spoke as if he knew Marty personally. Stephanie took that with a grain of salt. The Marty she remembered wouldn't have been on very good terms with a preacher. Monica broke down a couple of times, crying as elegantly as she did everything else. Kate sobbed noisily, hot tears running down her cheeks and spattering against the skirt of her blue dress.

Stephanie wanted to cry, but she couldn't. Her chest felt constricted, like someone had clamped an iron band around it. She closed her eyes, taking a deep breath. Would this service never end?

When the preacher started talking about Marty and heaven, Stephanie tuned him out. Whatever heaven Marty had coming would have been here on this earth. She didn't remember ever seeing him in church. Of course, after she was seven years old, she didn't see much of him, period. Now all she had was this bitter longing for the things they never got to do together.

The congregation rose to repeat the twenty-third psalm. Stephanie joined in, stumbling over unfamiliar places, but Brad surprised her by knowing all the words. Monica's voice rose above the others, sweet and clear, turning the psalm into a hymn of praise. She knew all the words too. Another surprise.

They drove to the cemetery a few miles down the road from the lodge. Marty's grave waited in a neat little plot under towering pines. A tent stretched above their heads, and a green rug kept their feet off the spring grass. Flowers from the chapel made a fragrant, multicolored backdrop.

Brad walked beside Stephanie, taking her arm as they strode over the uneven turf. She was grateful for his concern. His presence kept her from feeling so alone, but she didn't want to rely on him too much. Brad Wilson was nothing to her, and she intended to keep it that way. She joined Monica, Loralee, and Kate in the row of chairs in front of the casket, while the others crowded in behind them.

The edges of the canvas tent flapped gently in the breeze. Stephanie caught a faint whiff of Brad's cologne and knew he stood behind her chair, close enough to touch. Monica reached over and took Kate's hand. Loralee bowed her head, her hair swinging down to curtain her face. Stephanie sat dry-eyed, staring at the roses covering the casket and feeling desperately alone. Brad's hands rested on her shoulders, giving badly needed comfort. She reached one hand up to touch his in gratitude.

The minister read from First Thessalonians, chapter four, verses thirteen through fifteen. "Brothers, we do not want you to be ignorant about those who fall asleep, or to grieve like the rest of men, who have no hope. We believe that Jesus died and rose again and so we believe that God will bring with Jesus those who have fallen asleep in him. According to the Lord's own word, we tell you that we who are still alive, who are left till the coming of the Lord, will certainly not precede those who have fallen asleep."

Monica dabbed at her eyes with a tissue, as he continued. "Marty is in a better place today. Although we mourn his passing, we know he is at rest in the very presence of Jesus, our Lord and Savior." His voice dripped compassion.

He looked around at the people gathered under the tent, his voice ringing with a conviction Stephanie had never understood. She shut him out. It sounded good, but from what she knew about Marty's lifestyle, she doubted whether it was an accurate description of her father's destination. She'd absorbed enough church to know that heaven was a place prepared only for God's children. Unless Marty had made some drastic changes in his lifestyle, he didn't qualify. *Neither do you.* She shut that out too. Time to think about that later. Right now she had to say goodbye to Marty.

A young man with a trumpet played the haunting notes of "Amazing Grace." The hills flung back silvery echoes. The wind roared through the pine tree that shaded the raw earth of the grave. The solitude of this secluded little cemetery touched Stephanie.

For the first time, the iron band around her chest loosened. The tears she couldn't shed in the chapel stung her eyes, blinding her, and rolled down her cheeks. Someone put an arm around her waist and maneuvered her through the crowd of people to the car. Only when he opened the door and slid in after her did she look around to see Brad.

"Okay now?" he asked.

She nodded. "I'm sorry. It just hit me."

The flicker of sympathy in his eyes almost set her off again. She blinked away tears, remembering the last time she had seen Marty alive. A rising anger threatened her hard-won calm, as she remembered too, the way he had died. If it took the rest of her life, she would see that her father's killer was brought to justice. And tomorrow she was going to pay a visit to the local paper and have them run a correction of the obituary. She was Marty's only daughter. Someone had made a mistake, and she wanted it corrected.

Loralee and Lance joined them. When they drove past the reporters and their probing cameras, Stephanie leaned back so that she was partially shielded by Brad. Trees bordered the road—dark cedar, the swelling bud of the dogwood, and the pale fuchsia of redbud just starting to bloom. Spring had come early this year—a time of rebirth. Death had no right to intrude.

When they reached the lodge, Brad helped her out of the car. She liked the way his face crinkled into laugh lines when he smiled. He'd been nice to her today, and she appreciated it. She could almost forgive him for thinking she had murdered her father.

Back in her room, Stephanie changed into the brown pants and amber sweater she had worn her first day here, carefully folding Monica's dress and coat to be returned. She pulled off her earrings, dropping one, which rolled under the bedside table. Frustrated, she got down on her knees, groping for it. An edge of white caught her attention, and she dropped flat on the rug, straining until her fingertips touched the paper.

An envelope. The envelope she had found in Marty's room. She remembered tossing the jackets onto the bed before hanging them in the closet. Apparently the envelope had fallen between the bed and the table, where it had gone unnoticed.

Stephanie stretched out on the bed, pulled a pillow around to support her back, and slid a finger under the envelope flap. Yellowed newspaper clippings fell out. Large, black headlines caught her attention. She picked up the first clipping and examined it. Brad's face stared back at her. The headlines screamed their message: "Prominent St. Louis attorney arrested in murder of his wife."

Stephanie read through the clippings. Brad had spent time in prison? She looked at the date on the top one and did some rapid figuring. He served only a few years out of a life sentence? Why? And what was he doing here?

Stephanie leaned her head back against the pillow, thinking. It wasn't all that late, and she wanted to talk to him about this. Why did Marty have these clippings, and why hadn't the police taken them? She stood up and reached for her jacket. It was too early for dinner, so maybe she could catch him in his cabin.

When she reached the lobby, Clyde was standing by the receptionist desk, dressed in the same suit he'd worn to the funeral. He stroked his mustache with one finger, eyebrows raised. "Going out again?"

"Yes." She didn't want to talk about her reason. It struck her that he didn't seem to be all that interested in talking to her, either.

As if confirming her opinion, he raised his eyebrows. "Well, don't let me keep you."

"I won't."

As she pulled the door shut, she glanced over her shoulder to see him now standing behind the receptionist desk. As she watched, he pulled out a drawer and riffled through it.

Intrigued, she stepped around behind the facing, where she could watch without being seen as he systematically worked his way through each drawer. After closing the last one he straightened, looking frustrated.

Bonnie entered from the dining room, talking to a guest, but by the time she reached her work area, Clyde was standing in front of the fireplace, staring into the flames. Stephanie watched him for a minute but gave up when he started talking to one of the men who had entered.

Whatever he was looking for, he'd ended the hunt for now. She trudged down the narrow path to the cabin, wondering why Clyde Andrews was searching Bonnie McIntire's desk and why he didn't want to be seen.

Brad's cabin sat in a small clearing watched over by shortleaf pines and red cedar. Was she making a mistake in coming here? She was beginning to like Brad, but the clippings had jarred her alarm system. Maybe it wasn't a good idea to be alone in an isolated cabin with a former convict. Particularly since they'd had a recent murder.

Her steps slowed as she thought about turning around and going back, but she owed it to Marty to find out who had killed him, and Brad might have some answers that would help. She pushed aside her doubts and stepped up on the porch.

Brad answered almost as soon as she knocked, looking surprised to see her standing there.

"May I come in?"

"Sure." He stepped aside and let her enter.

She liked his cabin and the big stone fireplace and braided rugs. A large copper kettle held magazines, and a red plaid throw covered the couch. It was a man's room, void of all feminine touches, but comfortable. On the coffee table lay a worn Bible, an item she hadn't expected to see. She felt relieved, as though a man who read the Bible couldn't be a murderer. She was very much aware of the envelope of clippings she carried.

Brad pulled a high-backed wooden rocker close to the fire for her, and a Labrador the color of dark chocolate, lying on the hearthrug, stretched and pulled himself upright. He ambled over to put his head in her lap, and she let him sniff her fingers before gently running her hand under his chin.

"No, Caesar. Back." Brad commanded.

She stopped him. "Don't. I like dogs." Besides, scratching Caesar's ears gave her something to do.

Brad sat down in another rocker facing her, looking puzzled.

She smiled tentatively. "I supposed you're curious about why I'm here."

He nodded. "It had crossed my mind."

She flushed, wondering whether he was getting the wrong idea. "I'm doing detective work."

"Oh? I thought we were partners in that."

"We are. And I have something I want to talk to you about."

Caesar left Stephanie and slumped down on the hearth in front of Brad.

Stephanie curled her hand around the envelope in her pocket. "How well did you know Marty?"

"Well enough I guess. Why?" His manner was casual, but she sensed a tension about him that hadn't been there before.

The burning wood popped, throwing a flaming coal out onto the rug. Brad jumped to his feet. Stephanie gasped, startled, her hand flying to her throat. He kicked the glowing lump of fire back to the safety of the hearth and sat back down, seemingly unaware of her reaction. It took a minute to get her voice under control.

"Why did you come to the lodge?" His eyes were direct, challenging her.

She hesitated. "Marty wanted me to come."

"Oh, yeah? Why?"

"He said he needed someone to watch his back." She waited for his reaction.

He raised his eyebrows, looking stunned. "He said *what?*"

"You heard me. Someone was a threat to him. He wanted me to keep my eyes open. At first I refused to come, and then when I changed my mind, I got here too late."

"I see." He was silent for a moment, looking thoughtful. "I overheard your conversation with Monica. Your mother really did refuse to give Marty a divorce."

"I never thought about it, I guess. I just supposed if he'd asked for one she would have been agreeable."

"He asked all right. Begged on his knees, the way I got it. She said no. That's why they had to wait until your mother died to get married."

"I'm surprised they bothered. After all, they had lived together for years."

"You don't know Monica. Once she sets her mind on something, she never gives up, and once she gets something she wants, she never lets go. Getting married vindicated all those years she had lived in sin. At least that's the way she saw it. By the time your mother died, I don't think Marty cared whether he got married or not, but he didn't have a choice. What Monica wants, Monica gets."

A log collapsed in a shower of sparks, and the March wind howled around the cabin. A glance at the window showed clouds gathering overhead, darkening the sky. Dusk would come early.

Brad pulled on his lower lip, looking thoughtful. "Why did you come here tonight? I doubt if it's because I'm so fascinating you can't stay away."

Stephanie pulled the packet of newspaper clippings from of her pocket and handed it to him. "I want to know why he had this."

Brad took the envelope and opened it, sliding out the clippings. "You read these and you still came to my cabin? How could you know you would be safe?"

"I have trouble picturing you as a killer." She'd never claimed to be a good judge of character. She'd probably have trouble seeing Jack the Ripper as a killer.

"Anyone can kill if you push them far enough. Don't trust anyone. Not even me." He tossed the clippings into the fire and stirred the flames with a poker.

She uttered a startled yelp of protest. "Why did you do that?"

"They're old news. Why keep them?"

"Marty kept them. Why did he have those clippings?"

Brad's voice was harsh with anger. "He tried a spot of blackmail, but it didn't work. Pay a blackmailer once, and he never lets you stop paying."

She stared at him, appalled. Marty, *her father*, had stooped to blackmail? Something else occurred to her. "Blackmail is an excellent motive for murder."

"If you think that, why did you come to meet me?"

"I didn't know about the blackmail then." Her voice sounded as squeaky as a baby's pull toy. She cleared her throat. "What did Marty do when you said no?"

"Nothing. My past wasn't a secret. I wouldn't like to have it all dug up again, but I'm not about to pay someone to keep it quiet when all people have to do is read back issues of the newspapers. It's there for anyone who cares enough to look."

She didn't speak, thinking over what he had said. Maybe it was the truth, and maybe it wasn't.

Brad stared into the fire. "What did Rob want to talk to you about?"

"Mostly why I came to the lodge. He's trying to pin Marty's death on me, and I resent it. I don't think he's even looking at anyone else."

"Well, let's see. If I have it right, your story goes something like this. Marty just happened to drop by to see you, after who knows how long since his last visit, and as soon as he left you jumped into your car and drove for hours in one of the worst thunderstorms we've had for a long time, just to stage your own little surprise party. Can't say I blame Rod for not swallowing that."

Stephanie shook her head. "It wasn't like that. You make it sound like I'm lying."

"Aren't you? We knew Marty had a daughter, but you never came around. Five minutes after you hit the lodge, he's dead. What would you think if you were the sheriff?"

He leaned forward and picked up the poker, and she tensed, ready to run, but he only stirred the fire. When the flames leaped up again, he leaned back in his chair and resumed talking. His voice was low and rough with emotion. She wanted to look away, but her eyes were drawn to the pain in his expression.

"Since you read the clippings, you must have some questions. I came home from work and found my wife dead, beaten and her throat slashed. I got blood on my clothes when I bent over her. She'd been killed with my hunting knife. My fingerprints were on the handle, smudged, of course, but that didn't seem to matter."

He stopped, and she hunted for something to say, but he swallowed hard and then continued. "I was young and ambitious, determined to clean up the county, and I'd stepped on a lot of toes, including the sheriff's. I guess no one looked very hard for the real killer."

"You don't have to tell me this."

"If I expect you to trust me, I do. You saw those clippings." He drew a deep breath. "I got life. Two years later we had a new sheriff. An attorney friend of mine decided to go for another trial. Before we went to court, the cops caught the real killer, a guy who used to mow our yard. He had hit on Kelly and she fought him, and he got mad and killed her. They let me out and locked him up."

"I'm sorry." It was all she could manage. She stared at the fire, unable to bear the pain in his voice. A faint stirring of compassion warmed her heart. The silence lengthened until she had to break it or scream.

"How did you end up working for the Harringtons?" Lame question, but it was all she could come up with.

He looked down at his hands. "I called Lance and asked for a job. Something outside. I don't like being cooped up anymore."

Who could blame him for that? She thought of Brad locked in a prison and felt tears sting her eyes. What a terrible story. Prison would have been horrible for a man like him.

The isolation of the cabin and the story she had just heard unnerved her. She shifted positions and glanced at her watch. "It will be time for dinner soon. I'd better go back to the lodge."

"Yes, I suppose that would be best."

She got to her feet, feeling awkward. "Thank you for helping me through the funeral."

He stood beside her, solid, strong. For an instant she wished she had met him under different circumstances, but she pushed such foolishness aside. She didn't want to get involved with anyone. Love wasn't anything like what the sweet songs led you to believe. Love was crying alone in the night, watching for someone who never came. Broken promises and broken hearts. Who needed it? She turned toward the door, and he followed her, reaching for the doorknob.

"Be careful, Stephanie. Remember, someone killed Marty. Don't keep digging in things that don't concern you. It might be dangerous."

She heard and rejected the worried tone of his voice. "Is that a warning?"

"You can take it that way. Go back to Independence. Marty shouldn't have asked you to come. The killer is sure to be suspicious, and it isn't safe for you here."

Their eyes locked, and Stephanie felt herself sway toward

him. She stiffened. What was wrong with her tonight? She started to walk away, but he followed her outside.

"Don't be so stubborn. We have a murderer among us."

She didn't want to listen. Brad Wilson had no right to tell her what to do. She turned and ran toward the path leading to the lodge. A heavy mist and the lowering clouds had indeed caused an early dusk. The thicket of cedars threw black shadows over the path.

A sleepy bird, already gone to roost for the night, burst out of the trees in a muffled whirl of wings. Startled, she stumbled over a root, losing her balance. Something crashed against her head, and the world exploded in a blinding flash of light. She heard the faint barking of a dog and the sound of running footsteps before she lost consciousness.

* * *

"She's waking up." She would recognize Lance's voice anywhere. "Come on, Stephanie. Look at us."

"Let her alone," Brad ordered. "She'll open her eyes when she's ready."

"Light . . . bright . . ." she muttered. He must have understood, because someone immediately shaded the lamp. She cracked her eyelids open just enough to see their shadowy forms standing beside the bed where she lay. A parade with a lot of bass drums marched through her head. "What happened?"

"You got ambushed. If you weren't so hardheaded, you'd be dead." Brad sounded upset. "Caesar scared him off. Lance heard the barking and came running, but whoever did it was gone when he got there."

"Where were you?" She thought it was a legitimate question. After all, she had just left him.

"Are you accusing me of hitting you?" he demanded. "That's gratitude for you."

"I'll be grateful when my head stops hurting." She forced her eyes open. The two men stood solidly together, shoulders touching. She appreciated their concern, but how had they gotten there so fast and never seen who had hit her?

* * *

Brad looked down at Stephanie, thinking how vulnerable she looked. Whoever bashed her had meant business. Why had he let her walk back to the lodge alone? If she had been killed, he would be at fault.

Another thought occurred to him. If she had been killed this close to his cabin, suspicion would have turned on him. Had the person who had attacked her been aware of his past? Maybe he was being paranoid, but he felt like he had been set up.

Her eyelashes fluttered, and a rising flood of tenderness laced with anxiety filled him. In spite of himself, he was drawn to Marty's daughter.

He thought of Kelly, of the lonely days and nights since her death. His memories of her had faded with time. Now, more and more he found himself thinking of Stephanie. He was going to find out who had hurt her and make sure it never happened again.

8

Stephanie's head felt like it could split open with the slightest encouragement, but keeping her eyes closed against the light seemed to help. "Who hit me? You must have seen something."

"No one saw anything."

Brad's voice.

"Do you want to go back to the lodge, or are you going to spend the night here?" Her eyes jerked open, and he laughed. "Just kidding. Stay awake, Stephanie. Don't go to sleep."

"You'd better be kidding." She struggled to an upright position, then clung desperately to him as the room whirled like an out-of-control merry-go-round.

His arms cradled her. She blinked in surprise as something light as a rose petal brushed her forehead. She had a disturbing sensation that Brad had kissed her. That whack on the head must have been harder than she realized.

"Will you lie still?" His impatience banished any romantic imaginings she might have harbored. He pushed her down against the pillows. "You need to see a doctor. Someone really let you have it. Lance is calling the sheriff, and as soon as he gets back, we're taking you up to the lodge."

"I don't need a doctor, and why did he call Rob? I don't want to talk to him."

"What you want doesn't matter right now. If Caesar hadn't scared that guy off, you'd have been helpless." He pointed his finger at her for emphasis. "And as soon as you get over this knock on your head, you and I are going to have another talk."

His jaw had a firm line she didn't like. Brad Wilson didn't need to think he could push her around. The very thought sent the blood pounding in her temples, although at this point, she couldn't tell whether that was caused by temper or the knock on the head she had received.

Caesar made a rush for the door, barking a warning. Lance entered and gave the dog an absent pat. "I brought a wheelchair, but the path down to your cabin's so rough I left it at the gate."

"Forget it. I can walk," she protested.

Brad scooped her up in his arms. "Open the door. I've got her."

Stephanie glared at him. *Just like a sack of flour.* But his arms were so warm and comforting she decided not to protest. She let her head slump against his shoulder. He stumbled a little, and she tightened her hold around his neck.

He laughed softly. "Don't worry. I won't drop you."

"I know." Her imagination might people the night with monsters, both human and make-believe, but although she hadn't known Brad very long, she sensed something reassuring about him. Something dependable.

Dependable was good.

They reached the gate, and he dumped her in the chair and straightened to catch his breath. "You don't miss many meals, do you?"

"What's the matter pal, out of breath?" Lance taunted. "Should have let me carry her."

Stephanie gritted her teeth, her good opinion of Brad vanishing as quickly as it had come. She might have to ride in this stupid chair, but that didn't mean she had to put up with jokes about her weight.

"When you are through having fun at my expense, perhaps we could get on with it?"

"The lady wants a ride," Lance exclaimed. "Do I get to push?"

"As far as I'm concerned you do. I did the hard work." Brad walked beside the chair as Lance shoved it over a protruding tree root and started down the path. Stephanie reflected sourly that they were certainly getting a lot of enjoyment out of her being hit on the head.

Lance pushed her through the kitchen and down a hallway into a part of the lodge she had never been before. An elevator took them up to the family quarters. They came out around the corner from her room and at the far end of the corridor. She noticed they weren't joking so much now.

When they reached her suite, Monica was waiting. "Y'all go on, get out. I want to take a look at that head wound."

"We need to talk to her," Lance protested. "She's able to

answer a few questions."

"Well now, I don't know whether she is or not. I suspect her needs are more important than what you want."

Stephanie started to protest, then decided it wasn't worth the trouble. Trying to talk to Monica when she was in this mood had about as much effect as arguing with a bulldozer.

"Any blow on the head needs medical attention, and I'm going to call Doctor Harrison. He'll drop by the lodge if I ask him to. You could have a serious injury."

Stephanie rejected that argument. "I'm not going to see a doctor, and I don't want one coming here."

"We'll see. First let's get you out of that jacket."

Stephanie struggled to her feet, intending to demonstrate her ability to take care of herself. The room whirled, and she pitched forward into Monica's arms as the lights went out and they both hit the floor.

* * *

Stephanie woke in a hospital bed with Monica sitting in an uncomfortable-looking chair, her knitting in her hands. Knitting? The Queen of Country Music? She'd always had an exaggerated vision of Marty's wife as a superstar, glamorous and exciting. She was having a hard time adjusting to this real-life, ordinary woman.

"What are you making?"

Monica started at the sound of her voice. "I didn't know you were awake."

"You're knitting?"

She laughed, looking down at the fluffy yellow yarn in her lap. "Knitting relaxes me, so I knit baby blankets for the local churches to give out at Christmas. I suppose that would surprise my fans?"

"It surprises me. You're not at all what I expected."

Monica sighed. "You're not exactly what I had in mind, either. I wish we'd met earlier. I think we could've been friends."

"We'll have to work on that." Being friends with this woman would seem like a betrayal of her mother. She wasn't quite ready for that. Stephanie reached for a glass of water, wincing at the sudden stab of pain. She had a headache that wouldn't quit, and every time she moved too quickly, the room drifted in circles, giving the impression she was stranded in a whirlpool.

Monica reached out to steady the glass. "Are you hurting bad?"

"Yes! I don't understand why anyone would want to attack me. It doesn't make sense." She remembered the key and clutched her neck, relieved to find it still there.

"Maybe you know something you don't realize you know." Monica let the knitting rest in her lap. "Stephanie, why'd Marty go to see you?"

"He thought he was in danger." She might as well tell the truth. It was just a matter of time until Sheriff Rob tricked her into talking, and she was tired of keeping secrets. Besides, it might look better if it came from her instead of letting Rob find it out on his own. "I wouldn't come, so he took a diamond necklace I'd borrowed from my aunt and left a note that he'd see me at the lodge."

Monica laughed. "That sounds like Marty. He knew how to get his way." She sobered. "But when you reached here, he was dead. What happened to the necklace?"

"I don't know. I've looked, but I haven't found it. I'd guess he hid it somewhere."

"Or whoever killed him took it." Monica's forehead wrinkled in a puzzled frown. "Marty knew he was in danger? He never said anything to me about it, and what did he mean, anyway? Until his death, nothing ever happened here."

"Something did happen. Tara disappeared."

"Tara left three years ago. Are you saying he thought something happened to her?"

"Loralee thinks she's dead."

Monica dismissed this with a wave of her hand. "That girl isn't quite on board where Tara is concerned. I used to think Loralee wasn't all that fond of her cousin, but once Tara was gone, there was no holdin' her. She left too."

"Where did she go?"

Monica shrugged. "She never said. Just announced one day she was leavin'. I hated to lose her. Loralee is extremely efficient and creative. Or she used to be. Now she acts like she really doesn't care. I'm beginning to wonder if I made a mistake in findin' her and insistin' she come work for me."

"She showed me Tara's suite." Stephanie's head was killing her, but she didn't want to stop the flow of words while her stepmother seemed in a mood to talk.

Monica erupted in a ladylike snort. "I wish we had half the money Tara blew on those three rooms, and then she spent as little time here as possible."

Stephanie let that drift on past. "Why did she leave?"

"Who knows? She was here for dinner, and then no one saw her again. Of course, she didn't bother to leave a message."

"Did you report her as missing?"

"No, why should we? She had a habit of leaving. Tara never wasted any time explainin' her behavior. She'd just pack up and go without a word to anyone. She'll come back when she's ready to come and not a day before."

Stephanie leaned back against the pillows, willing the room to stop spinning. She took a deep breath. "Three years is a long time. Didn't you try to find her?"

Monica fumbled with her knitting needles, looking uncomfortable. "It's not easy to find someone who doesn't want to be found. I had a hard enough time locating Loralee, and she had no reason to hide."

And Tara did? Stephanie filed that comment away to be examined later. "How did you find her?"

Monica hesitated, a flush staining her cheeks. "I hired a private detective."

A detective to find Loralee but not to find Tara. Because she didn't want Tara found? Or because she knew Tara couldn't be found?

"I understand Tara spent a lot of time with Marty."

"That's not true." Monica clicked her knitting needles together, the sound sharp and overly loud in the small room. Her voice was just as sharp. "I guess Clyde knew her better than most. They both liked to tour with us, and since they weren't involved with the show, they were thrown together a lot."

When Monica spoke again, Stepanie could sense her reluctance. "Marty went through a bad time right about then, but it didn't have anything to do with Tara. This is not a subject I enjoy discussing."

"But maybe he knew something about Tara." Whether she enjoyed talking about it or not wasn't the point. If she could shed some light on whatever had worried him, she needed to say so.

"He didn't. Look, Stephanie. Some people, like Marty, think they can frolic through life doin' exactly as they please with no thought of the consequences. Three years ago, a young woman took her life because of him. She stalked him, I guess you would say. She was very unstable to start with, and when he brushed her off rather viciously, she couldn't handle the rejection. Her death hit him hard.

"He blamed himself, and I guess it was his fault in a way, but suddenly he seemed to remember everything he'd done to other people, and the entire load of guilt just sort of dumped on him all at once. He couldn't handle it. We both went through a very bad time."

"I see. And he never loved Tara?"

"He detested Tara." Her face flushed with sudden rage, and Stephanie remembered what Brad had said about what Monica wanted, Monica got. Surely she wouldn't give up her husband without a fight. Did she know more about Tara's disappearance than she admitted?

Her voice crackled with anger. "I don't know what nonsense Loralee has fed you, but my daughter-in-law is a very shallow, incredibly selfish young woman without a moral to her name. There isn't anything too dirty for Tara to pull if she thinks she can gain by it, and no one will ever make me think we got rid of her so easily. She'll turn up again one of these days and devote all her energies to making life miserable for us."

Monica looked at her watch, evidently wanting to change the subject. "I suppose I need to go home so you can get some sleep."

Stephanie's hand shot out of its own accord. "Oh no, you don't! You're not leaving me alone here. Whoever hit me might come back and finish the job."

"Rob thought of that. He posted a guard outside your door."

"He did?" Somehow that didn't comfort her as much as it should have. If Rob had decided to guard her, she must really be in danger.

The door opened and a nurse entered. "Are we awake? I just want to take your temperature."

Monica took advantage of the moment to shrug into her coat and head for the door. She turned around to wiggle her fingers in a goodbye wave. "See you in the mornin'. Sleep tight."

"No, wait." The door was already closing.

Stephanie slapped the bed in frustration. Drat. She had forgotten to ask Monica about the obituary. She'd know who wrote it, and she'd also know what to do to correct the mistake.

The nurse gave her a pain pill and waited until she swallowed it before leaving.

The phone rang and she reached for it.

"Stephanie? It's me, Brad. How you doing?"

"All right, I guess." She was surprised he would call, but it was good to hear his voice.

"I just wanted to check on you and make sure you're okay. Is Monica still there?"

"No, she left a few minutes ago, but Rob has someone stationed in the hall." She heard him sigh as if relieved.

"That's all right, then. I thought if you needed me I might come down and spend the night."

"That's not necessary, but I appreciate it." There was something she wanted to ask him, though. "Brad, why do you think someone hit me?"

He was silent for a minute. "Steph, I don't want to scare you, but if there is anything you know that could be a threat to anyone, you need to tell Rob."

"But I don't know anything."

"Someone seems to think you do, which is just as bad."

"*That's* comforting."

He chuckled. "You get a good night's sleep, and when you get back to the lodge we're going to take better care of you. That's a promise."

She remembered the way his arms felt around her and remained silent, not sure what to say.

"Stephanie?"

"What?"

"Don't worry, okay?"

She wasn't far from tears. "Brad... thank you."

"Sure. Go to sleep now. I'll see you in the morning."

Beyond her room the muted sounds of a busy hospital were reassuring. The pill took effect, and she went to sleep to dream of someone chasing her down the dark path to Brad's cabin. She pounded on the window to get his attention.

When he turned around, she realized it was Marty, not Brad. He waved and smiled but made no move to answer her. She could hear her unknown enemy plunging toward her through the underbrush, but although she screamed his name, she couldn't make Marty understand that he had to open the door and let her come in.

9

The sheriff dropped by the hospital while Stephanie was eating breakfast. "Hear you're going home this morning." He took the ever-present toothpick out of his mouth, looked at it, and put it back. "I'm tryin' to quit smoking."

"Good idea. It's a nasty habit."

"You want to tell me about what happened when you got hit?"

"Like what?"

"Like did you see anything, maybe?"

Stephanie pushed her tray aside, not hungry anymore. "It was dark."

"You could still see and hear, couldn't you? You notice anything at all?" He chewed on the toothpick, his manner nonchalant.

"Not a thing. Nothing. Believe me, if I had any idea who it was, I'd tell you."

"The way you told me the truth about why you came to the lodge?"

She met his eyes and felt herself blush. "All right. If I don't tell you, Monica will. . . if she hasn't already."

"No. I haven't talked to her about it." He allowed himself to look very disappointed.

Stephanie repeated her last conversation with Marty, and Rob stared at her out of those nice brown eyes that would probably look just as thoughtful and interested while he adjusted the tension of a hangman's noose. "You hightailed it right on down here? That what you're saying?"

She shook her head and then wished she hadn't, because sudden moves still hurt. "No. Actually, I refused to come, but I had a diamond necklace I'd borrowed from my aunt, and he took it when he left. He knew I'd come after him."

Rob looked skeptical. "What's this necklace like?"

Stephanie hesitated, trying to dredge up a picture that wasn't there. She rubbed her forehead. Why couldn't she remember? She paused, recognizing that while she could recall recent events, there were gaps in her memory. Had that knock on the head affected her more than she realized?

She covered her confusion the best she could. "I can get a detailed description."

"You do that." He tossed the toothpick in the general direction of the wastebasket. "So that's why Bonnie thought you were in a killing mood when you showed up that night."

Stephanie clamped her lips together and swallowed the sudden lump in her throat. She'd deal with this grinding remorse the rest of her life. "I wanted to hang him. Then when I got to his suite and found he'd been murdered, I felt so guilty. I can understand someone being angry at Marty, but why kill him?"

"People kill for a lot of reasons. Marty was too unpredictable. You never could guess which way he'd jump. His killer probably got nervous and made a move."

"That lets me out. I didn't have a reason to murder him." She cautiously sipped milk through a straw and took another bite of oatmeal, which she hated.

"Sometimes people just get mad and cut loose. You had a reason to be upset, seems to me."

Stephanie cocked a derisive eyebrow in his direction. "And then I whacked myself on the head to throw you off the trail? Good thinking."

"Believe it or not, stranger things have happened. I could tell you lots of stories."

"Well, don't. I'm not in the mood for them. Hand me my clothes and step outside. You can take me back to the lodge. I'm leaving."

"Not until the doc releases you, you're not." He grinned. "You've got a temper, all right. I can see you getting mad and bashing someone."

"You're going to see me bash the long arm of the law if you're not careful."

He laughed. "I can't dismiss anyone at this stage. Everyone's a suspect until I get more information, and that includes you."

Stephanie leaned back against the pillows, feeling exhausted and somewhat disoriented. "Clyde thinks you'll find the reason for Marty's death by digging into Marty's past."

"He's probably right," the sheriff conceded, sarcasm dripping off every word. "Unless someone just goes haywire and starts killing randomly, you almost always find the motive for murder somewhere in the victim's past. But you're all a part of Marty's past. You can't expect me to ignore that, can you?"

"Why do I get the impression you don't like Clyde."

Rob grinned. "Now why would you think that? I went to school with the guy, known him all my life, and he hasn't changed one bit."

"And you have?"

He laughed. "Probably not."

Stephanie changed the subject. "When Marty visited me in Independence, he hinted that he wanted to be more involved in my life. I didn't believe him, but Monica swears he'd changed."

Rob looked thoughtful. "She told me the same thing. Marty ran with a wild crowd, but I don't think he ever got involved in anything illegal, because he knew Monica would kick him out. She's pretty straightlaced."

"Oh yeah, right." Stephanie let the sarcasm roll. Straight-laced Monica, her father's live-in girlfriend.

Rob knew what she was thinking. "She took up with your dad, and you hold that against her, and that's natural, but she was on Marty's back a lot about his lifestyle."

"It didn't stop him, though, did it?" Stephanie didn't want to hear that some other woman had succeeded where her mother had failed.

"No, but it slowed him down. Without her, he'd have been out on the street, and he wouldn't have liked that."

Stephanie lifted a limp hand, then let it fall back against the bed. "So what's the problem?"

"A Marty with a conscience could be dangerous. A lot of people would've had to run for the border if Marty Walker ever started talking. Marty liked to collect secrets. I don't know how he did it, but he could talk anyone into telling him anything."

"What about blackmail?" She had to ask the question that had been burning at the back of her mind.

Rob looked suddenly alert. "You mean besides what he tried to pull with Brad?"

"How did you find out about Marty and Brad?"

He grinned. "Monica told me. Marty owed some gambling debts to people who wouldn't think twice about rearranging his face. Monica paid the debts, and I gave Marty a good talking to, and I didn't figure he would try that again."

"But what if he did and that's the reason he was killed?"

He fished a second toothpick out of his pocket and stuck it in his mouth. "Sure, it's something to think about. It's almost a done deal the guy was a threat to someone he knew real well. You don't usually find random killings in the victim's private quarters. Particularly when the quarters are on the third floor and you have to walk past a reception desk to get there. That pretty well rules out someone just passing by."

"So you think one of us killed him?"

"I don't know what I think at this point, but I don't want to overlook anything important just because I know the people involved."

Monica arrived and put an end to the conversation. Today, she wore jeans and an Irish-green hand-knit turtleneck. She looked about twenty-five, and she was in her dictator mode. "You can leave now, Rob. I'm going to help Stephanie get dressed."

Rob got to his feet. "We're through here anyway, and she's raring to go. Had all the hospital she wants. Talk to you later, Steph."

Monica started pulling clothes off the hangers, bringing them to the bedside before the door shut behind Rob. "Bet you'll be glad to leave. Lance is bringing a chair. He'll be here in a minute."

"A wheelchair! No way. We did that last night. I can walk."

"Of course you can, but there's no need to. Don't argue, Stephanie."

"Why are you in such a hurry to take me back to the lodge?"

She laughed. "Don't be so suspicious. It's just that I can look after you better at home, and Rob's taking his guard away this morning. You'll be safer at the lodge."

"I was at the lodge when someone hit me on the head, remember?"

"What's the matter, don't you trust us?" She picked up Stephanie's jacket and helped her into it.

"A whack on the head helps one see things in a different light. I'm a little more cautious now."

"I can understand that, but I think we can keep you safe."

"The way you kept Marty safe?" Stephanie regretted the words the minute they were out of her mouth.

Monica's normal color faded to a dirty gray. "I didn't know Marty was in danger. I realize you blame me for his death, but I would never have hurt him. When the person who killed my husband is caught, I will do everything in my power to see that he pays."

"Fair enough," Stephanie muttered. "I shouldn't have said that."

Lance arrived with the wheelchair. "Ready to go?"

Stephanie met him look for look. "I don't need that chair. Just give me your arm and I can walk."

He grasped her shoulders and helped her off the bed and into the chair. "Easier this way."

She frowned up at him. "You're a lot like your mother, you know that? Neither one of you hears anything you don't want to hear."

"Probably so." Lance pushed the chair toward the door, and Monica followed.

Stephanie knew she was being rude and cranky, but her head hurt. Her memory appeared to be defective at times, and underneath it all, she was scared. Her boring life in Independence was looking better every day.

Lance had brought the Lincoln, a far cry from the hard-used Ford pickup he usually drove. Monica got in the front passenger side, and Stephanie settled against the cushioned comfort of the backseat and closed her eyes. Her thoughts whirled like a hamster on a wheel. Until she got her strength back, she was vulnerable, and she didn't really know these people. Suddenly the hospital seemed a lot safer than the lodge. After all, that's where she had been when someone attacked her.

Lance stopped in front of the main entrance, and Stephanie opened the car door and started to get out. He hurried around to grip her elbow.

"It's possible to be too stubborn."

She rolled her eyes at him and made a face. "I am not stubborn."

"Right. You're just determined."

He started to lift her up the steps, and her eyes locked with his. "Don't even think about it."

He grinned. "Now, now. Be nice."

A wheelchair waited at the top of the steps, and Monica steadied it, then opened the door for them. Lance pushed the chair through the lobby, and a woman who looked strangely familiar approached them, but Brad cut her off. She looked so disappointed that it caught Stephanie's attention. Lance stopped in front of the elevator, the door opened, and he pushed the chair inside. Monica punched the button, and the door closed.

Stephanie gripped the chair arms. "Take me back to the lobby. I want to talk to that woman."

Monica ignored her, snapping at Lance. "I thought I told you to keep her out of sight."

"What'd you want me to do? Lock her in her room?"

The elevator jarred to a stop, and Monica went ahead to open the door to the suite. She led the way into the bedroom, switching on the table lamp and turning back the bedspread. "Your head hurts, doesn't it?"

"Yes, but . . . ."

"She'll still be here when you wake up. I promised the doctor you'd go straight to bed." Monica motioned for Lance to leave. "Take your shoes off and I'll get your pills."

Stephanie eased down on the bed, but her thoughts were still on the woman in the lobby. A niggling little doubt intruded. Monica and Lance hadn't been surprised to see her. In fact they'd known she would be here. Lance was supposed to keep her out of sight. A hard certainty came from somewhere. That woman had a claim on her father, and Monica had known. And put her name in the obituary.

"You knew!" the words burst from her with the violence of wind-driven hail. "You wrote the obituary."

Monica stood in the bathroom doorway with a glass of water in her hand, frowning. "Knew what?"

"That other daughter. . .the one in the obituary."

"Of course I knew. What difference does it make?"

"What *difference*? I can't believe you said that." Of course it made a difference. She'd had to share her father with the whole country, but in a private way he'd always been hers. She was special. His only daughter. Now this stranger threatened even that.

Monica took a prescription bottle from her purse, shook a small white tablet into the palm of her hand, and held it out. "Here. Take this."

"What is it?" Bitter anger coursed through Stephanie's veins as hot and swift as lightning. A knife-edge of pain stabbed behind her eyes. She tried to think what to do next, but her mind wouldn't work right.

"It's your pain pill. See." Monica held up the bottle. "Go on. Take it."

Stephanie wanted to refuse, but suddenly the anger was

gone, leaving only the pain, surging in red-hot waves through her head. Out of strength and too tired and emotionally drained to argue, she put the pill in her mouth and washed it down with a gulp of water.

Monica looked down at her. "Don't try to talk right now. You need to rest."

Exhaustion washed over Stephanie as she sagged against the bed. She heard Monica leave, but she was too tired to care. She tried to stay awake, drifting in and out of consciousness, but sleep closed over her like dark water.

10

Brad sat at the family table, nursing a cup of coffee. Lance joined him, carrying a cup of his own. Without asking, he pulled out a chair and sat down. "You see our new guest?"

"How could I miss her?" Brad sipped cautiously at the hot liquid. "They sure look alike, don't they?"

Lance looked surprised. "You think so?"

"Don't you?" Where were the man's eyes?

Lance shrugged. "Stephanie's all right, I guess, but that Heather's a knockout."

Brad suppressed a grin. So it was like that, was it? Well, to each his own. For his money Stephanie was the best-looking woman to hit these parts in a long time. He brought the conversation around to what was foremost in his mind. "Who do you think is behind our recent crime wave?"

Lance stirred sugar into his coffee. "I figured Marty had crossed the wrong guy, but that doesn't explain the attack on Stephanie. You got any ideas?"

"Not yet, but I'm working on it."

"You be careful." Lance warned. "This isn't anything you need to get involved in."

"You mean my past might catch up with me?"

Lance held up his hand, palm out in a placating gesture. "I'm just saying don't brush it off. The law don't always work the way it's supposed to."

"Which is exactly why I need to get involved. I don't want any mistakes this time." For either him or Stephanie. A cold knot of fear settled in Brad's stomach. He would do all he could to keep her safe. He just hoped it would be good enough.

* * *

Loralee knocked on Stephanie's door, bringing lunch. The denim dress and the orange scarf she wore at her neck made her look washed-out. She placed the tray on the coffee table in the sitting room.

Stephanie eyed the grilled chicken and salad with loathing. "I don't want anything. I'm not hungry."

Loralee sat down in one of the chairs, smoothing her skirt. "You'd better eat. Marty's lawyer called. He's coming at two o'clock to read the will. Besides, your long lost sister is pacing the floor, waiting to see you."

"My what?" Stephanie stared, bewildered. The fog cleared. "That redhead. She claimed to be my sister?"

Loralee shook her head. "If you're thinking she's an impostor, don't. She has her birth certificate listing Marty as her father. Quite a family reunion, don't you think?"

Stephanie frowned. A birth certificate? That sounded awfully definite. "What's her name?"

Loralee absently took a cracker and bit into it. "Heather. Are you sure you didn't know anything about her? Was she close to Marty?"

"He never mentioned her to me." Stephanie decided she didn't want to talk to Loralee about this. Whatever the outcome, it was Walker family business, and she'd never been one to talk about private matters.

She eased off the couch and stood up. "If I have to go downstairs, I need to change clothes. We can talk later."

Loralee raised her eyebrows, but she left, and Stephanie locked the door against any more visitors. She needed to shower and get ready for her meeting with Marty's lawyer . . . and her new sister. The sister she didn't want and wasn't ready to accept.

She didn't expect much from the will. Money never stuck to Marty's fingers for very long.

She peered at the bathroom mirror, making a face at her matted, dirty hair. She wasn't sure whether she was supposed to wash it or not, and she didn't really care. She wanted a shower too much to worry about her head. With the water adjusted to a warm, gentle spray, she leaned against the wall and let her fears wash down the drain. For a little while she could forget that someone had tried to kill her.

Feeling refreshed after her shower, she choked down a few bites of chicken and some salad before going down to join the others. The elevator glided smoothly enough, but she grunted with pain when it jarred to a stop. They were all gathered in the family part of the dining room, drinking coffee. Heather was a surprise, reminding Stephanie of a puppy, eager to be liked but not sure of her welcome.

She smiled tentatively. "Hello, Stephanie. I'm Heather, Marty's other daughter."

"So I hear." What should she say to a stranger who claimed to be a sister? This would have been easier if they'd had a chance to meet in private. Having people watching hampered any display of emotion. She waited helplessly for words to come, words that would bridge the awkward situation and put everyone at ease. Her mind was blank.

Heather flushed. "I hope you're feeling better."

"Yes, I am, thank you."

Brad pulled out a chair for Stephanie, and she sank gratefully into it, glad for a respite from that direct gaze of the woman who claimed to be her sister.

"How's the head?" he asked.

"I know it's there." She tried not to stare at Heather, which left her looking at Brad and the concern in his eyes.

"The doctor says you're all right?"

"He seems to think so."

He frowned. "I'd like something more conclusive."

"Well, he released me, so I guess I'll live." She glanced around the table at the others, making an effort to appear casual, although the close proximity to Brad was playing havoc with her desired level of cool. What was it about the man that made her feel all fluttery and warm inside?

Her roving gaze stopped at the stranger in their midst. Looking at Heather was like peering into a clouded mirror and seeing her own image. No point in trying to deny they had a strong resemblance, but a part of her still rebelled at having to share Marty with this woman who had just appeared out of nowhere.

Lance seemed to be trying to make their new guest feel welcome, and Kate sat beside Heather, hanging on to her every word, which was surprising, since Lance's daughter wasn't quick to accept anyone. Occasionally Heather would smile at the little girl, and Kate would sort of shine, as if they shared a secret. Neither Heather nor Lance glanced in Stephanie's direction. Evidently Stephanie had been dismissed.

Loralee sat to one side, watching them and wearing a brooding expression, her eyes flicking from Lance to Heather. Stephanie realized she'd never seen her pay much attention to Kate. As crazy as she seemed to be about Tara, you'd think the woman would show some interest in her cousin's daughter.

Mac leaned over Monica and said something too low to be overheard. She nodded, drained the last of her coffee, and stood up. "Shall we go to the library? I believe Tom Allison, Marty's lawyer, has arrived."

They filed into the elevator, and Stephanie was conscious of Brad's arm brushing hers. She was definitely aware of his presence, more than she liked to admit. It seemed she couldn't turn around without bumping into him. Was he following her? And would she mind if he did? The elevator doors opened, and Monica exited and turned toward the library.

Tom Allison, a small, thin man with a surprisingly deep voice, greeted everyone and waited until Brad and Stephanie took the last two remaining chairs.

He opened his briefcase and spread out the papers on the desk. "Marty made a new will in November." He peered at Monica over his gold-framed eyeglasses. "I assume you were aware of that."

She nodded, and he continued. "He called a while back, wanting to change a couple of things, but he never got around to it. So we will have to go with this one. If you're ready, I'll read it to you."

There was the usual statement about being of sound mind and the revoking of any previous wills or codicils. It directed for the prompt payment of his burial expense. Monica wiped away tears at that point.

The lawyer cleared his throat and waited for their complete attention. "He leaves Brad Wilson and Lance Harrington each a wildlife print of their choice, and his apologies for any problems he may have caused them."

Brad grunted in surprise, and Lance looked as if someone had hit him. Obviously they hadn't expected anything, and Stephanie wondered why Marty had left something so valuable to men who hadn't liked him and made no bones about it. She knew what those prints cost—anywhere from three thousand to five thousand dollars. Her father had spent extravagantly on his collection, more than he ever bothered to spend on his wife and daughter. Loralee got his jade cuff links and a print. He left Kate five thousand dollars for being his friend, and his two daughters split forty thousand down the middle.

Well, that settled it. She had a sister. Stephanie gripped her hands tightly in her lap, hoping no one could see how upset she was and think it was all about money. For some reason, Marty had chosen to keep this daughter a secret.

Another, more hurtful thought occurred. Maybe Heather hadn't been all that much of a secret. Monica knew about her. Maybe everyone else did too. Everyone but her? *Marty, why did you leave a problem like this for me to deal with?* She had thought he couldn't do any more to hurt her. She'd been wrong.

The last item brought an exclamation of pain from Monica. He left her the balance of his wildlife prints, all future royalties from his music, and the contents of a certain carved oak chest. He also left her his love.

Monica faced the others with tears streaming down her cheeks. "I didn't know about this. The royalties ought to go to his daughters. I'll do something about that."

"No." Heather stood up, gripping the back of her chair. "I never knew my father. He left me more than I expected, and I'm grateful. If he wanted the royalties to go to you, then that's what I want."

"You don't know how much they bring in," Lance said.

Heather tilted her chin. "I don't care. If Marty wanted Monica to have them, that's the way it should be."

Stephanie felt a faint twinge of respect for this new sister. If she was here just for the money, she wouldn't have been foolish enough to turn her back on the royalties from Marty's songs. She needed to make her own position clear. "I agree. If that's what Marty wanted, that's the way it should be."

"What about this chest?" Loralee demanded.

Tom Allison looked at Monica, but she shook her head. "I

don't know anything about it. I've never seen a chest that meets that description."

"If it's in the lodge, it'll turn up somewhere." Brad sounded like the bequest had shaken him. They sat in silence, like people who had nothing to say yet not wanting to be the first to leave.

Mr. Allison broke the silence by expressing his sympathy to Monica, then shook hands all around and left.

Everyone else drifted out of the room, until Monica and Stephanie were alone. She handed her stepmother a box of tissues and sat down on the couch. Although her head had started throbbing again, she had some questions, and Marty's wife was the lady with the answers.

When Monica stopped crying, Stephanie was ready for her. "How long have you known about Heather?"

"Marty told me about her four weeks ago. If I'd known earlier, I would've done something to help her. She's had a hard life."

That answered one of her questions anyway. He'd kept Heather a secret from his wife too. "Hard like what?"

Monica blew her nose. Her fans had probably never seen the Queen of Country Music with a red nose and tear-swollen eyes. "Heather's mother died when she was just a baby. An aunt and uncle raised her. I gathered from what Tom said that they kept her more out of duty than love."

"I see." And she did. Her mother had been strict, but Stephanie had never doubted her affection. She began to feel sorry for Heather, something she wanted to avoid because she had a hunch this new sister would want to be part of a family, and she wasn't ready for that.

"Why wasn't she at the funeral?"

"I tried to locate her, but she wasn't home. She showed up last night, and of course we asked her to stay."

"Oh, of course." Loralee had it right. This was definitely a family reunion. Stephanie rubbed her head. She wasn't up to handling all of these surprises.

"Why this change of heart from Marty? He had very little time for me, and evidently he had even less time for Heather. Why this business of the will?"

"I think he felt guilty about the way he'd neglected his daughters." Monica pushed her hair away from her face, using both hands. Tears beaded her eyelashes. "Marty was trying to get away from his previous lifestyle. I know old habits die hard, but I believe that with God's help, he would have done that if he'd lived."

Stephanie shrugged impatiently. Talk about irrelevant. "I never knew Marty to care much about God."

"Marty changed. I know it's hard to believe, but God had become an important part of his life. He became a Christian shortly before he wrote the new will."

"He what?" Stephanie gasped, feeling like the breath had been sucked out of her lungs. Selfish, egotistical Marty, a Christian? Monica had to be making this up. But then Stephanie remembered the Bible in his room.

Monica wiped her eyes and slumped against the couch as if exhausted, and Stephanie put the subject of Marty's conversion aside. It wasn't anything she had to deal with right now. She had more important questions to ask. "How did you feel when you learned about Heather?"

"I was surprised, of course, but she was born before I met Marty, so it didn't really matter."

Stephanie blinked. The words hit her like a blow to the stomach. "How old is Heather?"

Monica's blue eyes flashed with sympathy. "She's four years younger than you."

"I was just four years old and he was already cheating?" Ignoring the pain shooting through her head, Stephanie struggled to her feet, wanting to run away from everyone, try to hide her hurt the way she had done for all the years she had been Marty's daughter.

"Don't, Stephanie. It happened a long time ago. It doesn't matter now."

"Yes it *does!*" Her head throbbed, but the emotions assaulting her heart hurt even more.

"Listen to me!" Monica grabbed her shoulders. "He never talked about Heather, It was always you. I heard so much about you I was sick of the sound of your name. He did love you."

"Then why did he leave us?" It was a cry from the heart. They stared at each other, the question hanging between them. Monica started to speak, stopped, and started again, her voice faltering, then gaining in strength.

"Love isn't always enough. Two people can be in love and still tear each other apart. I don't know why it's like that, but I do know it is." She pulled Stephanie down on the couch beside her. "I'm the last person in the world who should talk to you about this, but I want you to listen. Your mother was a good woman, but she was the wrong woman for Marty. If you wanted to hold him, you had to learn to look the other way."

"My mother would never do that."

"No, she wouldn't do that, so she lost him. Living with Marty wasn't a romantic dream, if that's what you believe. Sometimes, I think your mother was the lucky one. She got out. I never could."

"Didn't you care what you did to us?"

Monica stared at her, stricken. Tears pooled in her eyes, her lips trembled. "I didn't at first, but then it ate at me. I lived with my sins for a long time."

"Lived? Like in the past? What about now?"

"What I did to you will never be all right. I tried to run away from it, until I almost had a breakdown. I finally had to face the wrongs I'd done to you and to your mother. God has forgiven me, Stephanie. I hope you can."

Monica buried her face in her hands. Her shoulders shook with sobs.

Stephanie struggled with her own emotions, thinking of her mother, of the silent grief that had turned Bess Walker into a shadow of her former self. She thought of the days, the months, the years she had spent yearning for a father. She had hated this woman, but she couldn't help a faint quiver of pity. Marty had left a lot of damaged lives behind, but perhaps Monica was the most damaged of all.

11

Brad sat on his couch and stared at the print of an eagle coming in for a landing. A legacy from Marty? Who'd have thought the guy would leave him anything? He'd even accompanied it with what amounted to an apology.

Monica claimed that Marty had become a Christian. A tough tale to swallow, but Brad knew that God could change even the most hardened sinner, so he had to admit it could have happened. What else could explain that print hanging on his wall?

He picked up his Bible and thumbed idly through it. He had another problem. For some time he'd felt that God was nudging him in a direction he didn't want to go. He knew God called out men to preach His Word. He just didn't think he should be one of them.

A disbarred lawyer, an ex-con, standing behind the pulpit telling everyone else how to live? He could get his license reinstated, of course, but he'd turned his back on the law, feeling it had let him down. Now he just wanted to live as quietly as possible. But God wouldn't let him alone.

He walked to the window, watching a cardinal eating sunflower seeds from the feeder he'd made. This was where he belonged. He couldn't get up in front of people and preach. His chest got tight every time he thought about it.

And there was Stephanie. At night when he sat by the fire, he liked to imagine her sitting beside him with Caesar sleeping on the hearth. He hoped in time she would get over her fixation about her parents' marriage. Maybe she would eventually see him as someone with whom she could share her life.

* * *

Stephanie headed for the kitchen to pick up a couple of blueberry muffins, planning to skip breakfast this morning. She had some thinking to do, and the outdoors called her. The path to Brad's cabin lay inviting in the morning sun. She thought about following it but couldn't come up with a reason for an early-morning visit, unless he could provide a dose of reality. She was still reeling from the brutality of Marty's death. Add the attack on her and now the unexpected and unwanted complication of Heather and she had about reached the point of no return. Surely nothing more could happen.

Her growing attraction to Brad Wilson was another problem, although she had trouble understanding why she would be attracted to an ex-con who had suspected her of being involved in her father's death. She guessed there was no accounting for tastes.

She almost made it to the stables before a voice called her

name. A quick glance over her shoulder revealed Heather hurrying down the path, her bright hair gleaming in the early-morning sun. Stephanie sighed. Why wasn't this new addition sitting at the family table with the rest of the gang?

She needed some time alone, and she had a feeling her new sister would be hard to shake. Putting off this meeting wouldn't make it any easier, though, so she might as well get it over with. Even though she was aware that her attitude might seem childish and petty, she still resented Heather. Part of that resentment stemmed from the way she had learned about Marty's other daughter. If she had known when she was young that she had a sister, it wouldn't have been such a shock. A new thought intruded. Had her mother known?

Stephanie stopped and faced her pursuer, forcing herself to be civil. "Good morning."

Heather paused for breath. "Is it all right if I join you?"

"You already have." Stephanie pointed out the obvious, but after seeing the hurt in Heather's eyes, she felt ashamed. "I'm sorry. I'm not at my best this morning."

"That's all right. I understand."

"No, you don't. I don't understand, myself. My life is getting complicated, and I'm not coping well."

"And I'm one of the complications?"

Unable to give Heather the answer she wanted, and ashamed of her own surliness, Stephanie handed her a muffin as way of compensation. "How do you like the lodge?"

Heather's expression lit up like a Roman candle. "I love it. I'm going to ask Lance for a job."

"Okay, if that's what you want." Definitely not something Stephanie wanted to have in her future. She started walking again, slanting sideway looks at Heather.

They were the same height, had the same coppery hair. Heather's complexion was the soft ivory of heavy cream, while her own was dusted with a generous handful of freckles. From a distance it would be difficult to tell them apart.

Heather smiled, her expression suddenly shy. "We look alike, don't we? I'm glad. I've never felt like I belonged anyplace."

"There must be a family somewhere that you're a part of, isn't there?"

"Not really." Heather shoved her hands into her pockets, her eyes on the horizon. "My mother's sister raised me, but she didn't want me."

"Why not?"

Heather flushed. "Aunt Flora thought my mother was sinful and I was the byproduct of that sin. I thought about taking the money Marty left and paying her back every cent she had spent on me, but then I changed my mind."

"You said you never knew Marty. Did you ever meet him?"

"No. I always wanted to, but you know how it is. He never made any effort to see me, so I wouldn't have felt right just calling him up."

"He knew about you, though, because he told Monica."

"Oh, yes. He knew. Once in a while he'd send money, but not all that often."

"Yeah, I know about that. Not regular enough so you could count on it."

"At least you knew him." Heather kicked a rock out of the path. "He cared enough to acknowledge you."

"He was married to my mother," Stephanie reminded. "He lived with us until I was seven."

"And my mother was just a passing fancy."

Stephanie listened for a hint of bitterness, but Heather sounded rather matter-of-fact.

"When did you learn you were Marty Walker's daughter?" Stephanie asked.

"I guess I've always known. I knew about you too. Aunt Flora made sure I knew about the family who didn't want me."

"That's terrible. Why would she do that?"

Heather shrugged. "Aunt Flora was pretty religious. Not a loving, caring kind of religion, but kind of rigid. Judgmental. She felt like my mother had disgraced the family name. Mom died when I was a little over a year old, and there wasn't anyone else to raise me, so my aunt got stuck with me. I guess she resented me from the beginning."

"I'm sorry." Stephanie couldn't imagine anyone blaming a child for the sins of the parents."

"I survived." Heather rejected Stephanie's sympathy. "As soon as I graduated from high school I left. I haven't been back since."

They reached the lake, and Stephanie sat down on a boulder. Heather tossed a rock into the water, then turned to sit on a limestone slab. "I know I'm a surprise to you, probably an unpleasant one. If it hadn't been for me, you'd have all of Marty's money. I won't interfere in your life. I just want us to be friends."

It sounded like a rehearsed speech. Stephanie looked across at the dark points of cedar and the newly leafed oak trees covering the opposite shore. A hungry fish shattered the surface of the water. Morning mist, fragile as a bridal veil, rose to meet the slanting rays of the sun. This new sister had endured a lot, and Stephanie felt guilty for having had so much when Heather had been left with nothing. She thought about how to answer, slowly feeling her way.

"Legally we're sisters, Heather. I don't want your share of Marty's money, but I agree we should get better acquainted. Just don't expect too much from me at first."

"I won't."

Stephanie cringed inside. Heather's look of happy anticipation made it clear she would. She couldn't help herself. Leave it to Marty. The least he could have done was to introduce his two daughters to each other. It would have spared them this awkwardness.

Heather leaned forward, her eyes compelling. "Tell me about our father."

Stephanie raked her fingers through the small, water-smoothed rocks littering the shoreline, trying to find a nice way to put it. "Marty had the smile of a choirboy and the heart of a con man. His motto was move fast and travel light."

"Why did he remember us in his will?"

"According to Monica, he'd found God."

Heather actually glowed. "I'm so glad. I never had the chance to get to know him here, but now I'll meet him in heaven. Thank you for telling me that."

Well, great. It looked like every member of the family was a believer except her. "It doesn't sound like you've had such a wonderful life. Why didn't God help you?"

"He did help me." Heather's voice held that confidence that Stephanie had never understood and halfway suspected as being phony. "Every day of my life. How do you think I found the strength and the will to survive? The day I accepted Jesus as my Savior was the day I really started to live. Aren't you a Christian, Stephanie?"

She wasn't ready to answer that. Her beliefs were no one's business. "If you're going to stay here, you need to remember there's still a killer out there."

"Why would anyone hurt me?"

"Someone hit *me*. At least you weren't here when Marty was murdered, so you're not a suspect."

Heather looked uncomfortable.

"You *were* here!"

Heather kept her attention turned toward the horizon as if searching for inspiration . . . or weighing her options. "I received a letter from his attorney. It seems, after all these years, Marty was curious about his number-two daughter. I decided to check him out, and I was in the dining room having dinner when the police arrived."

Stephanie grinned at her discomfort. "Welcome to the list of suspects. Does Sheriff Rob know you were here?"

"No. Are you going to tell him?"

"I won't, but someone will. You had to order a meal; the waitress saw you. You paid for your dinner; the cashier saw you. Did you have a car?"

Heather nodded. "The parking lot attendant saw me. I'd better tell him myself."

"Either that or hope no one will remember."

"No. I don't want to lie, and hiding the truth is a form of lying, isn't it? Besides, I didn't have a motive."

In spite of her better judgment, Stephanie was beginning to like this new sister. "You did have a motive. You were in the will, and Mr. Allison was making inquiries about you."

Heather looked appalled, and Stephanie laughed. "That's irony for you. Probably the nicest thing he ever did for either of us, and now we're suspected of killing him."

A voice sounded from behind them. "There you are. I've been looking for you."

They whirled at the sound. Kate approached across the rocky shoreline. "You promised to walk with me this morning."

Heather got to her feet. "I'm sorry. I forgot. We can go now if you like."

"Do you want to come?" Kate asked Stephanie.

"I don't think so. Enjoy your walk."

"We will." She reached for Heather's hand. "Come on. I want to show you where the spring beauties grow."

Stephanie watched them walk away to search for the pink blossoms of the spring beauties. Prickly little Kate had accepted Heather. Like recognized like. They had each known rejection.

Stephanie stared out across the lake, thinking of her new sister and the story of her past. So she had grown up without a father. At least she'd had a mother's love, not like Heather, who knew that no one wanted her.

The question Heather had asked bothered her. No, she wasn't a Christian. She didn't hate God or anything like that. She knew He existed, but somehow they'd never gotten together. She walked back to the lodge feeling she'd missed out on something important.

The family wing was deserted, and on an impulse Stephanie tried the door to Lance's suite. The knob turned easily, and after a quick glance around, she stepped inside.

The rooms reflected his taste: beige carpet, off-white walls, brown leather couch and chairs. A Navajo blanket in a pattern of red, black, white, and gray hung on one wall. A large, bronze figurine of a bucking bronco, the rider swinging his hat in a molded display of exuberance, sat on a low table of dark wood.

Stephanie doubted whether Lance owned anything small or dainty enough to fit the key hanging on a chain around her neck, but it wouldn't hurt to look. A quick search revealed nothing interesting. No small cabinets or chests. If Lance had anything to hide, he apparently didn't keep it in his suite.

Photos of Kate and Monica were scattered through the sitting room and bedroom. No picture of Tara, his wife, though. Which said precisely what? Nothing as far as she could tell. If Tara had lived up to her reputation, Lance probably had plenty of reasons not to display her picture.

The quiet of the suite got to her. She wasn't the kind to sneak around among someone's personal effects. All she wanted right now was to get out of there before she got caught in Lance Harrington's rooms. She blushed at the thought.

Stephanie eased the door open a crack and then quickly closed it again at the sight of the tall, aristocratic man hurrying toward the stairs. She counted to ten before checking to see if all was clear, but she had something new to add to her list of unanswered questions: What was Clyde Andrews doing in Tara's room?

Later, dressed in jeans and a sweater, Stephanie sat down on the couch to try to figure out who had killed Marty. Scribbling notes about where everyone was at the time proved useless, since she didn't have enough information. She tried listing motives.

Monica? According to Loralee, Marty had cheated with his daughter-in-law, although Monica had denied it. Motive for murder? She hesitated before putting a check mark beside Monica's name as a possible suspect. It wouldn't be the first time a ticked off wife had killed a cheating husband.

Lance? Practically the same motive as Monica. Brad? No known motive. The blackmail attempt was a washout, but he sure didn't like Marty. Clyde? Ditto.

Mac seemed to have tolerated him better than the others, but that could be an act to divert suspicion from him.

Loralee? Who could guess? Maybe she knew more about Tara's disappearance than she was telling and Marty found out. Heather had been in the area, and she had a strong reason to resent the father who had rejected her.

Stephanie read her notes, which provided motives for everyone except Kate. As a detective, she was a definite bust. She yawned and leaned back against the cushions, trying to focus on what she knew about the people in the lodge, but her eyes kept closing.

The notebook slid off her lap, crashing to the floor. She snapped awake, every nerve sharpened, every muscle tense. The silence of her suite mocked her, but still she waited, locked in the suspended state between dreaming and reality. Finally, her breathing slowed to normal. She picked up the notebook and slid her hand down between the back and the seat of the couch, trying to retrieve the pen before it stained the soft peach fabric. Cold, sharp steel sliced her fingers. She jerked her hand back, staring at the blood flowing from a fresh cut.

Stephanie probed with her other hand and found a cloth-wrapped bundle. She pushed back the soft folds to reveal an ivory-handled, thin-bladed knife, which she immediately recognized. Marty's letter opener. He'd bought it at a craft festival in Independence. The carved handle was encrusted with a dark stain that had pooled in the crevices. She looked up to see Loralee standing in the doorway.

"That's Marty's knife! *You* had it. No wonder Rob couldn't find it."

"No, that's not true! Someone hid it in the couch."

"Don't bother. I'm not the one you have to convince."

Loralee whirled away from the door, and Stephanie heard her footsteps pounding down the stairs. The only reason Rob hadn't arrested her was the absence of a murder weapon. Well, he had one now. She could hear them rushing up the stairs. Lance filled the doorway, blocking off escape. Behind him Stephanie saw Loralee and Brad.

"I didn't do it," she stammered. "You have to believe me."

The condemnation in their faces was as cold and as final as a prison door slamming shut.

12

Lance used the phone in Stephanie's suite to call the sheriff's office. When he hung up, he spoke to Brad. "He'll be here in a few minutes. Don't disturb anything."

Stephanie braced her hands on the arm of the chair. "I didn't *have* that knife. Why won't you believe me?"

"It's not that we don't want to believe you," Lance said. "But look at the evidence."

"Any one of you could have planted that knife on me." She heard the panic in her voice and tried to control it, but fear filled her chest in a rising tide that threatened to drown her.

Brad took the chair across from Stephanie, keeping his voice low, but the others could still hear him. He caught her hands in his. "Calm down now. You need to be alert."

She nodded, seeing the concern in his eyes.

He leaned closer. "Look at me. You're innocent. You don't have to be afraid."

"That coming from you? You were innocent, and you went to prison." She stared at him, wide-eyed, suddenly aware of what she had just said.

"That was different."

She could see the anxiety in his expression. "No, it wasn't," she cried. "I was there. I had blood on me. The knife was in my room. Just the way it was with you."

Brad brushed her hair off her forehead. "Take it easy. No one's going to frame you. Trust me."

Trust him? He was the one who first pointed the finger of suspicion at her. How could she trust him? She clung to his hands anyway, drawing strength from his presence.

He lowered his voice almost to an inaudible murmur. "Listen to me. Someone put that knife there. I'm going to find out who did it. I promise you I'll dig out the truth."

She wet her lips. "You'll help me?"

"All I can. You tell Rob exactly what happened."

She nodded and listened as the elevator door slid open and then closed. Rob entered, looking grim. He barred them from her suite, and they gathered in Lance's office.

Lance dropped into his desk chair, but the sheriff stopped him. "I'll talk to Stephanie alone. I'll call when I need you."

"Now see here, Rob . . ." Brad protested.

The sheriff cut him off. "I'll get to you later. I want to talk to her, and I aim to do it without any help. And stay away from her rooms. My men will be working there."

They left protesting.

Rob lowered his bulk into the chair behind the desk. "Now. Where did you find the knife?"

"In the couch . . ." Her voice quavered. She stopped and

started over. "It was hidden in the couch. I didn't put it there."

"I didn't say you did." Rob shifted his weight, and the chair squealed in protest, causing him to look momentarily startled. "You don't have any idea who could have?"

"Anyone could. The door wasn't locked, and even if it had been, I assume there are keys available."

"I would imagine so." He stared at the desktop, apparently thinking before indicating a chair on the far side of the room. "You sit over there. I'm going to call Loralee in and ask her some questions."

When Loralee entered, Stephanie watched her closely. You never knew where you were with this woman. Sometimes she was quiet and unassuming. Other times she was . . . different. Like that time in Tara's room. It was almost as if she had a split personality. Today was she was in one of her different moods?

Her eyes were bright with excitement. "I found Stephanie with the knife. She killed him. It's so obvious."

Stephanie leaped to her feet. "No, I didn't." She had to make them listen.

Rob pointed at her, his face stern. "You sit down and keep quiet, or I'll put you under guard in another room."

She sat, silent but seething, anger overcoming her fear.

Loralee smiled, her expression triumphant. "I opened the door to Stephanie's room, and she was just sitting there with the knife in her hand. Like it was a souvenir or something."

"You didn't knock on her door before you opened it?" Rob's voice showed nothing at all about what he thought.

Loralee didn't seem quite so sure of herself. "Of course I did, but she didn't answer."

"So you opened the door and walked in? Why?"

"Why? I don't know. I just did. Is that important?"

"What did you do then?"

"I ran to get Lance, of course."

"I see. And that's all you know about this?"

"What more do you want? Bonnie said Stephanie was spoiling for a fight when she arrived. Brad found her kneeling over Marty's body. She had the knife in her room." Loralee ticked the facts off on her fingers. "I'd think that would be enough to make an arrest."

"Maybe, maybe not," Rob said.

One of the other policemen came to the door, and the sheriff stepped outside to talk to him. When he came back he said, "Well, Stephanie, it looks like I'll have to take you with me. "I have some questions to ask."

Brad appeared in the doorway. "Aren't you moving a little too fast, Rob? She didn't have a knife in Marty's room. I ought to know. I was there."

"We found bloodstains inside her jacket," Rob said. "Looks like that's where she hid the knife."

Inside her jacket? How did blood get *inside* her jacket? Stephanie knew there were smears on the outside from where she had tried to help Marty, but *inside*? Like the knife, the bloodstains had to be a plant.

"I'll get her coat," Brad said. "It's cold outside."

"Wait a minute." Rob stopped him. "I can't let you take anything out of that room. Stephanie, did you have more than one jacket with you?"

"I had a brown suede and a green corduroy."

"Have you worn the green one since you got here?"

"Just the night I came."

"There's blood on the inside lining. Quite a bit on the outside, too. You got another coat in your car?"

"No. It's all right. I'll be fine." Her lips were stiff, barely forming the words. Held for questioning? How could this be happening to her?

"Here. Take mine." Brad thrust a denim jacket at her.

Stephanie took it, too numb to protest. Brad's looked worried. Stephanie stumbled after the sheriff. The deputy took her arm and escorted her through the lobby. From the looks on the faces of the people they met, she might as well have been in handcuffs.

They drove through the gate, Stephanie in the front seat with the deputy, and the sheriff seated behind. The crowd of reporters blocked their way, but most of them ran for their cars.

Stephanie fought back tears. She'd get a lawyer. No, she'd call Aunt Margaret. It was just possible this time she'd managed to find a problem her aunt couldn't fix. They reached the jail, and the reporters swarmed the car.

Rob spoke to the deputy. "Go around to the passenger door. I'll get on the other side of her. Don't answer any of their questions. I'll have a statement later."

He eased out of the car, yelling, "No comment! Stand back! Move out of the way!"

The reporters inched back from the car, still shouting questions. The deputy opened the door and helped Stephanie out.

Flashbulbs went off in her face. The sheriff grabbed her other arm, and between them they shoved her through the crowd. When she stumbled, they lifted her up, pushing her toward the door. She tried to keep her head down, letting her hair obscure her features. A blond-haired woman shoved a microphone at her face.

The sheriff knocked it back. "I said no comments," he roared.

They ignored him, pressing closer. The door to the jail opened, and the sheriff and deputy staggered inside, dragging Stephanie with them. Someone slammed the door, shutting out the clamor of the reporters. The silence hurt her ears. Rob led the way to a small room and offered her a chair. She fell into it, and he brought a glass of water.

"They're like a mob." Still shaken from running that gauntlet, Stephanie took a shuddering breath, her voice trembling.

Rob slumped down in a swivel chair behind the battered desk and gave her a few moments to calm down. "It's their job, but they kind of overdo it."

"That has to be the understatement of the year." She breathed deeply, counting to ten. Using both hands, she pushed her hair out of her eyes. "Now what?"

"Now we talk. I can't force you to tell me anything, but there are some things I need to get straight."

Was it a good idea for her to talk to Rob at this point? Someone was doing his best to frame her, and she didn't want to do anything to help him. If only there was someone she could trust for advice.

Rob waited, watching her.

"Can I stop the questions at any point and ask for a lawyer?"

"You got my word on it." He leaned forward, putting his elbows on the desk. "There's a lot I don't understand here. How long has it been since you've seen Marty?"

"Three years."

"That long?"

"Yes." She looked away from the question in his eyes, rejecting his pity. "You knew Marty. He gathered no moss."

"No, I guess not. That's part of the problem. I can't see how you could have been such a threat to him, or why after not seeing him for three years you would follow him down here and kill him. Doesn't make sense to me."

She waited, letting him talk it out. At this point nothing she said could possibly help.

"Another thing, it kind of hurts my pride to think you smuggled that knife out of Marty's bedroom and had it on you while I questioned you in Monica's suite. I'm a better cop than that. Or at least, I think I am."

"I didn't see that knife until today. I found it just like I told you."

"You say you'd been out of your room most of the morning. Did you see signs someone had searched your room? Anything out of order?"

Stephanie stopped to think, then shook her head. "Nothing I noticed."

Rob scribbled a few notes. "We talked to your neighbors. One in particular was very helpful."

Stephanie's mouth dropped open in shock. "You talked to my

neighbors about *what?*"

"Marty's visit, when he came, when he left, when you drove away to follow him."

"So my neighbors know I'm the prime suspect in a murder case? Thanks a lot."

"Well, now, no need to get your back up. One of them lives across the street. . . ."

"Mrs. McCleary," Stephanie said in resignation.

"Yeah, that's the lady. She confirmed what you told us."

Stephanie was only partly mollified. "I don't see why you had to talk to her. She's the biggest gossip in Independence."

Rob had a shrewd look in his eyes, and she realized he was studying her reaction. "I'm not in the habit of believing everything I'm told," he said. "You should have known we'd check it out."

"I've not had a lot of experience with the police. I'm just beginning to realize how much I've missed in life."

Rob grinned. "Don't be bitter."

"I do not find this funny."

He sobered. "Neither do I. But it's my job to ask questions."

"Ask someone who has the answers."

A deputy brought in a plastic bag and unpacked it, putting the items on the desk: her jacket, with a dirty brown smear on the green satin lining, and the knife.

Rob pointed at the knife. "You recognize it?"

She nodded. "Marty bought it in Independence on one of his visits home. It's actually a double-edged dagger, more weapon than letter opener."

"It made a good weapon, all right." He offered her coffee, and when she refused, he filled his cup and sipped gingerly at the tar-black liquid. "You weren't wearing that jacket when I talked to you that night. I wouldn't have missed seeing those bloodstains."

Stephanie thought back. "No. I took it off and dropped it on the floor. It had Marty's blood on it."

He nodded. "Thing is, every murderer leaves something at the scene of the crime, and he takes something away. In this case we know he took the knife, but a stabbing like this leaves a lot of blood. Some of it would have splashed on the murderer. You didn't have enough blood on you."

"What did he leave?"

He shook his head. "We don't know yet. The lab people are working on it. I couldn't tell you if I did, but DNA testing will bring out some surprising things—hair, fingernail clippings, fibers. They're all there. We just have to find the right source."

"You took samples from me." She remembered.

"I took samples from everyone."

"What if you don't find anything? Do I get elected in lieu of better evidence?"

"I've never railroaded anyone yet." He drained his coffee cup and pushed it aside.

There was the sound of voices in the outer room, and someone pushed open the door. A man she had never seen before entered and grinned at them.

The sheriff shoved back his chair. "You looking for someone, Harry?"

"I guess so, Rob. Brad Wilson retained me as Miss Walker's

attorney. I thought I'd join the party."

"Brad?" Rob looked thoughtful. "Now why do you suppose he did that?"

"He seemed to think she needed help, so I told him I'd do my best." He held out his hand. "Harry Patton, Miss Walker. Take my advice and don't talk to anyone until we have time to discuss the situation."

She took his hand and smiled, feeling relieved. He was tall and thin, balding, with hazel eyes and a wide, amiable smile. His jeans, black sweatshirt, and denim jacket weren't the garb she expected from an attorney, but she was glad to see him.

"You have a reason to hold her, Rob?" he asked.

"No, I guess not." The sheriff didn't seem too unhappy. "Looks like we're through for the day, Stephanie."

"Those reporters," Stephanie began. She'd rather spend the night in a cell than face them a second time.

"My car is close to the side door," Harry said. "We can go out that way. Maybe miss a few of them."

"Sure, I guess you can do that," Rob agreed. "I still have some questions I need answered."

Stephanie pulled Brad's jacket closer around her. "I didn't kill Marty. You need to look somewhere else for your answers."

"I'll look," he promised.

Stephanie waited until Harry was in the car with the passenger door open. Rob stuck his head out and looked around. "You'll make it if you run." He pushed her toward the road. "Go. Now."

A sharp-eyed reporter saw them. "There she is."

The shout sent chills up her spine. She leaped into the passenger seat, slamming the door as Harry spun out of the parking space.

He left her at the lodge. "Don't talk to the police about this case unless I'm there. All right?"

She nodded. "I really appreciate this, Mr. Patton. I'd like you to send your bill to me."

He grinned. "You'll have to take that up with Brad. He's the one who hired me."

He drove away, and she went inside. Clyde was sitting at the family table, and at first she started to walk on by, but then she changed her mind. He looked wary when she pulled out a chair and sat down.

"You're here? I thought Rob had arrested you."

The sleeves of Brad's jacket were too long, and Stephanie rolled them above her wrists. "Brad got me an attorney."

"Why would he do that?"

"I haven't a clue, but I intend to find out." He'd promised to help, but she hadn't expected that assistance to include hiring a lawyer.

"Loralee said you hid the knife in your room."

"Correction, someone *put* the knife in my room." Anger flicked across her nerve ends like an electric shock. She intended to find out who had tried to frame her. Rob had his investigation, and she had hers.

As far as she could tell, Tara's disappearance was the only major thing that had happened at the lodge. She thought of all she had heard about Clyde—proud, prude, starstruck. "We haven't had an opportunity to get acquainted. What do you do for a living?"

He looked startled. "I have an insurance office in Eureka. Why?"

"I just wondered. I didn't remember hearing anyone say." How did he have time to run a business and hang out here? "You know Tara?"

"Of course I know her. Why?"

She noticed with surprise the way his eyes shifted away from her. "I just wondered. No one seems to like her much. What did you think of her?"

"Why this interest in Tara? I shouldn't think she would be any of your business."

"I suppose I'm just curious." And getting more that way all the time.

A muscle in his face twitched. "We'd be better off if she never came back." He looked at his watch. "If you'll excuse me, I have to run."

He got to his feet, one hand gripping the back of his chair. "You like to ask questions, don't you? If you'll forgive me for saying so, that could be a dangerous habit."

She watched him walk away, thinking that Brad had been wrong. Clyde had known Tara very well, and he hadn't liked her.

Stephanie met Mac at the elevator. "You going upstairs?" he asked.

She nodded.

"Do me a favor? Take this tray up to Loralee?"

"What's the matter? Isn't she feeling well?"

He shrugged. "All I know is she called down and ordered it

delivered to her. We're shorthanded today."

"Sure, I'll be glad to help out. She's probably in one of her moods about Tara. She gets depressed at times." Stephanie had some questions to ask, and she wanted some straight answers.

"Yeah, whatever."

"What's that supposed to mean?"

"She didn't used to be so crazy about Tara."

"Absence makes the heart grow fonder."

"Or maybe guilt." He punched the up button and strode off without waiting for the elevator door to open.

Stephanie turned her head to watch Mac. What was eating *him*? What did Loralee have to feel guilty about? Stephanie recalled the long hours spent working in the office with Lance and the way Loralee seemed to resent Heather. Did she want Tara's husband for herself?

Loralee looked surprised when Stephanie knocked on the door and carried in the tray. "Are you waiting tables now? I thought Rob had arrested you."

"No, he took me in for questioning. Brad got me a lawyer, and Mac asked if I minded helping, so here I am." She set the tray down on a low table. "Are you all right?"

"I'm fine."

"You look upset." Actually she looked like she was about to burst out crying.

"Oh, I just get depressed sometimes."

Stephanie sat down in the rose-colored chair facing the couch. This room was a far cry from the elaborate suite Tara had created. It was comfortable enough but decorated with the same lack of taste Loralee showed in her dress. The blue couch and rose chairs, the blue print draperies, and the few scattered ornaments seemed to have been chosen haphazardly with no thought of harmony. However, three large photographs of Tara were prominently displayed.

"You seemed rather anxious for Rob to arrest me. Why?"

Loralee looked down at her hands. "I really thought at the time you were guilty."

"And now you don't? What changed?"

"Well. . . Brad seemed so sure you were innocent. I guess he persuaded me."

And turtles fly. Something was going on here, but Stephanie didn't have a clue what. "You practically accused me of murder, laid it out for Rob, told him he had all he needed to arrest me."

"Yes. . .I did all that. I was wrong." Loralee held out her hands, her expression beseeching. "I'm sorry, Stephanie. I want this nightmare to end. You were holding the knife, and I just jumped to a terrible conclusion. Please forgive me."

"Someone has been telling everyone I'm guilty. Was that you?"

Loralee shook her head, her eyes wide. "No, of course not. I would never do anything like that. Never."

Stephanie eyed her, not sure what to believe. She had an idea the apology was as phony as a three-dollar bill but decided not to pursue the discussion any further right now. Maybe later when she had calmed down some.

She let her eyes roam the room, looking for something that might fit the key hanging around her neck. Nothing seemed to jump out at her in the sitting room, and she couldn't think of a reason to visit the bedroom. She made a note to come back later when Loralee was working.

"Do you have any pictures of you and Tara together?"

Loralee stared at the photographs for a moment. "No, we never had our picture taken together."

"Oh. I thought perhaps . . . ."

"I never liked to have my picture taken, and what few I did have I destroyed."

"Why?"

"I don't know. Or yes, I guess I do. I hated my pictures, the way I looked."

Stephanie shot her an assessing glance. "Don't you ever look in a mirror? You're very pretty, you know."

Loralee's voice was hardly more than a whisper. "But I'm not Tara."

13

Stephanie went downstairs to breakfast the next morning, glad she could sit down to linen placemats and blue-and-white china instead of having breakfast in a jail cell. A low, green glass vase shaped like a cannonball held purple lilacs. She leaned close, breathing in their clean, spicy fragrance.

Brad joined her, carrying a cup of coffee and a Danish. "Got a minute?"

"All the time you need. Thanks for getting me an attorney. I'll reimburse you for expenses."

"That's okay. I haven't received a bill yet." He finished off the Danish in short order. "On second thought, let's get out of here. I want to talk to you without someone interrupting us."

"Where are we going?"

"My place. We won't be bothered there."

The air was brisk with the sun burning away the last wisps of fog. Fat, little white clouds played tag with the wind. A bed of pink tulips and grape hyacinths made a pool of color under a clump of white birch. Stephanie drew in a lung full of crisp, cold air, and almost strangled.

Brad pounded her on the back so enthusiastically she promptly lost what breath she had left. "What's the matter, city girl? Can't handle a little fresh air?"

"Let me alone." She wheezed, mopping the tears from her eyes between coughing spells. She was probably turning blue from lack of oxygen, but what did he care?

Brad pushed open the gate and dug the key out of his pocket. "Come on in and I'll fix you a cup of tea. That'll make you feel better."

He tossed a log on the fire and headed for the kitchen while she settled down on the couch in front of the fireplace. His Bible lay open on the coffee table, and she eyed it askance. Although she'd noticed it on her previous visit, the printed pages gave her an uneasy feeling, and she flipped the cover closed.

Caesar put his head in her lap and moaned with delight when she scratched behind his ears. She decided to get a dog of her own. A dog was always glad to see you and it didn't take much to make him happy. If more women kept a dog instead of a husband, the divorce rate would drop faster than the stock market on a rocky day.

Brad returned carrying a tray loaded with tea and sweet rolls. He wore a red plaid shirt and well-fitted jeans, and his smile and the light in his eyes when he looked at her blew away her theories about dogs and men. A dog was nice, but some things couldn't be replaced.

She chose a plump Bismark with a tangy raspberry filling. "If I keep eating like this, I won't be able to wear anything I own."

"You look fine to me." He squeezed lemon into his tea. "I like my women to have a little flesh on their bones."

"I am not one of your women."

"Just say the word and you can be," he invited.

She decided it was time to change the subject. "What did you want to talk about?"

He sobered. "About Marty. Someone killed him, and if you didn't," he held up a hand to still her outrage, "then someone here at the lodge is a murderer."

She shivered. That was the frightening part, that people who seemed so normal could do something so terrible.

Brad picked up an apple fritter and bit into it. "So let's talk about motives. Someone had a reason to kill him. Find the reason, and you've got your man. Let's start with you. Why did you come to the lodge, and how about giving the real reason for a change."

"I'm your first suspect, right?" She relented. "Oh well. I've already told Monica and the sheriff."

He raised his eyebrows when he heard about the necklace. "Rob know this?"

"Yes."

"And he hasn't arrested you? I can't believe it. I would have hauled you in first thing."

"Perhaps that's why he's the sheriff and you're just a list maker. Besides, he did haul me in, as you put it. That's why you got me the attorney."

He ignored that. "Let's try to figure it out. I was in the room with you, and I'm sure you didn't have that knife."

"But later it turns up in my room hidden in the couch."

"Where it would be easily found if someone like Rob looked for it."

"There's a flaw there," she pointed out. "Why would anyone search my room a second time?"

"I don't know, but I have a hunch that if you hadn't found that knife, Rob would have gotten an anonymous call. Are you *sure* you don't know something dangerous to the killer?"

She shook her head in exasperation. "What am I supposed to know? People keep asking me that, and I don't have an answer. I hadn't seen Marty for three years, and I'd never met any of you. I'm no threat to anyone."

"Because he came to Independence and you followed him down here. The murderer has to wonder why."

Put that way, she suddenly saw another option. "Try this. Suppose Marty told the person who killed him that he had talked to me about whatever the problem was."

Light dawned in Brad's eyes. "And if anything happened to him, you'd see that they got theirs. But wouldn't he have known he was putting you in danger?"

"Do you think he would have cared?"

"Not a whit. Self-preservation would come first."

She watched the flames flicker light across Caesar's dark brown coat. Brad waited, giving her time to think.

"We're back to where we started," she said. "I wish I knew his real reason for wanting me to come."

"Doesn't make sense. Nothing happened here."

"You have an extremely short memory. What about Tara?"

Brad stared at her. "Are you out of your mind? Tara's been gone for three years."

"No, but think about it. No one knows what happened to her. Loralee thinks . . ."

"I know all about what Loralee thinks, and Loralee is nuts. To hear her tell it, Tara is every man's dream."

"Wasn't she?"

"Not unless you're talking nightmare."

He refilled his cup and absently waved the earthenware teapot in her direction. She shook her head, and he set the pot back on the tray. "She kept something stirred up all the time."

"Like what?"

He didn't answer for a moment, then he shrugged. "It's no secret. She had a bigger ego than Marty. It's not that Tara liked men. It was more as if she thought all men should be crazy over her. She picked them up and put them down like a spoiled brat in a toy store."

"How did Lance take that?"

"Very badly at first. Then he either got to where he didn't care or he got good at hiding how much he really did care. Mostly he ignored her. She didn't stay here very much anyway, and it was a relief to everyone when she'd leave. We'd settle down, and then she'd blow in like a tornado and get us all riled up again."

He tossed the lemon slice into the fire. "When this new guy throws her over or runs out of money, she'll come wandering back home."

"Why would a man like Lance put up with that sort of treatment? He couldn't enjoy being humiliated."

Brad chose a doughnut from the tray and bit into it. Caesar, who had moved back to the hearthrug, thumped his tail, and Brad broke off a piece of the pastry and tossed it in his direction. The dog caught it in midair.

"Why did Monica put up with Marty?" he asked. "I doubt if they knew themselves. It seems to me that a lot of us reach a point where we 'put up' with something. Maybe we're too proud or too stubborn, or too helpless, to break out."

She thought about it. "Do you think that's why there are so many murders? People do get tired of their situation, and they do break out. You know, Mac said something about Loralee feeling guilty where Tara was concerned. Do you think she's interested in Lance?"

"Not that I know of. I'd say he's not interested. Never has been, never will be."

"What about Clyde? Did Tara make a play for him?"

"Are you kidding?" He roared with laughter. "Clyde is so straightlaced he would probably faint if anyone suspected him of an impure thought. A little tramp like Tara would have ruined his vision of himself and put an indelible blot on the sacred Andrews name."

"No, but wait. I was talking to him about her, and he got upset and said everyone would be better off if she never came back."

Brad looked thoughtful. "You mean Clyde and Tara. . .? Nah, I can't believe that."

"Humor me. Suppose Clyde really had a thing for her. Clyde's good-looking in a dignified way. He wouldn't be bad if he'd quit being so stiff, learn to bend a little."

"He's not made of bendable material," Brad said. "He'd break before he bent. What do you mean he's good-looking? You like the way he looks?"

She caught the gleam in his eyes. "I never said that."

"Don't get ideas about Clyde. He's not your type."

She started to ask him just what he knew about her type, but his expression stopped her. She held her breath for a moment, strongly aware of the blue of his eyes, the teasing quality of his smile. She had made a resolution to never let a man get close enough to treat her the way Marty had treated her mother, but a prolonged exposure to Brad Wilson might be a serious threat to her good intentions.

She took a deep breath. "If Clyde had been seeing Tara on the sly, could Marty have known?"

"You think Clyde killed him?"

"I don't know, but if I had a choice, I'd rather it would be him."

"You can't call a guy a murderer just because you don't like him. No proof, no case."

Stephanie stared at the fireplace, mesmerized by the dancing flames. Why would any woman leave a man like Lance and a sweet kid like Kate? What could she possibly find out there that could be more important than her home and family? The same question could be asked of Marty, of course.

She realized with relief that she hadn't inherited the roaming trait from her father. She had her mother's desire for a home. If she couldn't see sharing her home with a man, that was probably her mother's fault too. She was just beginning to understand how much all of that unrelenting grief and anger had influenced her own life. Stephanie couldn't recall her mother ever badmouthing Marty, but she must have absorbed the unhappiness through the pores of her skin.

"If Tara is what you claim, why did Lance marry her?"

"Tara could be pretty spectacular when she chose. Lance fell hard. He'd never met anyone like her, and he didn't find out what he'd done until too late. As for Tara, she probably took one look at the lodge and thought 'money.' Have you seen her suite?"

"Loralee showed it to me."

"What was your reaction?"

"Too elaborate. I felt stifled."

He took her hand, running his fingers around her wrist. "No, that wouldn't be your style."

Her flesh tingled from his touch. The fire, the cozy room, even the dog, set an intimate mood she knew was dangerous. Too aware of Brad, she pulled her hand away.

He wasn't upset. Instead his eyes flickered with amusement. "What are you afraid of?"

"I'm not afraid of anything."

"Yes you are. You're afraid of love."

"Love is an illusion. It doesn't last. I've seen what love does, and I don't want any, thank you."

"You mean it didn't last for Marty and your mother. That doesn't mean it wouldn't last for you. Are you going to spend the rest of your life running?"

She set her cup down. Enough, already. "I'm getting a little tired of being psychoanalyzed."

"I'm not psychoanalyzing you. But it doesn't take a genius to see you're carrying around a load of problems caused by your parents' broken marriage."

He put his arms around her. She felt the warmth of his body, smelled his aftershave, and fought an unreasonable urge to put her head on his shoulder and yield to the pressure of his embrace. Instead, she pushed him away.

He dropped his arms, and she ran for the door. His voice jolted her. "When you get tired of running, I'll be waiting."

* * *

Stephanie walked down to the lake, wanting to get away from the lodge. She was surprised to find Loralee sitting on a boulder looking out over the water. One glance at her eyes revealed she had been crying.

"Sorry if I'm intruding. Can I help?"

She shrugged. "No. I don't guess anyone can."

"Okay. I'm not trying to stick my nose in where it's not wanted."

Loralee threw a rock into the water with unnecessary force. "It's just Brad and Clyde talking about Tara."

"Oh? What were they saying?" Was Brad following through on her idea? Maybe he had taken her seriously.

"Tara wasn't like they say. She was special. The rules didn't apply to her."

"I think you're wrong. The rules apply to everyone."

Loralee turned her head away, blinking back tears. "Do you

realize how hard it is for me to sit and listen to them run her down that way?"

"I can imagine how you must feel. I'm Marty's daughter, remember? The truth is, both Marty and Tara weren't what they should have been. Look at the way your cousin treated you. Can you say that was right?"

Loralee's expression tightened. "You don't know anything about it. Tara was just a year older than me. When I moved in with them, she had to share her mother, share her room, share her toys. It wasn't easy for her."

"And Tara didn't share."

Loralee got to her feet. "You don't understand. You never could. I should have known better than to try to talk to you or anyone else. I know what Tara was like. I know
better than anyone. You never knew her."

"No, I didn't," Stephanie agreed. "I'm not sure I would have wanted to, if she was anything like they say."

"She wasn't. She was Tara. People like you *couldn't* understand her." She walked away, back straight, head high, but a pitiful figure for all of that. Tara might be gone, but Loralee was still in bondage.

14

Brad drove toward Eureka with a list in his pocket of Marty's favorite watering holes. Mac had sworn the five lounges were the main places where they used to go for impromptu jam sessions. Bars like this used to be Brad's favorite hangouts before he became a Christian. Back then it had seemed natural to him. Now he felt out of place.

At the first lounge the bartender looked at Marty's picture and shook his head. "I know who he was. Sure, he wrote good music. I'm new, just been here a few weeks, and he didn't come in when I was on duty. Sorry, I can't help."

At the second place, the guy behind the bar said, "Yeah, Marty used to come in here a lot, but then he quit. I heard he got religion or something."

"Did he have any problems with anyone?"

"You mean anyone who was mad enough to kill him? I've thought about it, but I can't point a finger."

"You can't always tell who'll kill and who won't."

The bartender leaned against the bar. He was big and muscular, with a well-trimmed black mustache and beard and a tattoo on his beefy forearm of an eagle holding an American flag. He looked tough enough to double as a bouncer. "Were you a good friend of Marty's?"

"No, I guess I wasn't," Brad said.

The man grinned. "Me neither. Self-centered little jerk, wasn't he?"

Brad laughed. "I guess that about covers it."

"Sorry I couldn't help you."

"That's okay." Brad hesitated. It was a long shot, but Stephanie had brought up the subject, and it wouldn't hurt to ask. He pulled out another picture, a group photo. "Anyone here you remember coming in with Marty?"

The guy tilted the picture to catch the light from a beer sign. He pointed a thick finger at Mac.

"Him and Marty used to play with the band. But I think it was mostly because of the music. They didn't seem to be all that fond of each other."

He pointed at a couple of other people in the picture. "These two used to come in together, but not with Marty, which I guess is what you're interested in."

Brad stared at the picture. This wasn't what he expected to hear. "Together?"

"Yeah. Seemed to have a thing going. Couldn't see what she saw in him. Not her style at all."

"No, probably not." He'd have to agree to that.

Tara and Clyde? The last two people in the world he would

have suspected to "have a thing going." It looked like Stephanie's hunch might have some substance, although at this stage, he wasn't sure what.

He flipped the picture against his free hand. "Thanks a lot. See you around."

"Sure. Drop in anytime."

Brad hadn't expected to find out anything, and he wasn't happy with what he *had* found. Tara was a match for Marty when it came to causing trouble. If she had set her sights on Clyde, he wouldn't have stood a chance.

He started the motor and adjusted the heater. Clyde wouldn't have wanted Lance to know he was fooling around with Tara, which was probably why they met in a bar in Eureka, a place Lance wouldn't frequent.

Tara had tried to come on to Brad too, but even if he'd been tempted, which he wasn't, he owed Lance too much to fool around with his wife. He didn't see how her affairs could have had anything to do with Marty's death, but he had a feeling something had been set in motion that would be hard to stop, and while it wasn't macho to admit it, he was scared.

* * *

Stephanie stood by her window watching as Heather and Kate took the path to the stable. Since the way they crept along showed they didn't want to be followed, she immediately started after them.

They were out of sight by the time she rounded the corner of the stable, but she could hear Kate giggling. The noise seemed to be coming from an empty box stall at the end of the room. She tiptoed across the straw-littered floor to peek inside.

Heather was on her knees, watching Kate play with a long-legged, brown-and-white puppy. His long-silky ears and big feet hinted at a touch of hound. Stephanie snickered at his antics, and Kate whirled, ponytail swinging, her expression showing shock and what . . . anger?

"What are you doing here?" she demanded.

"I followed you. Where'd you get the puppy?"

"I found him. He needs a home real bad, and if you tell my dad, he won't let me keep him."

"We don't know that, Kate," Heather said. "Your father is a reasonable man. Let's give him a chance to make his own decision."

Kate fondled the pup's ears, and the puppy tried to chew on her fingers. "I had a dog once. No one would tell me what happened to him. I don't want to lose Sam, so don't you tell."

"I won't. Is that his name, Sam?" Odd name for a puppy, but he was Kate's dog, and she could name him what she liked. Stephanie squatted and held out her hand. "Here, Sam. Come on, boy."

Heather sat back on her heels. "You know, your dad will find out about Sam anyway. It would be best to let him hear from us, don't you think?"

Kate didn't look like she thought much of the idea, and Stephanie was inclined to agree with her, but she was willing to go along and lend moral support.

They started out trying to lead the pup, but he sat down and refused to budge. Stephanie was the lucky one who got to pack him into Lance's office. Unfortunately, a meeting was in progress.

Loralee noticed them first. "What's that dog doing here?"

Kate looked worried, Heather was defiant, and Stephanie struggled to keep Sam from licking her chin. Monica grinned, and Brad laughed outright.

Lance smiled at Kate. "What's all this?"

"He's my dog, and I want to keep him." From the way she stood, feet apart, fists clenched on her hips, it was obvious she meant to fight for the pup. Her jaw was set in a pugnacious angle, making her look even more like a miniature copy of her father.

Stephanie adjusted her grip on Sam. "Kate found the dog, and she and Heather have been taking care of him. They want permission to let him stay."

Brad winked at her and reached out to scratch Sam's ears. The pup struggled to climb into Brad's lap, and Stephanie handed him over, glad to get rid of him. She shook her arms to get the circulation moving again.

Kate tried to bargain. "We need a watchdog to bark at burglars, and he's a good dog."

"I can see that," Lance said. "You'd have to feed him and take care of him."

"I can do that, and Heather will help me."

"What happens when Heather leaves?" Loralee asked. "After all, she isn't here to stay."

Heather spoke for the first time. "I wanted to talk to you

about that. I need a job. I can wait tables or wash dishes or clean rooms. I'm strong, and I'll work hard."

Stephanie realized that Heather had probably worked her share of minimum-wage jobs. Evidently she didn't intend to squander her inheritance, nor was she playing on her connection to the family. The jobs she asked about would be hard labor.

Lance smiled at her. "We can do better than that. I've been thinking about hiring someone to help in the office. Loralee's supposed to work with Mom, and I need someone full-time."

"I've been doing all the work with no problem," Loralee said. "I really think I can keep up by myself."

"Not if I can talk this son of mine into building a theater, you can't," Monica said. "If I get what I want, we're going to be busy."

"I think Mom can keep you occupied, Loralee. I'll need someone who can work full-time here," Lance said. "If you're interested, Heather, we'll talk about it later."

She smiled, and the room seemed to light up. "I'm very interested."

Stephanie hoped she was talking about the job. How much of the fascination Heather felt for the lodge involved Lance Harrington? Her baby sister needed to be careful.

Kate got back to the main point. "May I keep Sam?"

"I suppose so," Lance said. "But I don't want to see him inside the lodge. Some people don't like dogs."

Kate hurled herself at Lance, her arms in a stranglehold around his neck. He loosed her grip and pulled her onto his lap. "What's this? There's no need to cry."

"She was afraid you would say no," Heather said as a look of understanding passed between them.

Lance set Kate on her feet and gave her one final hug. "Don't worry. Nothing will happen to Sam. I promise. Run along now and let us get back to work."

They left the room, with Kate's eyes shining and Sam hanging from her arms like an extremely contented ragdoll.

Heather and Kate took Sam back to the stables, and Stephanie headed for the library. She sat down behind the desk and thought about the way the people who lived at the lodge were getting on with their lives. Even Heather had made a place for herself. They seemed to have forgotten about Marty.

Another thing that bothered her was the way the whole family trooped off to church every Sunday morning, leaving her behind. Sometimes they even went back on Sunday night. But if her suspicions were correct, one of those fervent churchgoers had brutally murdered her father.

Stephanie riffled through the desk drawers, looking for anything pertaining to Marty, but found only neat records of bookings for Monica, which she had apparently canceled after Marty's death. So maybe she wasn't getting back to normal all that fast, after all.

In one of the bottom drawers she discovered a handful of newspaper clippings. She glanced at them, casually interested. Most seemed to be about performances in various cities. A couple of items were circled in red, but she couldn't see anything relevant.

Stephanie felt guilty going through private papers. What excuse could she give if someone came in and caught her? She shut the last drawer and thought about what to do next, but nothing came to mind. After selecting a couple of books from the shelves, she escaped to her suite.

An hour later, Kate came and bounced up beside her, ponytail swinging and a worried look in her brown eyes. "You have to go find Heather."

"No I don't. She can take care of herself."

Kate knelt on the bed, hands braced on her knees. "Heather had a fight with Loralee, and ran away and she hasn't come back."

"She's probably walking around the lake cooling off, or sitting on a rock somewhere."

Kate's lips quivered. "She might not come back."

Stephanie watched her for a minute. The poor kid was really upset. Kate had a lot of issues to deal with right now—Marty dead, her mother gone.

She didn't give up, either. "You'll have to wear Heather's jacket. She took yours."

"She did what?"

"She grabbed yours off a chair in the library and ran out." Kate let her eyes plead for her.

Stephanie sighed. "Okay, I need a walk. I'll go with you." She shrugged into Heather's jacket, which Kate had thoughtfully brought with her.

* * *

Brad stepped off his cabin porch and whistled for Caesar. He'd planned to check on the stand of young pines north of the lodge, and the Lab could use some exercise. The dog came running, and Brad paused for a moment, just enjoying the quiet of the afternoon.

The thick barrier of cedar between the lodge and the highway muffled the noise of passing cars. A red-tailed hawk rode the wind currents over the ridge behind the lodge. Brad never ceased to be thankful for the blessing of freedom. God had been good to him.

A gunshot punctured the silence.

Brad froze in midstep, head twisted around, listening. Nothing. The natural background sounds had ceased. No birds twittered in the trees, no hum of insects. The hawk fled over the ridge, leaving the stretch of sky as bare as if he'd never been there.

Brad hurried in the direction of the lake. Someone potting frogs? Lance didn't allow hunters on lodge property—too great a chance of a stray bullet hitting the wrong target.

He topped the slope leading down to the lake. A crumpled form lay facedown on the rocky shingle. A brown suede jacket, copper hair. Stephanie!

He ran down the path, sliding in loose rock. Blood gleamed red in the sun. Dear God, no! Please! He reached the inert body, grasping her shoulder, pulling her over, face up.

A white face, a smear of blood. Not Stephanie. The burst of relief left him weak.

Reality hit.

Someone had shot Heather.

* * *

Stephanie and Kate were halfway down the final flight of stairs when a commotion at the lodge entrance brought them to a stop. A flurry of kicks rocked the door. People screamed and scurried away from the front desk. Lance jerked the door open, and Brad staggered in carrying Heather. Her bright hair hung in a copper waterfall over his arm. Her face was dead white. His voice echoed through the lobby.

"Call an ambulance! She's been shot!"

Brad eased Heather onto a couch in the lobby and straightened up. "I found her down by the lake."

"Is she . . . ." Stephanie couldn't finish.

"She's alive, but she's lost a lot of blood." He stepped back out of the way. "An awful lot."

Lance dropped to his knees and groped for Heather's wrist. "There's a pulse, but it's weak."

Heather's chest barely moved with each fragile breath. Her lashes made a dark smudge against her cheek. Stephanie gripped the back of the couch so tightly her knuckles looked like hard, white bones. Every resentful thought she'd ever had about Heather marched through her mind.

How could she have been so foolish? She, who had no one except one aunt and had mourned her lack of family, had rejected the love Heather tried to offer. If she lived, they would truly be sisters. *I'll change, Lord. I promise. Give me another chance. Please.*

Monica ran to the desk and grabbed the phone. As soon as she finished talking, she hurried back. "The ambulance is on its way, and I called Rob."

Stephanie rushed to the dining area and brought back a folded napkin. She dropped down beside Heather. "Pressure points," she muttered. "Where are they?" Why couldn't she remember?

"Here, let me." Monica nudged her out of the way.

Lance got to his feet and stood behind the couch, looking worried. Kate pressed close against him, her face pinched and white. "Why would anyone want to hurt Heather?"

He sheltered his daughter under his arm. "I don't know, but until we find out, you stay close to the lodge."

Loralee ran into the room, followed by Mac. She stopped, hand to her mouth. "Oh, my word! Is she dead?"

No one answered, but she didn't seem to mind. Like everyone else, she was drawn to the drama being played out in the lobby.

Mac hovered on the edge of the little group, his expression stolid. Stephanie watched them all, looking for some unwary speech or action that might betray a murderer. Her mind echoed Kate's cry. Who would want to hurt Heather?

Monica was still on her knees, pressing the napkin against Heather's shoulder. A spreading crimson blotch seeped across the brown suede. Stephanie caught her breath. She had forgotten that Heather was wearing her jacket. The hair on the back of her neck furred. Had someone shot the wrong Walker sister?

The ambulance arrived with the sheriff's car right behind it. Monica moved out of the paramedic's way, going to stand by the desk, her lips moving in prayer. Clyde, who had entered with the ambulance crew stood beside her.

Rob rushed through the door. "What's happened now? I'm spending more time out here than I am at my office."

Lance pushed past him. "Ask Brad. He knows more than I do. He found her. I'm going to the hospital." He hurried after the stretcher. Mac hesitated before leaving too. Loralee watched them go, a thoughtful expression on her face. She moved as if to follow, but Rob intervened. "You stay here. I want to question all of you. Let's go to the library, where we'll have more privacy," he added, as the guests who had crowded back into the lobby showed no sign of retreating.

We trailed after him to the elevator. In the library, they each chose a seat as far from the others as possible. Stephanie looked around the room to meet eyes cold with suspicion. No one knew whom to trust anymore. She could read it in their expressions.

Clyde had entered the hotel as the attendants were loading Heather into the ambulance and immediately came looking for Monica. She clutched his hand, more like holding on to a lifeline than anything else.

Loralee bristled at being included in the interrogation. "I didn't even know she'd been shot. Why must I stay for this?"

"Because right now, this has knocked down all my ideas, and until I get a handle on this development, every one of you is under suspicion, except for Kate. But I want you where I can see you, okay honey?"

"Okay." She perched on the arm of Stephanie's chair and gave her a curious, scared little smile. Stephanie wanted to pull Kate into her lap and promise her that everything would be all right. She didn't, though, because Kate was too smart to believe her.

"What happened here?" Rob asked.

Brad leaned against the edge of the desk and folded his arms, staring down at the toes of his boots, as if getting his story straight in his mind. "I had just stepped out of my cabin to start my rounds when I heard the shot. It seemed to come from the lake, and I knew no one should be shooting in that direction. I walked down, expecting to find someone potting frogs or hunting squirrels out of season. When I got to the top of the slope, I saw her at the edge of the water. At first I thought it was Stephanie, until I turned her over and realized it was Heather."

Rob watched them each in turn, openly assessing their reactions. "Why did you carry her to the lodge?" he asked.

Brad shot an impatient glance in his direction. "I should think that would be obvious. I didn't want to leave her there while I went to get help."

"Do you think whoever shot her was still there?"

The room hushed as they waited for Brad's answer. "You mean he might have been waiting for me to leave so he could finish her off? That's sick, Rob." Brad shook his head at the thought. "I didn't consciously think that, but maybe I had it in the back of my mind."

"Rob, that's horrible." Monica twisted her hands in her lap. "Heather didn't arrive until after the funeral. Why would anyone shoot her?"

"I don't know, but I'm going to find out." He looked at Loralee. "When did you last see her?"

"About three-thirty. She left to take a walk."

"How well did you know her?" Rob asked.

Loralee shrugged. "She's only been here a few days. I had my work to do. I rarely saw her." She stared at Stephanie with hard, bright eyes, warding off any contradiction.

Rob turned to Stephanie. "Did you know Marty had another daughter?"

She braced herself against the intensity of his gaze. "No. I found out about Heather the day I came home from the hospital."

"The day Tom Allison read the will," Loralee murmured.

Rob gave her his full attention. "What was in that will? He leave anything to Heather?"

"We all got bequests," Loralee said. "Marty was very generous. We were surprised to meet Heather, but I guess Monica knew about her."

"It's true I knew about Heather," Monica admitted. "I also knew about the will, and I won't get one penny of the money if she dies, so why would I bother to shoot her."

"Who does get her part of the estate?" Rob asked.

"Why, I don't know," Monica faltered. "I guess . . .I suppose if Heather dies, Stephanie would inherit, but that's ridiculous. She had no reason to kill her sister."

Stephanie thought she had just been handed a very good reason. Rob had a faraway look in his eyes, already building his case against her. She tried to think of something in her defense. She didn't want to see the inside of Sheriff Rob's jail again. One experience like that was enough.

Before she could speak, Brad came over to lean on the back of her chair. "Now just a minute. Stephanie didn't shoot anyone, and if you're planning to accuse her, you had better have some proof."

"Oh yes, I forgot." Clyde favored him with a cold smile. "You used to be a lawyer. I don't think you can act for Stephanie, though. You're not allowed to practice anymore. Isn't that right?"

"That's right, and Rob knows all about it," Brad agreed. "I wasn't planning to represent her, but I can give her some advice."

Clyde dismissed this with a wave of his hand. "So where was Stephanie when someone shot Heather? Has anyone bothered to ask?"

It was time she took part in this conversation. "I don't know when she was shot. I spent some time in the library and then I went to my room to read. Kate wanted me to go with her to find Heather, and we were on our way downstairs when Brad carried her inside."

"Why did you want to look for Heather?" Rob was gentler with Kate than he was with the rest of the group.

Stephanie reached up and grasped her cold, little hand. Kate's voice was steady. "Because she had a fight with Loralee and ran outside. I waited and waited, but she never came back."

"That's a lie!" Loralee leaped to her feet, moving fast toward Kate. "You take that back."

Brad stepped in front of her. "Hold it. Why did you fight with Heather?"

"It wasn't a fight." Loralee rested her delicate, white hand on his arm, her eyes pleading with him. "Kate is exaggerating. I didn't like the way Heather had pushed herself into the lodge.

Why, she even talked Lance into hiring her to help in the office."

"Heather didn't ask for an office job," Stephanie pointed out. "She offered to wait tables or wash dishes if she could just work here. She felt like she had finally found a family and she wanted to stay."

"She has no claim on Lance. No right to expect him to accept her as family. Lance is Tara's husband." Loralee's lovely face flushed with anger.

"Heather is Marty's daughter and my stepdaughter," Monica said. "We were glad to accept her into the family because she is a well-mannered young woman who is a joy to have around, and we'll not be talking about rights."

"I suppose you mean I have no right to be here." Loralee burst into tears. "I guess Marty's daughter is more welcome than Tara's cousin. That's what you're saying, isn't it?"

"For heaven's sake, Loralee. Don't read anything into my words that I didn't mean." Monica sounded as exasperated as she looked. What little grasp she had on her temper was slipping fast. "You've always been welcome here and always will be. We're happy to have you as part of the family, but you can't expect us to turn Heather away just because you're jealous of her."

Clyde put his arm around Loralee and led her to the couch. "I think this has gone far enough," he rebuked Monica. "Loralee has been a faithful worker for you, and she can't be expected to stand by and watch as someone else takes her place."

"Oh for . . ." Monica caught herself before saying what she thought, but Stephanie caught the flare of blue fire in her eyes. Her lips tightened as she swallowed hard, then started over. "I think we're all too upset to make sense right now. What else do you need to know, Rob?"

"I need to know a lot of things. For instance, I need to know why Brad here thought Heather was Stephanie when he first saw her. I know there is a family resemblance, but not that much when you know them."

Brad wrinkled his brow, evidently puzzled at what Rob was getting at. "I don't know. I just immediately thought of Stephanie, and that scared me too much to think clearly about anything else."

Stephanie figured that remark didn't endear her to Loralee, but she didn't care. Her heart sang at the look in Brad's eyes. It was plain he had been shaken when he thought she was lying in the mud with a bullet in her. She shouldn't feel so happy at just that moment, but she couldn't control her feelings.

Kate brought everyone down to earth. "Heather was wearing Stephanie's jacket."

"What's that?" Rob turned to stare at her. "You sure?"

She nodded. "Heather was so upset she grabbed the wrong jacket and ran outside. I took hers for Stephanie to wear."

Stephanie looked down at the forest-green jacket she had pulled on before leaving her room. Had someone intended to shoot her and hit Heather instead? If Heather had been wearing her own coat, would she be in the hospital now, fighting for her life? Rob got to his feet. "I'm going to look around. Brad, you come with me, and the rest of you stay in this room. That means you, especially, Stephanie. If someone is gunning for you, and I'm not saying they are, I don't want you out wandering around on your own. What time did you get here, Clyde?"

"I arrived as the ambulance pulled away." Clyde replied stiffly. "Are you insinuating that I could have shot that girl? If so, I think I'll be leaving. I have no intention of staying here to be insulted."

"You don't go until I say you can," the sheriff ordered. "Don't make me come looking for you. If you do, I won't be happy."

"We'll all stay here, Rob." Monica was back in control. "Just let us know what you find out."

"I'll be back in a little while. In the meantime, I'm depending on you to see that no one leaves. And I'm calling for help to search the lodge for a gun. We'll try not to disturb your guests."

"All right," Monica nodded. "I'm sure everyone wants to cooperate with you on this. The sooner we find out who is responsible for these terrible things, the sooner we can all get back to normal."

Rob and Brad left the room, and Clyde got to his feet. "You can't be serious about expecting us to stay here. I haven't had my dinner, and I intend to do so now."

"You can have it in this room. I'll call someone to take your order." Monica reached for the telephone beside her. "I am very serious. So serious that I will instruct one of the employees to guard the door if I have to. Now, what do you want to eat?"

15

Brad led the way down to the lake, followed by Rob and the crime team. What was going on here? After he got out of prison, the lodge had seemed like a peaceful haven. Now it was turning into something right out of a horror story.

He stopped and pointed to a spot on the lakeshore. "I found her right there. You can see the blood from here."

"Okay," Rob motioned to the people behind him. "Let's get busy."

Jake Hogan, one of the deputies, approached the crime scene, moving deliberately. Brad watched Jake as he inched around the area, taking pictures of the spot from all angles. Jake shot a couple of rolls of film before stepping aside and letting the others go to work.

Two men whom Brad knew by sight but whose names he couldn't think of, measured the area, writing down the results. It took a long time, but when they were finally done, Larry Jackson and Sharon Vinson, long-time members of the police force, moved in, searching for evidence. They gathered up every rock and pebble that had a smear of Heather's blood. Larry searched, and Sharon bagged evidence and labeled it.

Rob and a couple of men stood together, eyes scanning the tree-covered slope behind them and talking in low tones. Brad strained to hear what they were saying, but a breeze was kicking up a racket, rustling the leaves and stirring up a lot of background noise.

Rob waved for him to join them. "We're figuring whoever shot her had to be standing up on that slope somewhere. You heard the shot. Which direction do you think it came from?"

Brad thought back. "I came out of my cabin, heard it, stopped, and listened." He pursed his lips, thinking. "From my left."

"Your cabin sits over there. Left would be about right. You come with us, but stay behind me. I don't want you walking over any evidence."

"I'm not stupid."

"You're not a trained officer, either."

Rob walked away, and Brad followed, figuring he'd better not argue or the sheriff would send him back to the lodge. If he wanted to hang around, it would be a good idea to do what he was told and keep quiet.

They tromped around in the brush for a while, and Brad was about to give up when one of the deputies gave a shout. "Over here."

When they reached the place where the deputy waited, Brad saw a trampled place in the grass, a bunch of bird's-foot violets crushed underfoot. A broken twig dangled from a sumac bush.

Someone had stood there, all right.

Rob, puffing a bit from his climb, paused for breath, and motioned to the young deputy. "Tucker, you stay here until I can get the rest of the bunch to go over this spot."

Tucker nodded. "We're not going to find anything much. That grass didn't take any footprints."

"I suspect you're right, but we'll give it a try." Rob sent one of the other men down to the lake to give orders to check this spot next.

Brad turned and looked down the hill. His heart chilled. He was staring right at Sharon Vinson, who was helping Larry look for evidence. No one who knew how to use a gun could miss a shot like this. If he had a rifle in his hands and pulled the trigger, Sharon wouldn't have a chance.

* * *

Stephanie called the hospital the next morning. The nurse on duty told her that Heather had had a peaceful night and her condition was stable. Feeling grateful, Stephanie hung up the phone. Another fatality averted. But their attacker's luck was bound to eventually turn. Maybe Rob would solve the case before anyone else got hurt.

Lance met her as she left the elevator. "How's Heather?"

"She's stable. What time did you leave her last night?"

"Around midnight. I thought I'd go back today."

"Monica's going in this morning, and I'm going later in the afternoon. Want to come along?"

"I might do that." He thought for a minute. "Would four

o'clock be too late?"

"That will be fine if we can stop someplace and let me buy a jacket." Rob still had the bloodstained green one, and now the one Heather had borrowed was stained with blood and had a bullet hole through it.

"Meet me right here. I'll drive."

Stephanie noticed the worry lines around his eyes and the way his shoulders slumped. Murder and a couple of near fatalities were wearing him down.

He strode away, and she joined Kate for breakfast and then walked with her to the end of the driveway and waved until the bus vanished around a curve in the road.

After lunch curiosity drew her down to the lake where Brad had found Heather. Yellow crime tape marked the spot. The breeze had died, bringing an oppressive silence. The leaves hung like limp banners, and even the clouds were motionless. The sound of running footsteps ruptured the silence. Stephanie whirled, a sudden rush of fear-induced adrenaline surging through her veins like high-octane fuel.

Brad advanced over the rocky shingle. "What if I had been a guy with a rifle? I thought Rob told you to be careful. Someone shot your sister, and it's not at all clear whether he meant to get her or you. I'm walking you back to the lodge, and you stay there."

Her temper, egged on by the sudden scare, boiled over. "You have no right to give me orders."

His expression softened. "Maybe not, but I never again want to feel the way I did when I thought you were lying there with a bullet in you."

She stared at him, lips parted, seeing the truth in his eyes. He had been frightened . . .for her.

He took her arm. "I'm sorry I yelled at you, but I'm taking you back to the lodge. It's not safe out here."

"You don't know the gunman meant to shoot me," she protested. "He could have meant to hit Heather all along."

"Maybe so, but until we know for sure, we have to keep in mind that there's already been one attempt on your life. I think this was another one."

The thought frightened her so much that she let Brad walk her back to the lodge and the shelter of her room.

* * *

Brad walked beside Stephanie, close enough to smell the spicy fragrance of her perfume. Some kind of flower. Carnation? The top of her head reached his chin. Just the right height to be easily kissed.

He let his thoughts dwell on the rosy curves of her lips, the perfect way she had felt in his arms, the way she had of invading his dreams. His mouth twisted in a smile.

"What's so funny?"

He came back to the present with a jolt to meet the question in those green eyes. What would it be like to see them glow with tenderness?

"Nothing. Just thinking."

"About what?"

"Just things in general."

Let her get one whiff of his thoughts and she would be gone like a scared rabbit. Those parents of hers had done a job on her. It would take a miracle to change her mind and her heart. But he was praying, and he believed in miracles.

* * *

Monica came home at two o'clock and reported that Heather was doing as well as could be expected. She'd lost blood. The bullet had chipped her collarbone and done some damage to tissue and muscle, but barring any unforeseen setbacks, it looked like she would be all right.

Kate got home from school about a quarter to four and came looking for Stephanie. "Are you going to the hospital?"

"Yes, did you want to go?"

She nodded. "But Dad says not this time. Will you take something to Heather for me?"

"Of course. What do you want to send?"

She had been holding her hands behind her back but now she brought forth a card she had made. The crayoned letters were crooked, but the words came from her heart. She flushed. "It's not as pretty as I thought it would be."

Stephanie read it aloud. "I miss you." Hearts and flowers cut from typing paper and colored with care were scattered generously over the front of the card. She didn't open it to read the inside, but she knew it contained a message of love. "I think it's really neat. No one ever sent me one half as nice. She'll like it."

"Do you really think so?" Kate smiled, reassured. "I didn't have an envelope. Will it get wrinkled?"

"No. I'll put it right here, inside my purse." Stephanie smiled at her. "You must think a lot of Heather."

"Oh, I do. I wish . . . ." She stopped and ducked her head as if she had just said something wrong. "I'd better go now."

"All right. I'll tell Heather you sent your love." Kate smiled and ran away, and Stephanie wondered about the sentence she never finished. She wished what? That Heather was her mother? Poor Kate. How much did she remember of Tara?

Lance was waiting when Stephanie got downstairs. They left at five minutes till four, and it was a good thing she was ready to leave, because he was in a hurry. He took the curves on the road to Eureka Springs at a clip that left her breathless.

"Isn't the speed limit fifty-five?"

"Oh, right. Too fast for you?"

"I don't want you to get a ticket, but then, I guess Rob would fix it if you did."

He laughed. "Don't you believe it. Rob doesn't hand out any favors. He arrested his nephew last month for selling pot. Really upset the kid. He thought Rob would be too embarrassed to arrest him. He knows better now."

"So okay then, you'd better slow down. Righteous Rob may give you a ticket."

"Righteous Rob. He'd get a kick out of that."

"Don't tell him. I'm already at the top of his list of suspects. I don't want to make him mad at me."

Lance stopped at a small boutique before they reached the hospital. He waited in the pickup while Stephanie ran inside. She chose a black suede jacket with pewter buttons, gulped at the price, whipped out her credit card, and was back at the car in less than twenty minutes. Lance eyed her with approval.

"That was fast, and it looks good too."

She preened a little, glad he approved of her choice. Black was a good color for her, and she knew it. Lance parked in the nearly empty parking lot at the hospital, and they walked inside. Stephanie hesitated at the door of Heather's room, not sure what she would see. Heather smiled when they entered, but her face was white and drawn. Her hair spread over the pillow, as rich as molten copper, and her eyes glowed like newly cut emeralds. Lance blinked as if someone had turned on a bright light.

"Stephanie! How nice." Heather reached out with her good arm. "Thank you for coming."

Stephanie gently returned the hug, careful of the bandaged shoulder. "How are you feeling?"

"Not too bad, a little sore. God must have been watching over me, and I know you have all been praying for me."

Stephanie felt guilty because she hadn't thought of praying, but she doubted whether any prayer of hers would have accomplished much anyway. A vase of red roses almost filled the window ledge, and from where she stood, she could see that they were from Monica and Lance. She needed to send flowers.

"I have something for you." Stephanie fished Kate's card out of her purse and handed it to Heather. From the way she carried on, she must not have received many cards. She insisted Lance put it on the table at the foot of her bed so she could see it.

"Has Rob been to see you?" Stephanie asked.

"He came this morning. I wasn't much help. I was so angry at

Loralee I wouldn't have seen anything that didn't jump directly into my path."

Lance shed his jacket and tossed it over a chair. "Loralee's okay. She has a temper. She was just mouthing off. Doesn't mean half of what she says. Tara's the same way."

"Half is enough." Heather made a face. "She sure has it in for me. I wonder why?"

"She's jealous." Stephanie moved around to perch on the window ledge beside the bed after first shoving the roses aside. "Kate follows you around, and Lance gave you a job in the office. She thinks you're crowding her out."

Lance sat down in the nearest chair and leaned his elbows on his knees, his face troubled. "I hadn't thought of that. Tara brought her here. She might have the idea that if Tara doesn't come back she won't be welcome."

"Is that the way it is?" Heather asked.

"No, that's not the way it is," Lance said. "Is that what you think of us? We wouldn't toss Loralee out because of something Tara's done. Loralee made her own place. She belongs here."

"Perhaps you should tell her so," Stephanie suggested. "Maybe it would cut down on the temper tantrums."

"I might do that." He grinned. "You know for years it seemed like Loralee didn't have any life of her own. She was just an extension of Tara. Now that her personality is emerging, it's surprising to see how much they have in common. Must be a family thing."

"I'm sorry you got hurt," Stephanie said, feeling guilty. She should have been the one in the hospital bed.

"Don't worry. I'll be all right." Heather's expression was calm, unworried. "I'm a lot tougher than I look, and God's always taken care of me. He will now. But you be careful, big sister. I don't want anything to happen to you."

Yes, Heather was tough. She'd had to be, Stephanie thought ruefully. Marty should have done a better job of taking care of this daughter. Evidently she'd pretty well raised herself. Done a good job of it too.

The three of them talked for a while, and when Lance and Stephanie stood up to leave, Stephanie hugged Heather. "Hurry up and get well. We miss you."

Lance took Heather's hand. "They're keeping you here for a few days. You do what the doctor tells you."

Heather smiled up at him as if they were the only two people in the room. Lance held her hand a little longer than was necessary. Stephanie watched from the doorway, feeling more than a little alarmed. Tara might be gone, but Lance was still very much a husband. Stephanie couldn't think of a worse scenario than for Heather to fall in love with him, only to have his wife come home.

Traffic in Eureka Springs was heavy for this time of year, and Lance threaded the narrow streets with care. The main wave of tourists would arrive with warm weather. The town would take on a summer carnival atmosphere, with pedestrians crowding the streets, shopping, sightseeing, and just enjoying Ozark down-home hospitality.

The afternoon sunlight gilded the hills. Redbud trees dotted the hillsides with a deep rose pink. Wild plum foamed against the dark pyramids of cedar. Stephanie stretched like a contented cat.

They were getting close to the lodge before Lance spoke. "You haven't given us the benefit of your opinion. Who do you think shot Heather?"

"How should I know? The general consensus seems to be that someone mistook her for me. Although why everyone should assume that people would just naturally go after me with a gun is beyond my comprehension."

Lance shot her an appraising glance. "If you and Marty were mixed up in something that would cause anyone to come after you, you'd better tell Rob."

Stephanie swiveled her head to face him. So what was this? Guilt by association? Marty was her father, so she had to be mixed up in what he was doing? "That is the most insulting thing I've ever heard. When do you think I'd have seen enough of him to be mixed up in anything?"

"It's a logical conclusion, knowing Marty. He visits you, and you follow him to the lodge. Some unknown person kills him, tries to kill you, and shoots Heather. Either this guy is awfully mad about something, or he's carrying out a vendetta against the Walker family."

He drove with two fingers resting on the wheel, his voice a lazy drawl, just an interested bystander voicing an opinion. She turned her head slightly, watching him. Lance always seemed so even natured. What would it take to set him off?

He grinned. "What's wrong?"

"You didn't like Marty."

He still sat easy, but his hand tightened on the steering wheel. "And you've decided I had a motive to kill him? Let me guess. He was supposed to be fooling around with my wife." The pickup sped up.

"Was he?" Stephanie asked, giving him a chance to answer the question she would never have the nerve to ask if he hadn't brought it up.

A muscle quivered in his jaw. "If he was, it was probably her idea."

She didn't know what to say. After a few minutes he relaxed. "Sorry. I didn't intend to get off on that."

"It's not a pleasant subject for me, either." She kept her eyes on the road, her voice casual.

"No, I guess not. Your father, my wife. I'm thinking we've both paid enough for something we couldn't control. Marty's dead, and I have a private detective looking for Tara. If she's out there, he'll find her."

"Why the decision to find her now? Do you think her disappearance is connected with Marty's death in some way?"

"No, I'm doing this for me. I've lived under a cloud of uncertainty long enough."

"How can you be so sure she's all right? Wouldn't she care enough about Kate to keep in touch?"

He snorted. *"Her* care about Kate? You've never seen anything like the fit she threw when she found out she was pregnant. She'd have gotten an abortion, except she knew I'd have divorced her for sure if she did that."

"What about Loralee?"

He shook his head. "Forget that. Loralee would never cross Tara. She was afraid to show any interest in Kate, and now it's too late to forge any bonds. Kate doesn't trust her. In fact, Heather's the first person she's opened up to, and she seems to be accepting you."

"Loralee will be glad to hear about the detective. Half the time she thinks Tara must be dead because she hasn't heard from her."

"As much trouble as Mom had finding her, I don't know how she'd expect to hear from anyone."

It sounded like Loralee had deliberately shut herself off from old friends and family. Yet she had been willing to leave her new life and return to the lodge. "So why did Monica bring her back?"

"She's smart, and she's a good worker. Mom likes her. I don't know how long she'll stay around, though. Maybe she has too many bad memories of the lodge."

Lance speeded up to pass a car. "What are you planning to do when this is all over?"

"I haven't had much time to think about it. I'll probably go back to Independence and look for work." The idea depressed her more than it should have.

"Why not stay here? Heather wants to keep in touch with you."

"What would I do? I don't think Loralee could handle another of the Walker sisters working in the office."

Lance laughed. "I wasn't thinking of the office. Marty collected music memorabilia, and I need someone to catalog it and throw away the junk. You interested in the job?"

"If you really mean it, I am." After being left out of Marty's life for so long, she'd jump at the chance to be involved in this.

"I mean it. Want to swing by the barn and see what you're up against?" Lance turned off on a narrow lane.

The barn, as he called it, was a long, metal building within walking distance of the lodge but hidden by a thick stand of cedar trees. Stephanie stepped over the threshold and stopped, stunned at the sight of boxes and bags stacked higher than she could reach. Sequined jackets spilled out of cardboard cartons. Guitars, banjos, dulcimers leaned against piles of sheet music.

"Oh, my!" Words failed her. It would take forever to go through this accumulation.

Lance laughed. "You have to see it to understand."

"Where are you planning to put all of this?"

"That's up for grabs. I wanted to build a museum here, but Mom wants to build a music theater in Branson and have the museum next door."

Stephanie moved a stack of *Country Music* magazines from a chair and sat down, looking around at the collection Marty had amassed. "Maybe I can find the chest he left Monica."

"Now that's an idea. It might be here at that." He nudged a pile of sheet music with his foot.

Stephanie didn't get a chance to talk privately with Lance very often. He was always busy. She wanted his version of something that had been bothering her. "Loralee said Marty and Tara were close."

Lance didn't say anything at first, and then he shrugged, as if it didn't matter. "I don't think Marty was interested in Tara.

They were too much alike. He did try to get something going with Loralee."

"Marty was interested in Loralee?"

"Oh, probably not. She was there and would have been a challenge, if nothing more than to get Tara stirred up. She never allowed anyone to get close to Loralee."

"Didn't Loralee have dates, or anything?"

"Not that I can remember." He looked thoughtful. "Mac swears she had a fight with Tara over Clyde, but I always figured he was just jealous. Mac was crazy over Loralee, but Tara broke that up, and since Loralee's come back, she ignores him."

"When did she have this fight?"

"The day Tara left. He's always thought that was the reason, but I can't buy it. If Loralee ever had her sights set on Clyde, she sure got over it. She barely talks to him now." He looked at his watch. "You ready to go? I need to get back to the lodge."

Stephanie followed him outside and watched as he locked the door. If she had any sense she would get in her car and head back to Independence and safety. Instead, she climbed into the cab of Lance's pickup and rode back toward the lodge and whatever problems awaited her there.

* * *

After dinner Stephanie avoided the family gathering in the library and went to her room. Something had been nagging at the back of her mind all evening. She stretched out on her bed and stared at the ceiling.

Something she had seen or heard lately? She closed her eyes, thinking. A picture fluttered at the edge of her memory. Something she had noticed on a clipping in the library desk drawer that hadn't seemed important at the time. Now she wanted a second look.

She stayed in her room, reading until the clock hands pointed to one-thirty. Surely everyone had gone to bed by now. She turned out the bedroom light and inched open the door. The corridor seemed deserted, and she tiptoed down the hall to the library.

With the door closed behind her, she clicked on her penlight and opened the drawer. Someone had shoved the clippings to the very back. She pulled out the crumpled pieces of newsprint and spread them on the desktop until she found what she was looking for.

Two items had an area circled in red. What was so important that someone had taken time to mark it? A sound in the hall brought her heart into her throat.

Moving swiftly, she separated the two clippings she wanted and shoved the others back into the drawer, pushing it shut. She grabbed a book from the shelf and inserted the clippings inside it just as the door opened and the light flashed on.

Stephanie whirled, to find Loralee framed in the doorway, her forehead puckered in a frown. "What are you doing in here?"

"I couldn't sleep. Thought I'd get something to read."

"Why didn't you turn on the light?"

"I didn't want to disturb anyone. Did I wake you?"

"No."

Stephanie waited, but no explanation was forthcoming. She

held up the book. "Well, I don't want to keep you. I'll just run on back to my room. See you in the morning."

For a minute Loralee blocked her way, then moved aside. In her room, Stephanie switched on the bedside light and examined the clippings, each written by the society editor of the *Kansas City Star*. "What lovely daughter-in-law of a famous female singer didn't show up for her first booking at a prestigious club? No-shows soon get a bad reputation."

The second clipping was more of the same. Someone had missed an important booking. Stephanie stared at the newspaper article. Daughter-in-law? Tara? She had a booking to sing, and she didn't show? From what she had heard, Tara wanted to perform. So why hadn't she shown up if she was the person mentioned here. And why had someone thought it was important enough to save and mark the clipping? Someone who knew Tara wasn't coming back?

A sound, real or imagined, caught at her, and she turned out the light. A killer walked the halls of Harrington Lodge. Had Tara been the first victim?

16

Brad leaned against the front desk, watching as Bonnie handled an irritated guest. The guy was ticked because he couldn't get adult channels on the TV in his room. Brad could have told him he was fighting a losing battle. Lance refused to indulge a guest's taste for watching filth, and Bonnie had handled tougher guys than this one. She finally convinced him he'd have to wait until he got home for his favorite viewing experiences.

The man left, and Bonnie wandered over to talk to Brad. "Hi. What's going on?"

"Not much. Just want to ask you some questions. Did you see Marty come in the night he was killed?"

"Sure." Bonnie picked at the polish on her index fingernail. "He was in a good mood. Said he ate on the way down and he was going to shower and watch TV for a while."

Brad frowned, thinking. "The television wasn't on when I was in his room, but he was wearing a robe. Wonder if he'd had his shower or was going to take one?"

"I wouldn't know," Bonnie said. "Does it matter?"

"It might help us track his movements between the time he came and when he was killed."

"He came maybe an hour or so before Stephanie. I'm sorry I can't give you a more definite time. Clyde might know. Ask him."

"Clyde was here?" Had he heard that right?

"Sure. Came to eat his dinner, same as always."

"Did you tell Rob that?"

"He didn't ask. Is it important?"

"Everything's important in a murder investigation." A guest approached the desk, and Brad left, thinking that while Bonnie apparently didn't realize it, she had just blown Clyde's alibi.

* * *

Stephanie woke to a sky full of sunshine. Today would be a good time to look through the stuff in the barn, identify what she could, and leave the rest. Lance knew her qualifications were nil, so surely he wouldn't expect too much.

Loralee was already hard at work when Stephanie wandered into the office after lunch. Today, she wore a blue silk blouse and jeans. Not high fashion, but a little fancier than usual. Her hair, however, was back in the ponytail. Her eyebrows lifted in a questioning manner.

"Would you get me the key to the barn where Marty kept his collection? I promised Lance I'd start on it today." Stephanie waited for her reaction.

She frowned. "Start on it? What do you mean?"

"He wants me to sort and catalog everything for display in a music museum. I assumed you knew about it."

"I knew Marty wanted to do something like that, but I never dreamed Lance would take it seriously. You really intend to prowl around over there? I'm surprised Monica would allow that." Her fingers tapped her irritation on the polished surface of her desk. Their eyes locked, and Loralee's face flushed in sudden anger, but she had herself under control.

"I have no intention of prowling, as you put it. Lance hired me to put the collection in order and get it ready for display."

"Hired you? First he makes a job for Heather in the office, and now he manufactures a job for you. I wonder why?"

"Why don't you ask him? The key, if you don't mind." After hesitating long enough to make Stephanie wonder what she would do if the other woman didn't cooperate, Loralee got up and walked over to Lance's desk.

"This is against my better judgment, but if he doesn't like it, he can take it up with you." She brought out a key, neatly tagged "barn," and handed it to Stephanie. "If you find anything pertaining to Marty or Tara, I would appreciate it if you brought it to me first."

"Come off it, Loralee. You just work here like the rest of us. If I find anything I think is important, I'll take it to Lance. He's in charge, remember?" She didn't answer, and Stephanie left before she demanded the key back.

Kate met her in the hall. "Heather's home from the hospital."

"Aren't you supposed to be at school today?"

She grinned. "I'm sick. Can't you tell?"

"I tried that trick too when I was your age. So your dad let you get by with it?"

"He knew I wanted to be here when she came home." Kate grabbed Stephanie's hand, pulling her along. "Hurry. She wants to see you."

Heather lay on the couch in her room, with Lance in one wing chair and Monica in the other. She was still pale, but her smile was as brilliant as ever. As Stephanie hesitated on the threshold, Heather motioned for her to come in. "Oh, Stephanie. I'm home. Isn't that wonderful?"

Home? She called the lodge home? Was Heather assuming too much too fast? "It certainly is. You look great, too."

Heather laughed, and it was the happiest sound, like a brook bubbling over stones.

"Don't you feel strange complimenting me on my appearance, when we look so much alike?"

"I can't see it. Sure we have the same coloring, and we're about the same height, but that's where the resemblance ends." Heather had almost a classic beauty. Not one freckle marred her creamy complexion. Wild rose pink bloomed in her cheeks.

"You look alike until one gets to know you, and then your personalities color one's perception," Monica said. "I never dreamed I would have two such delightful daughters."

Stephanie pretended she hadn't heard that. Monica had no right to call her daughter. Stephanie would never allow anyone to take her mother's place, particularly the person who had destroyed her parents' marriage. That would be a betrayal of the lonely woman who had done her best to give her daughter a normal childhood.

She held out the key for Lance's inspection. "I'm going to the barn to work if that's all right with you."

"You are? How marvelous! You're braver than I am to tackle that mess."

Monica didn't seem to notice that Stephanie had ignored her comment. She didn't show any sign of being upset about someone working in the barn, either. So much for Loralee's remarks.

"What's in the barn?" Heather asked, and her face shined with excitement when Stephanie explained. "Oh, I want to help."

"When you're up to it," Stephanie promised. "There's enough stuff there to keep us both busy, if Lance can spare you from the office."

"She can do whatever she pleases," he said, "as long as she doesn't push herself too hard. Stephanie, take a phone with you. Maybe this isn't such a good idea. It's pretty isolated over there."

"I'll be all right." Working on the collection was something she really wanted to do. She'd never had an opportunity to be part of Marty's career. This was her chance to get involved, and while she was working, maybe, just maybe, she might find something that would throw some light on his death.

"Lock the door and don't stay over there after sundown," Monica ordered. "I'm not sure I like this, now that I think about it."

Stephanie left them arguing over when Heather would be able to get back to work. Sam, Kate's pup, was sleeping in the sun, and Stephanie didn't need to exert much effort to get him to follow her. She would rather have had Caesar, but at least Sam would be company. He might scare away the rats and mice, if any lived in the shadowed interior of the building.

The door to the building where Marty's collection was stored opened smoothly, and Stephanie stepped inside. Sam whiffed at a couple of boxes, and Stephanie wondered whether the boxes were full of mice. She waited just past the door, listening intently. Her nerves were shot. Since the attack on Heather, she'd been jumping at shadows, almost afraid to go outside.

She was here today because she'd finally convinced herself that hiding in the lodge would let their attacker win. On the other hand, getting herself shot couldn't exactly be considered a victory for her side. She carefully locked the door behind her.

Stephanie hefted an old banjo and put it back, trying to decide where to start working. A sequined jacket was draped over the top shelf of a wooden bookcase. Some of the costumes entertainers wore were worth a lot of money. If Marty had collected many of those, they would need special handling. She felt more and more unqualified for this job.

What she needed was a loose-leaf notebook so she could use a separate page for each type of material. She lifted a box to the top of the desk and opened it to find pictures of Monica in costume, apparently publicity photos.

She knew now that if it hadn't been Monica, Marty would have found someone else. He would never have stayed in Independence. The lure of the road and the fast-paced life of the entertainment business would have taken him sooner or later. The wife and daughter he left behind were just so much collateral damage.

The knowledge didn't hurt as badly as it once would have,

maybe because she was growing past the pain of being Marty's daughter. That didn't excuse Monica, though. She had known Marty had a family. She hadn't cared. If she had been so ruthless then, could she be just as ruthless now? All that talk about God forgiving her could be just that—talk.

Time passed, and she rose from her chair and stretched. Her back and shoulders ached from sitting still for so long. She decided to check the contents of the desk drawers and then quit for the day. Sam had scratched at the door long ago and been let out, apparently not finding anything interesting in the barn.

The shallow top drawer held an assortment of pens and paper clips, nothing worth saving. The side drawer on the right was empty except for a calculator without batteries and a pair of scissors. The deep bottom drawer was crammed with newspaper clippings about Monica and letters pertaining to bookings.

Underneath all of this clutter, Stephanie found a shorthand notebook that seemed to have no relationship to the other contents of the drawer. When she flipped it open, she discovered Marty's handwriting: notes for songs, unfinished stanzas, notations for chords. She started to toss the notebook aside when she saw Tara's name. On closer inspection, some of the notes seemed to be written in code.

Stephanie tucked the notebook under her arm, turned out the lights, and locked the door. She had felt reasonably safe in the well-lit building, but alone under the darkening sky, her apprehension returned. An owl hooted from somewhere behind her, and she spared a moment to sympathize with the small woods creatures cowering under inadequate shelter. Danger walked the night.

Twilight dropped softly, throwing a veil of shadows over the surrounding woodland. Sam, who had been prowling in the underbrush, joined Stephanie, hovering so close underfoot she almost tripped over him. She hesitated between wanting to tiptoe so she could hear stealthy footsteps if they came and making a run for it.

Although the barn wasn't far from the lodge, it seemed an eternity until she saw the lights gleaming in the parking lot. She plunged up the front steps, leaving the pup whining outside.

Loralee met her in the lobby. "Well, you're in a hurry. Where have you been?" Her paisley shirt and gray pants were dressier than normal, but her hair was skinned back in the perpetual ponytail.

"At the barn. I've been working."

"What's that you've got? You aren't supposed to remove anything without permission."

"Just a notebook I found."

Loralee's eyes narrowed. "That's Marty's."

Clyde joined them. "Is everything all right?"

"Stephanie has Marty's notebook. She's just supposed to catalog the collection, not remove anything."

Clyde laughed, as if he thought she was making a fuss about nothing. "If she finds anything interesting, I'm sure she'll let us know. Right, Stephanie?"

Loralee didn't give in gracefully. "If that notebook contains anything about Tara or Marty, I want to see it."

Stephanie looked up to find Lance and Monica entering the

lobby. Brad waited in front of the registration desk, and Mac stood at the entrance to the dining room. They were all staring at the notebook in her hand.

* * *

Brad ate his ribeye steak and baked potato while trying to watch the others without seeming to. He didn't know what was in that notebook Stephanie found, but it had sure created tension around the dinner table.

Lance and Loralee sat in silence. Clyde stumbled through a longwinded lecture on insurance rates. Stephanie kept her eyes on her plate, not looking at anyone, but every so often she shot a simmering glance in Loralee's direction. Only Kate and Heather seemed unconcerned.

Monica chattered about her plans for a theater, but the conversation seemed stilted. "Loralee, I'd like to use you in a number. You have a lovely voice."

"I'm not good enough." Loralee protested. "Tara had a good voice. She was a better actress, though."

"No." Monica tapped the table for emphasis. "Tara has a nice little voice, and while she did a competent job in the local little theater, I doubt whether she could have made it on the stage. Your voice, however, is very good."

To Brad's surprise, Loralee's face emptied of expression, except her eyes glowed with something curiously close to anger.

"You used to always be singing, Loralee," he said. "I've missed it."

"We all have." Mac appeared at her elbow, carrying a pitcher of tea. Brad shook his head, indicating that he didn't want more, and Mac moved on around the table.

"I talked to the bank today about getting a loan on the lodge," Lance said. "We oughta know by the end of the week."

"Oh, Lance. Really?" Monica exclaimed. "Are you sure you want to do this?"

"I'm sure. This way you can keep working, but we'll see more of you. Kate needs her grandma."

Clyde raised his water glass. "Here's to Monica's new theater. I'm looking forward to having a lifetime pass."

"Look out, Shoji Tabuchi," Brad laughed. "There's a new theater coming." It was good to see Monica excited again. Marty's death had left her looking wounded.

"Oh, mine won't be like Shoji's," she protested. "I can't afford anything like that, but it will be as nice as I can make it. I want a picture of Marty in the foyer and some sort of tribute to him. Don't you think that will be all right?" she asked Stephanie.

"I think it will be great. He would have been proud."

Brad had to agree to that. Marty would have been in his element. He would have chucked the little girls under the chin, hugged the older girls, kissed the women, and joked with the men. He was good enough with strangers in short encounters. He just didn't wear well for the long haul.

Monica shoved back her chair and stood up. "I have some phone calls to make. Loralee, why don't you come to my room and we'll start pickin' out music, and we've got PR stuff to talk about."

"What about me?" Kate asked. "Don't I get to help?"

"Of course you do, sweetie. You have a lovely voice. Perhaps I can use you in a number, too." Monica glanced challengingly at Lance. "How do you feel about your daughter bein' a performer?"

"I think I'm outnumbered." He laughed. "I'm going to feel mighty proud sitting out in the audience watching the women in my family outshine all the stars in Branson. We'd better get started drawing up plans if we're going to have a building ready for you."

"I have some ideas on that too," Monica told him. She and Loralee left the room, chattering excitedly.

Heather looked exhausted. Lance pulled out her chair. "I'll take you to your room. We can't have you overdoing."

Kate snuggled close. "Let's have breakfast together in the morning."

Heather smiled and put her uninjured arm around Kate. "I think that would be great. Come to my room when you're ready to eat."

Everyone left the dining room, and Stephanie hurried to her suite to get the notebook. It was still early, just eight-thirty, and she wanted to talk to Brad. She scurried down the path to the cabin, notebook tucked securely under her arm. The dark was her friend. If she couldn't see anyone, they couldn't see her, either. The stars were cold, yellow spangles against the deep black of the sky. The fragrance of wet earth and new grass tickled her nostrils. The flicker of firelight warmed the windows of the cabin.

Brad answered her knock. "What are you doing out alone at this hour?"

"What better time to come? No one would expect me to go visiting this late. I have something to show you." She pushed past him, anxious to get out of the yellow glare of light spilling out the door. Sam was curled up on the hearthrug. Apparently he had conned Brad into taking him in.

"The notebook you were determined to keep?" Brad took it from her and turned the book over in his hands. "What's so special about it?"

"For one thing, it mentions Tara. Trouble is, I can't read it. I thought maybe you could help."

"If you're serious about this, I'll see what I can do." He took her jacket and draped it over a chair. "I warn you, though, I can't see this fixation of Loralee's that something happened to Tara."

Stephanie sat down on the couch, and Caesar came to lean against her, begging to be petted. Sam nipped at her ankles with a cheerful abandon. The warmth of the fire and the relaxed atmosphere of the cabin welcomed her.

Brad sat beside her on the couch, trying to decipher Marty's handwriting. Stephanie inhaled the warm, spicy scent of his cologne, conscious of his nearness. It was hard to concentrate on the notes.

He suggested they start with Tara's name, as it was the only word they could recognize. "This reminds me of the secret codes we used to make up when I was a kid."

They stumbled through several theories, but nothing worked. Stephanie, aware of the clock hands ticking slowly, knew she needed to go back to her own suite, but she was reluctant to leave the safety of Brad's cabin to walk the dark path back to the lodge.

Brad ran his fingers through his hair, something she had wanted to do for the past fifteen minutes. "He sure didn't intend for anyone to read this." He tossed the notebook over onto the coffee table and gulped a mouthful of tea. "Monica wants me to go out to her farm tomorrow and check a stand of young pines. Want to come along? We can take a picnic basket."

A picnic with Brad? Just the two of them? Her internal radar emitted a warning, which she decided to ignore. "Is there a house?"

"No house, no outbuildings. Just a gorgeous view, a brook, and maybe we'll see a few deer."

"It sounds great. What time?"

"About eleven. Dress warm and comfortable, and don't tell anyone we're going. Let's keep it just the two of us."

He took her hand, and she didn't pull away. "I don't like your getting involved in this mess we have at the lodge. I'm afraid it's going to get worse before it gets better."

"I didn't choose to get involved. It was sort of forced on me."

He stretched out his legs and settled into a more comfortable position, still holding her hand. "I'd encourage you to go back home, but you wouldn't."

"No. I can't leave. Rob won't let me."

"Is that the only reason you stay?" His eyes questioned her.

"No," she whispered.

The fire crackled. Sam whimpered in his sleep. Brad leaned closer. Stephanie swayed imperceptibly toward him, knowing he was going to kiss her.

A log fell in the fireplace, breaking the spell. Stephanie

pulled back. "Brad . . . don't."

He sat very still, his eyes searching hers. Then he sighed. "All right, Stephanie. I won't rush you."

He stood up and helped her into her jacket. "Come on. I'll walk you back to the lodge."

"You don't have to do that."

"I do if I plan to sleep tonight. I don't choose to lie awake wondering whether you made it back okay."

He held her hand as they walked the rough path. The stars glimmered like new diamonds. The night was warm for March, and spring peepers sang their froggy songs from the lake. They reached the lodge much too soon.

Stephanie felt a faint stirring of disappointment, knowing how much she had wanted Brad's kiss. Why couldn't she let go of the memories of her parents and their miserable failure at love? Brad was right, she was afraid of commitment. Afraid it wouldn't last.

He rested his hands on her shoulders. "I want you to go inside and stay put. I have enough to worry about without having you wandering around loose."

He placed one finger under her chin, tilting her face up toward him, and this time she didn't pull away. His lips brushed hers, soft and gentle. A kiss to dream on. She floated upstairs in a rosy fog of happy confusion.

The minute she stepped inside her suite, she knew something was wrong. She stood by the door, the hair on the back of her neck prickling. The couch cushions were crooked, the vase of silk flowers had been moved.

Stephanie sat on the couch, watching the shadowed corners of the room reflected in the gilt-framed mirror. Thanks to Loralee's performance in the lobby, everyone knew that Stephanie had Marty's notebook, and someone had searched Stephanie's room.

17

The next day, Stephanie dressed in jeans and hiking boots and a moss-green sweater to match her eyes and compliment her red hair. She realized she was thinking about Brad in a way she had never intended. Was the feeling she had for him love? She honestly didn't know, and it wasn't anything she wanted to face right now. She brushed her hair until it gleamed with highlights, grabbed her jacket, and headed for the stairs.

Brad waited for her in the lobby. "How about that—right on time."

"Did you get the picnic basket?"

"Sure did, and now let's get out of here before someone decides to crash the party."

They ran out to the truck and were soon speeding away from the lodge. Stephanie leaned back in the seat, enjoying the scenery. Brad didn't drive as fast as Lance, and he kept both hands on the wheel. She liked that. She also liked the way his dark hair waved back from his forehead and the way his smile warmed her heart. She felt relaxed, with no pressure to talk.

He turned his head to smile at her. "All right?"

"Fine." Very fine.

"We'll soon be there."

"I'm in no hurry." And she wasn't. It was good to get away from the lodge, if just for a few hours.

* * *

Brad enjoyed being alone with Stephanie. Seemed like at the lodge someone was always around. Today he meant to bring the conversation around to a personal level. Maybe make a start at chipping away at the wall she had built around her heart.

It didn't take long to drive the distance to Monica's property, which was situated on top of a tall hill. They could see for miles. The Ozark Mountains lined up one behind the other, stretching into the distance until the blue of the farthest hills became a smoky smudge against the lighter blue of the sky.

Stephanie sat down on a large chunk of limestone and leaned back against a sturdy oak tree. "What a beautiful place. I wish I had a house here, with a wide front porch and a flower bed in front."

"No picket fence?" Brad spread a cloth and started unpacking a lunch of grilled chicken and vegetables, marinated salad, croissants, and, for dessert, fresh fruit compote.

"Picket fences have to be painted. Haven't you read your Tom Sawyer?"

"Mark Twain? Used to be a favorite of mine. I go in for more serious reading now. I like mysteries and Westerns for fun, and I read my Bible a lot." He poured ice tea into plastic glasses. "I've been watching for you in church. Guess I've missed you."

"No, I haven't been there. I don't go anymore."

Caught unawares, his mouth gaped open. "You don't? I thought you went all the time. At least that's the way Marty told it."

"Sure. I was the only kid in my Sunday school class with a perfect attendance record. It didn't take. I guess I have more of Marty in me than I do of my mother."

A red-tailed hawk floated overhead, riding the air currents. Lazy, fluffy little clouds drifted past. Brad was almost afraid to ask the next question.

"You are a Christian, aren't you?" He waited, fighting a prickle of apprehension. She had to say yes.

Stephanie looked out over the hills, a thoughtful expression on her face. "No, I guess I'm not."

"Not?" He couldn't believe this. The one woman he'd wanted since losing Kelly, and she was off-limits to him. His hopes for the future were just dreams without substance. He tried to compose his features so she wouldn't realize what he was thinking.

He said the blessing, and they finished eating, but for Brad the day was ruined. Stephanie seemed unaware of how he felt, and he tried to act natural, as if she hadn't just shot down his dream.

After lunch he got to his feet. "Want to walk back to the pines with me?"

"No. I think I'll just stay here and enjoy the view, maybe do some exploring."

He hesitated. "Why don't you wait until I get back, and I'll help you explore?"

"Get along with you." She leaned against her tree, smiling up at him. "I'll be all right. Probably I won't even stir from this spot. Has anyone told you that you worry too much?"

"Sure. I know. You're a modern woman, and you can take care of yourself. I won't be long."

* * *

Stephanie smiled as he walked away, enjoying the way his shoulders filled out his sweatshirt. Having someone worry about her was a novel experience. No one had been very concerned about her since her mother had died, except Aunt Margaret, who was mostly worried she would never find a man. Aunt Margaret would like Brad. For that matter, *she* liked Brad.

She sat for a while, enjoying the sunshine, but the call of her dream house was too strong to be denied. She wandered around the clearing, placing the living room here, the kitchen there, planning the landscape design. It all seemed so real she almost expected to turn around and find the house she had built in her mind waiting for her.

The spring rains had softened the ground, so she tried to stay on the grass to escape the mud. A straggly bush growing beside an irregular mound of earth caught her eye. A French lilac, she was sure, the kind her grandmother used to grow. She stepped closer, so intent on the lilac she didn't think to watch her footing. The ground dropped from under her.

She plummeted straight down, clutching at brittle lilac branches that broke off in her hands. A spate of rocks and wet dirt showered around her. She landed in a crumpled heap, her left hip hitting a large stone. The impact drove the breath from her lungs.

Stephanie pushed up to a sitting position, dazed from the fall. She had dropped into an ancient cistern that had evidently been used as a dumping ground for trash. As her eyes adjusted to the dim light, she could see the remains of an old suitcase and several rusted tin cans.

Vacant eye sockets peered from the shadows. A grotesque grin from bared teeth. Bones. A human skull lay about three feet away. Her heart rocked in a sudden surge of terror. She threw back her head and howled, her scream echoing off the walls of her prison.

"Stephanie! Stephanie? Where are you?"

"Here! Brad! Hurry!" She scrambled to her feet, putting as much distance as she could between her and that pile of bones.

"Where?" He was almost over her head.

"Down here! I fell in the cistern."

"How did you get down there?" He sounded exasperated. "Turn my back on you for just a minute . . . ."

"*Get me out of here!*" The rising hysteria in her voice finally got through to him. His face appeared in the opening, looking scared and blocking most of the light, which didn't help her state of mind. Something small and moving fast skittered across her foot. She screamed even louder, and he winced as if in pain.

"If you can yell like that, you're not hurt too bad. Calm down before you bust my eardrums."

"There's someone dead down here, you idiot. Get me out." But his words, while not exactly soothing, had brought her around. She was ashamed of her panic. That poor wretch, whoever he might have been, had lost the power to harm long ago. Just the same, she wanted out, but if she felt calmer, Brad was definitely rattled.

"What do you mean dead? How dead?"

His question struck Stephanie as devastatingly funny. She whooped with laughter until she cried. "Long dead," she gasped between guffaws. "Just bones." To her horror she couldn't stop laughing. The sound bounced around the walls and inside her head until she covered her ears with her hands, trying to turn down the volume.

"Stop that," Brad yelled. "Stop it now!"

The sudden silence was deafening. Stephanie wiped the tears from her face with muddy hands. Her breath came in shuddering gasps. "Get me out of here," she pleaded.

"Look, Steph. I have to get a rope out of the truck. It'll just take me a minute, I promise. Okay?" He sounded like he expected her to explode into hysterics again.

An aching loneliness settled around her as he hurried away. Each second he was gone seemed like an hour. Half convinced he had left her, she was just getting ready to yell for help when she heard him coming.

"I'm dropping the rope down. Can you climb out?"

"Just watch me." The rough fiber burned her hands. Her legs flailed as she tried to grip something, anything. Somehow she managed to get high enough for Brad to grab her wrists and haul her out. Her new sweater was ruined, mud gritted between her teeth, but a cool breeze fanned her face, the sun warmed her back, and she just wanted to lie there, hugging the friendly earth forever.

Brad yanked her to her feet. "Are you all right?"

She nodded.

"Were you serious? There are bones down there? Animal or human?"

"Human. At least there's a skull."

He released her and moved toward the hole. She grabbed his arm. "Don't! I can't get you out."

He pulled away but stopped to wipe the mud from her cheek. "Dirty face. I have to see what's down there. It's all right. I can climb out."

He released her and sat down on the wet ground, lowering himself into the hole. She noticed a flashlight sticking out of his back pocket. He dropped lightly, not at all like the bone-jarring way she had fallen. She shuddered and turned away, unable to look. She had never been claustrophobic, but the dank, dreary confines of that narrow hole and its macabre contents had brought out fears she never knew existed. Nothing would ever induce her to go back down there. After a few minutes, Brad's head and shoulders appeared in the opening as he pulled himself out.

"Well?" Stephanie demanded. "Was I right? It's human?"

"You were right." He looked sick. "Do you know what you found?"

The idea must have been forming somewhere in the back of her mind, because she was suddenly sure what he was going to say. "Don't tell me . . ." she began.

He nodded. "I think you've found Tara."

* * *

Stephanie sat in the pickup, staring at the hills, which didn't seem so pretty now. Tara, beautiful Tara, had been in that cold, dark cistern for three years, while the flesh rotted away from her bones.

Brad climbed into the pickup and pulled her close. She leaned against him, drawing comfort from his strength. "Rob will be here soon, and he's bringing Lance with him."

"Oh, Brad. Poor Kate. And Loralee, what will she do?" This would be devastating for her.

He took out his handkerchief and wiped her face. "Hold still. You look like you've been dragged through the mud."

"I have," she gulped. "You pulled me out of that hole I wish I had never fallen into. The Harringtons will have to go through the media nightmare all over again."

"Do you think it would be better for them to go on wondering what happened to her?"

"You make it sound like I've done them all a favor." She sniffed, grateful for his arms around her. "They have a horrible time ahead of them."

"Yes, they do," he agreed, "but with God's help they'll get through it. At least they'll know the truth, and not stay in limbo wondering about her."

Stephanie ignored his comment about God. She knew from experience you got through the rough spots in your life by putting one foot in front of the other and plodding ahead. God had precious little to do with it. She knew that Brad was right about the rest of it. Tara had been a blight on all of their lives. How sad to leave such bitter memories behind.

The wail of sirens echoed from the surrounding hills, and the sheriff's car came into view, followed by a police van. Lance had ridden with the sheriff. Brad went to meet them, and they talked for a few minutes before Rob came over to the pickup. Stephanie rolled down the window.

"I'm going to have to ship you back to Independence. I've had more business since you came than I've had all the rest of the year, put together."

"Don't joke, Rob. I'll have nightmares about this day for a long time to come. Brad thinks we've found Tara." Her lips trembled, and she knew she was about to cry.

"He might be right." He patted her hand. "Don't take it so hard. We need to wrap this case up and forget it. People can grieve for only so long without turning bitter."

"I guess so. How's Lance taking it?"

"Hard to tell. He's smart enough to know he'll be a suspect, of course." He unwrapped a peppermint and popped it into his mouth. At her look of surprise, he muttered, "Ran out of toothpicks. Stick around, Steph, I want to talk to you about how you found the body."

Rob walked over to join Brad and Lance at the cistern. Stephanie reflected sourly that her testimony would sound good in court. I found the body by falling through a hole. It sounded like something from *Alice in Wonderland*. No, Your Honor, I'm not sure if it was a rabbit hole.

The sun dropped behind a tree-covered hill, and the air cooled rapidly. Stephanie shivered and pulled her jacket around her, wishing she had thought to ask Brad for his truck keys. The heater would have felt good.

* * *

Brad waited with Lance as a couple of deputies went down into the hole. They set up flood lamps to illuminate every inch of the cistern. The bones were visible now—chalk white rib bones, long bones, and a grinning skull.

Jake went down the rope ladder as soon as the lights were set up, recording the scene with his camera. When he was finished, the two cops went over the ground inch by inch. The bones were bagged, labeled, and hauled to the surface. The police spread out a sheet of plastic and placed the suitcase on it. The sides were rotten, the contents spilling out. One of the policemen drew on latex gloves and went through the case item by item.

Brad noticed a tattered piece of a dress Tara used to wear. A large purse, the leather dry and cracked, yielded nothing important, just odds and ends of makeup: a lipstick, a bottle that had held foundation.

The men folded the sheet of plastic, securing the ends, and slid it into a separate bag to be hauled up. After the more obvious items were cleared away, Rob went down, and Jake came out to join Brad and Lance as the other three did a thorough search of the cistern.

Brad sensed tension building in Lance. This had to be tough for him. Tara had been mostly an absentee wife, but he had loved her once, and they'd had a child together.

Lance squatted at the rim of the cistern. "Rob?"

"Yeah? What?"

"Tara had a pendant she wore all the time. Never saw her without it for about a year before she came up missing. You finding anything like that?"

Rob peered up at them. "No, I don't believe we did." He glanced at the other two cops, and they shook their heads.

"That's funny," Lance muttered. "I can't see her not wearing it."

"What'd it look like?" Rob asked.

"It was on a gold chain, a good-sized chunk of ruby, with some diamonds."

Brad remembered it now. Maybe Tara's killer took it.

"Sounds expensive," Rob said.

Lance's voice had a hard edge. "I wouldn't know. I didn't pay for it."

* * *

Brad drove around to the back of the lodge. He and Stephanie got out of the truck and entered through the service door, passing through the kitchen area where Tom and his helpers were chopping and sautéing ingredients for dinner.

One of the cooks called, "Hey, man, you all right?"

Brad shook his head. "I'll be right back."

He walked with Stephanie to the elevator. "I'll see you later. All I want right now is a hot shower. I feel dirty, not just muddy, dirty inside, you know?"

She knew. She felt the same, as if they had been tainted in some way by today's discovery. The elevator stopped, and she stepped inside and pushed the up button. The doors slid shut, leaving Brad behind.

In her room, Stephanie stripped off her muddy clothes and turned the shower on as hot as she could stand it, scrubbing her skin so hard it tingled, as if she could wash away what she had seen. Later, dressed in jeans and a rust-brown sweater, her hair twisted up in a Grecian knot, she applied makeup with an unsteady hand.

Someone knocked on her door, and she went to open it. Monica stood there, her face white and drawn the way it had been too many times in the past weeks. "May I come in?"

"Sure. How's Kate?"

"She'll be all right after the shock wears off. I think Kate had given up on her mother ever coming back, and they really weren't all that close. She has Heather to help her past this period of grieving. It's Loralee I'm worried about."

"How's she taking it?"

"She's locked herself in her room and refuses to come out. I thought maybe you could get her to listen to you."

"I'll do what I can. Do you want me to try now?"

"If you will."

Monica led the way to Loralee's door and stood back while Stephanie knocked. No answer. She twisted the knob. "Loralee?

It's Stephanie. Let me in."

After a few minutes, the latch clicked and the door opened. Stephanie looked over her shoulder, but Monica had vanished. She took a deep breath and stepped inside. Loralee was a mess. Her eyes were swollen and red, her skin blotchy, her face wiped clean of all expression.

Her lips barely moved. "They said you found her."

Stephanie nodded. "Let's sit down and I'll answer your questions."

Loralee stretched out on the chaise lounge. "Lance said you were out at Monica's farm. How did you find her?" Her hands moved restlessly, rearranging the afghan, touching her hair, as if she couldn't be still.

"I fell into the old cistern and landed right beside her. Brad got me out and then went down to investigate." She shuddered at the memory.

Loralee stared at her. "What did she look like?"

"She was just bones. They found her suitcase. You were right when you thought she was dead." She waited for Loralee's reaction. When it came, it surprised her.

"Then someone who knew of that cistern put her there. It had to be Lance or Monica. They killed her."

"There's no evidence of what happened. We don't even know how she was killed. You can't jump to conclusions."

"It's Monica's farm. They both knew about the cistern. Lance and Tara didn't get along, and Monica hated her. It fits. You know it does."

"The same so-called facts that fit Lance and Monica fit all of you."

"You can't suspect me!"

"I understand the way you feel, but this is the same thing I went through when Marty died. You have to accept that everyone, including you, will be under suspicion."

Loralee started crying again, and Stephanie hugged her, trying to offer comfort. She could barely hear the frightened whisper. "I'm so scared."

"There's nothing to be afraid of. Tara's gone, and the waiting is over, Loralee. It's ended."

"You don't understand." Her eyes were wide with fear. Suddenly she relaxed, her shoulders slumped as she breathed deeply, fighting for control. "What am I going to *do*?"

Stephanie thought fast. "You're going to learn to walk, in a manner of speaking. Don't try to solve all your problems at once. I think you'll find out what most people have known all along. You're not like Tara. You're better."

"Better than Tara?" She bowed her head, letting her hair fall softly around her face, hiding her expression.

Stephanie pulled her to her feet. "Go wash your face and comb your hair. It's time for dinner, and you are going downstairs with your head up and your shoulders straight, and you're going to carry this through with dignity." Her mother's teaching would work for this occasion, too. "Don't forget, you're not alone. You have friends."

Loralee stared at her without speaking, her expression blank and unreadable. Then she turned and left without a word. Stephanie heard water running in the bathroom and relaxed, wondering what she could have done if Loralee had refused to listen. Locking herself away to brood over her memories was the worst thing she could do right now. She needed to be around people.

Someone knocked on the door, and Heather entered, just as Loralee came out of the bathroom, looking more in control. Knowing how the two women felt about each other, Stephanie expected fireworks.

Heather reached out to hug her. "I'm sorry. I know what it means to lose someone you love. I've been praying for you. If there's anything else I can do, just tell me."

Loralee freed herself and moved away. Heather raised her eyebrows and let her arms drop, but she didn't say anything.

Monica tapped on the door frame. "May I come in?"

"Always room for one more." Stephanie leaped into the breech. "Is it time for dinner?"

"Yes. I hate this, but we have to go downstairs and face all those people. We could order room service, but it would look cowardly, and I'm determined to not give the media anything more to gossip about. If you're ready, we'll go together." She hugged Loralee. "I'm sorry about Tara. I never listened when you were so sure something had happened to her. I apologize for that."

"That's all right." Loralee accepted the embrace but made no effort to return it. "I guess I'm ready."

All sound died when they walked into the dining room. Lance and Kate had joined them at the top of the stairs. Kate was calm, but her eyes showed that she had been crying. Brad was already seated at the table.

They made their way through the silent room, heads high, faces grave, but composed. Mac was their waiter tonight. He took orders, delivered glasses of water, and disappeared into the kitchen, saying little.

They had just started eating when Clyde arrived. "I came as soon as I heard. What a terrible thing."

"Hello, Clyde," Monica gestured toward an empty chair. "Join us? And yes, it is terrible. Here's Mac. He'll take your order."

His ordering finished, Clyde looked across the table at Loralee. "I'm sorry about Tara. I want you to know that, and to offer my help for anything you need."

Stephanie stared at him. Was it just her imagination, or did he look relieved?

Loralee bowed her head and choked back tears. "I appreciate it, but there's nothing anyone can do. We'll just have to get through it the best we can."

"When's the funeral?" Clyde sipped water. "But I guess you haven't had time to make arrangements."

Stephanie looked up, surprised that the thought of a funeral hadn't occurred to her, maybe because Tara had been dead for so long.

"We'll have to wait until Rob releases the body." Lance glanced at Kate as if to see how she was taking this. "You're right, though. We haven't had time to make plans. Loralee will have a say in what we decide."

Clyde chewed a bite of steak. "Of course. Does Rob have any leads?"

"He didn't say." Lance looked like he wanted to change the

subject. "He promised to keep us informed."

Stephanie glanced around the table at the people seated there. A sudden trick of light threw unexpected shadows on their faces so that they looked different, as if a mask had slipped, revealing what they were really like, sly and secretive. She carefully placed her fork in the center of her plate. She had lost her appetite.

18

When Stephanie came downstairs the next morning, she found Rob waiting in the family dining area. "I need to talk to you where we won't be disturbed. Brad said we could use his cabin."

They wandered down the path, and Rob held the door for her. Brad had built a good fire before leaving. Crackling flames flooded the room with warmth. Rob sat down on the couch and opened his notebook. "Look, Steph, I have a feeling we're rushing toward an explosion on this thing that will make Mount St. Helens look like a piker. Tell me what happened yesterday."

"There isn't much to tell. Brad went to check on a stand of pines, and I explored the clearing." She thought of the dream house she had built in her mind and dismissed the idea. "I stopped to look at a lilac and stepped on the wrong spot and fell. You saw the hole."

"Yeah, I know about the hole. I don't know what you decided not to tell me just now." He stuck a toothpick in his mouth and waited as she fidgeted.

"Oh, all right. I know it's silly, but the more I looked at that view, the more I wanted a house there. I was picking out where I would put the rooms."

He grinned. "There's a hill overlooking my favorite fishing spot. I've dream-built on that several times. Someday if I get rich enough, I might buy it and build for real. Tell me about yesterday."

She forced her mind to remember what it wanted to forget. "The fall knocked the breath out of me. When my eyes adjusted I could see that skull grinning at me. I screamed loud enough to bring Brad running and the longest fifteen minutes of my life were spent in getting me out of that hole and back into the sunlight."

"Yeah. I get a little claustrophobic myself. You've been here for some time now. I want you to tell me what you've heard people say about Tara. Did Lance mention her?"

"You know Lance. He doesn't talk much, particularly about his problems. He had a detective looking for Tara."

"He told me that." Rob scribbled in his notebook, drawing a house, complete with a chimney and front porch.

"You've known these people longer than I have. What good is this?" Stephanie asked.

"You might have gotten onto something I missed. Did Monica like Tara?"

So what was this, a trick question? Stephanie slatted a glance at him. "You know she didn't, but if she killed her daughter-in-law, would she have been quite so vocal about how she felt?"

"I don't know. Might make a good cover. Whoever put Tara in that cistern didn't aim for her to be found."

Stephanie slumped down in her chair, stretching her feet to the fire. She couldn't see how this was getting them anywhere. Apparently solving a murder in real life wasn't much like solving one on TV. "How could anyone have taken her out there without being seen?"

"It could have been done at night. Not much traffic on that road. It dead-ends at Homer Garrison's, and Homer don't go anywhere after dark. It would have been safe enough if the killer picked the right time."

"Do you really suspect Lance?"

"I suspect everyone. Hear you found Marty's notes. How about letting me see them?"

"As if I have a choice? Brad has them, but they won't do you any good. They're written in code." She grinned at him. "Unless you list code breaking among your talents."

"I don't, but I know a guy who does." He flipped the toothpick toward the fireplace. "The way it looks now, Marty got too close to someone, and they got rid of him. And Heather was shot with Brad's rifle." He closed the notebook and put it in his pocket.

That knocked the breath out of her. "You're serious?"

He nodded. "The problem is, Lance borrowed it to shoot a skunk and left it in his suite. We found it in the stable, wiped clean of fingerprints, of course."

"Then you don't know who used it?"

"Not yet, but we're working on it."

"One thing you might not know, but I don't see how it could be important. Clyde and Tara were an item."

Rob looked surprised. "Now that's interesting. Guess Clyde had more on the ball than I suspected. I'd better have a talk with him."

After another half hour of discussing ideas that seemed to lead nowhere, Stephanie followed Rob back to the lodge. They were standing on the porch as Lance and Loralee came up the steps, with Monica trailing behind. Loralee's eyes brimmed with tears, Lance was grim-faced, and Monica looked spitting, scratching mad.

"What happened to you?" Rob asked.

"Reporters." Lance spat out the word. "We went to Eureka Springs to make funeral arrangements. They were on our heels like a pack of yapping dogs. Isn't there a law to make those people leave us alone?"

Rob shook his head. "Nope. None I can think of. They call it the people's right to know, or some other such malarkey."

Monica's anger boiled over. "You keep them away from this lodge, or I'll go after them with a shotgun. I'm not going to have Kate subjected to what we went through today. You'd think we were criminals. That reporter from KOCD shoved a microphone in my face and asked me how I felt. How does she think I feel? We have had nothing but grief for one full month now, and I'm sick of answering questions." She glared at Rob. "When are you going to solve this case?"

"As soon as possible. I got things to do." He rammed his hat onto his head and broke for the parking lot.

Stephanie trailed the others to the elevator, wishing she, like Rob, had someplace else to go. Lance motioned for her to join them when they reached Monica's suite, and she reluctantly followed him inside. Loralee's eyes were wide. Apparently she had never seen Monica so wild. Once inside the sitting room, Lance lowered his bulk into an overstuffed chair after tossing a couple of lacy pillows to the floor.

"Sit down, Ma, and let's talk it over."

Monica prowled the narrow confines of the room with the controlled stride of a caged lioness, lips tight, eyes narrowed, and so consumed by the heat of her anger she gave the impression she would sizzle if touched.

"I don't feel like sittin' down. People should be able to bury their dead without it turnin' into a circus."

"You court their favor when it suits you," Lance said. "There's no way to turn it off when things go sour. Publicity put you where you are."

"And where is that, pray tell?" She stopped prowling and sat down on the edge of the chaise lounge, still managing to look ready to go to battle. "My husband was murdered, my daughter-in-law's bones have been found in a cistern, and my two stepdaughters have been attacked. Are you thinkin' of nominatin' me for the 'woman who has everything'?"

Stephanie noticed her drawl became more pronounced when she got angry.

"I know, Ma." Lance rotated his shoulders. "Life gets rough sometimes."

"It sure does." She rubbed the back of her neck. The anger

subsided, leaving her as deflated as a leftover party balloon. "And don't call me Ma."

"Anything you say." His lips curved into a half smile, and Stephanie could see how tired he was. Marty's death had been horrible for her, but the Harringtons had the added burden of the discovery of Tara.

"Did Rob say when they would release the body?" Loralee asked.

Stephanie shook her head. "I know he sent the DNA samples to the Joplin crime lab, but I don't think they've heard anything."

"It all seems so terrible. There is no body, just a bunch of bones." Loralee's voice cracked. "She was so beautiful. I can't bear to think of her like this."

"She was beautiful," Lance agreed. "I understand how you feel. But we'll fill the chapel with flowers, make it as pretty as we can for her."

Loralee clasped her hands together. "Monica, I know you got upset when that reporter asked if you were going to sing at the funeral, but it would mean a lot to me if you would."

Monica removed her hat and tossed it over onto a small table. "After all we've been through, I don't feel much like singin', but if that's what you want, I'll try."

"I just thought I'd like to make it as small and as dignified as possible." Loralee ducked her head, fighting tears, and Stephanie reached over to put an arm around her shoulders.

"I like that," Lance said, getting to his feet. "You're right. We don't need anyone else."

After he left, the women all just sat there, too dispirited to say much of anything. Stephanie couldn't imagine what they were going through. She'd stopped reading the newspapers, but according to Brad, they'd made *Good Morning America*. Diane Sawyer had been appropriately horrified.

The door flew open, and Kate rushed in, flinging herself on her grandmother.

"Look out!" Monica fought to regain her balance. "You almost knocked me over." After getting a look at her granddaughter's face, her expression hardened. "What's wrong? What happened?"

Heather had stopped just inside the door. Now she advanced into the room. "Kate was bored, so we slipped out for a drive. We stopped at Wal-Mart and bought a game and then went to the ice cream shop. The best I can figure is that someone there called the reporters. It was a mob scene." She took a deep breath. "You might as well know. There was one man who was very obnoxious. He wouldn't get out of the way, and I kicked him. I suppose it will be on the news tonight."

"Good!" Monica's temper flamed again. "I wish I'd kicked someone." She tightened her arms around Kate. "Don't cry, sweetie. We'll see they don't bother you."

Kate raised her tear-stained face to look at her grandmother. "Who killed my mother? I want to know."

"We don't have the answer to that." Monica smoothed her granddaughter's hair away from her forehead. "We're going to find out, though, and when we do, I'll tell you. That's the best I can promise right now."

Heather sat down in the chair Lance had vacated. "If it's all right with you, I would like to keep Kate with me. The rest of you have a lot of things to attend to, but Lance won't let me start work yet, so I have plenty of free time."

"I think that would great." Monica's eyes thanked her. "If you run out of anything to do, I have a box of pictures and clippings I need organized into scrapbooks."

Heather hugged Kate. "How about it, sweetie? Would you like to help me with that?"

Kate nodded. "Can we have lunch up here? I don't want to go down to the dining room. People stare at us."

"Of course. Just call Tom and tell him what you would like. I think there's strawberry tart with whipped cream."

"Do I get two?" Kate asked, the beginning of a smile touching the corners of her mouth.

"Sure." Heather laughed. "Come on. Let's go play your new game."

They left, and Monica sighed. "How wonderful to be young enough that strawberry tart can take your mind off your problems."

Loralee pushed herself off the couch, moving slowly, as if it took a great effort. "I think I'll lie down for a while before lunch. I have a headache."

Monica fished in her bag. "Here. Take two of these. Best headache cure I've found. I carry them with me all the time. Entertainers are like the postal service. Come headaches or heartaches, the show must go on."

Loralee took the tablets and left, with Stephanie following. At the door of her suite, she stopped with her hand on the knob. "If you don't mind, I'm very tired."

"This won't take long." Stephanie had some questions about Tara, and who better to answer them than the cousin who adored her.

Loralee shrugged and entered her sitting room. Once inside, she ignored her visitor. Stephanie watched in the mirror that half covered one wall as Loralee fished the tablets Monica had given her out of her pocket and tossed them into the toilet.

"Why did you do that? I thought you had a headache."

Loralee came out of the bathroom, closing the door behind her. "I'll take my own medicine. At this stage of the game, I don't trust anyone."

So that sweet behavior in Monica's room was all an act? And why bother? If Loralee thought Monica had killed her cousin, why beg her to sing at the funeral?

"I don't know what to believe." Loralee pushed her hair away from her face. "I'm Tara's cousin. You're Marty's daughter. What's to stop the murderer from coming after us? We may be next on the list."

"I seem to be on his list, but so far, nothing has happened to you. What makes you think something will? Do you have information you haven't given to Rob?"

It was time to get the secrets out in the open, especially if Loralee really thought she was in danger. After all, she knew Tara better than anyone else. "Most people seem to think Tara had run off with another man," Stephanie continued. "Everyone but you. Why?"

Loralee sighed and closed her eyes. "At first I thought she might have just left. It was nothing for her to pack her bags and leave for whatever city they were playing on tour, but Monica claimed she hadn't seen her."

"Why would she follow Monica? They didn't get along."

Loralee opened her eyes and stared past Stephanie. "She hoped for a chance to sing with the show. No matter what Monica claims, Tara had a lot of talent. She could have been a star if she had just had someone to help her."

Her face had that closed look again. Stephanie wondered what she was hiding now. She was learning about Loralee. Behind that pretty face was a shrewd, efficient mind that revealed only what she chose.

"One thing. When they found the body, Lance was surprised that a pendant Tara evidently wore all the time was missing. He didn't seem to know who paid for it."

Loralee closed her eyes. "I really do have a headache, and I don't know anything else. Just go away. Please."

"All right, I'll go, but if you are as afraid as you say you are, you need to tell Rob who Tara was seeing at the time she disappeared."

Loralee lifted her shoulders in a gesture of weary resignation. "Whoever it was, she was going to break up with him, like always. She just told the guys it had been fun but she couldn't leave her husband. They got the message."

"You mean they just walked away? They weren't angry?"

She shook her head. "No one ever crossed Tara."

"Someone did. She's dead."

* * *

Brad looked out his living room window to see Stephanie walking the path down toward the lake. That woman! Trying to keep her out of trouble was a full-time job. If he hurried he could catch up with her, and she would probably be in a bad mood. Everyone was these days.

He called her name, but she kept on walking. If anything, she walked faster. So all right, she didn't want to talk to him. Who cared? He clattered over the rocks in the path. "Didn't you hear me calling?"

"Yes. If I had wanted company I'd have invited you."

"It sounds like someone must have done something to upset you."

"You'd be upset too, if you had to put up with a bunch of temperamental females. It must be nice to work outside and not see anyone if you don't choose to."

"Are you one of those temperamental females?" He held up his hands in mock defense. "It's all right if you are. Feel free to fall into my arms and have a good cry."

"Don't be ridiculous." She started walking. "If you can't talk sense, go away. I want to think."

"I'm good at thinking. Maybe I can help." He took her hand, drawing it through the crook of his arm. She tried to pull away, but he only held tighter.

"Thing is, it's dangerous for you to be out here alone. I'm trying to take care of you, so go right ahead and think. I'll just walk along, ready to fight dragons—or would-be assassins."

She shivered. "Don't. I can't joke about it. There's been too much horror."

"That's why it's time to find out who's responsible for all this violence. I just wish we could smoke him out into the open before anyone else gets hurt."

"We can. I'm the one this idiot wants. We set a trap for him, using me as the bait."

He couldn't believe what she was saying. Didn't she know how much he wanted to protect her? "Are you crazy? That's a good way to get yourself killed. Of all the idiotic, ill-conceived, utterly stupid notions . . . you beat all, you know that? You just beat all."

"I'm glad you expressed your opinion so fluently. How nice that you think I'm so intelligent."

The look in her eyes told him he'd gone too far. He backpedaled, fast. "I didn't say you weren't intelligent."

"You think I'm a silly female, right? In that case, you can go back to the lodge. I never wanted you to follow me, anyway."

"You don't know what I think of you."

She stopped talking and took a good look at him. "What did you say?"

"I said you have no idea how I feel about you. For the record, I don't think you're a silly female. I think you're funny, smart, and beautiful. I'd like to keep you around a little longer if you don't object."

"I don't object," she muttered.

"What?" Had he heard right?

"I said I don't object. Now can we change the subject?"

"You're always wanting to change the subject just when it gets interesting," he complained. "So let's get it out in the open."

He never thought he'd care about a woman again after Kelly, but Stephanie wasn't like other women. He thought about her all the time. He even dreamed about her. He didn't have a right to those dreams, and he knew it, but he didn't seem to have any control over his thoughts.

When he was with her, she was all he wanted. When he was alone he wrestled with God, knowing he was wandering into forbidden territory. It seemed as though for most of his Christian life he had struggled between what was right and what he wanted. Was it that way for everyone, or just him?

He looked down at Stephanie thinking of how he'd like to take her in his arms and keep her safe. He chose his words carefully, not wanting to give a hint of his inner turmoil. "I know that after we catch this creep, you'll go away and I'll probably never see you again, but I'd have a hard time sleeping nights if I let you get killed. So until we nail this monster, where you go, I go. Is that clear?"

She stared up at him, her eyes intent and searching. Her expression softened. "You worry about me?"

He grinned. "Amazing, isn't it."

After a long pause, she said, "I planned to walk around the lake. Are you coming?"

"All the way around? That's five miles!" He looked at the sky. "It'll be dark before we get back. Don't you think we ought to stay closer to the lodge?"

She smiled, as smug as a cream-fed cat. "Since you put it that way, we'll only walk halfway around and then come back."

All right, if that was the way she wanted to play it. "I have a better idea. The sheriff drove up just as I set out after you. Why not go back and see what he wants?"

"I'm not in the mood to talk to Rob today."

So what was she in the mood for? Certainly not for heart-to-heart talks with him. Women! Who could understand them?

He bent down to pick up a flat rock, just right for skipping. "Bet I can skip this five times." The rock hit the surface, wobbled through a couple of skips, and sank.

"Is that the best you can do?" Stephanie jeered. "Watch this." She selected a smooth, white rock with very few jagged edges, held it between her forefinger and thumb, brought her arm back into throwing position, and let fly. The rock skimmed the surface of the lake while she counted. "Four, five, six! Let's see you match that."

He tried, but five skips was the best he could do. She couldn't match her first effort, either. After walking about twenty minutes, they gave up and started back to the lodge. Rob had left by the time they reached the main entrance, and Mac was setting up the buffet for the evening meal.

"Where's everyone?" Brad asked.

"In the library." Mac arranged a stack of plates and filled the bread tray. He stepped back and viewed his handiwork. "No more reservations than we have tonight, this is a waste of time. A few more weeks like this and we might as well close down."

"That bad, hey?" Brad asked.

"The only good thing about slow nights is that I get out early enough to go to the Possum House. You ought to come hear us play sometime."

"I've heard you," Brad said. "You guys make good music."

"I wasn't talking to you," Mac said.

"Oh." Brad didn't like the way the guy was smiling at Stephanie. Not that it was any of his business, of course.

"I'd like to come," Stephanie said. "I wish I could have heard Marty playing with you."

"Marty was some musician. Really could play that piano." Mac changed the subject. "I think the sheriff had some news about Tara. Loralee seemed upset, anyway."

"She has a right to be upset," Stephanie pointed out. "Tara's death was a shock to her."

"Maybe so," Mac said.

"You don't think so?" Brad asked. "Why such a skeptic?"

Mac shrugged. "She hasn't always been so wrapped up in Tara."

"That's not the way I got it." Brad pulled out a chair and sat down. "What exactly do you mean?"

"Nothing. Forget it." Mac walked away.

Stephanie stared after him. "What was that all about?"

Brad stood up and slid the chair under the table. "Who knows? Mac lives on his own planet. Let's go see what the sheriff has to say."

When they reached the library, Loralee was sitting in a miserable little heap in the wing chair, her face even paler than usual, and her eyes looked like they had been smudged in with a stick of charcoal. She jumped when they entered, as if her nerves had reached the breaking point. Monica huddled in the desk chair. Lance stood by the window, his back to the room.

At Stephanie's look of inquiry Monica explained. "Heather went into Eureka to pick up some cilantro the chef thinks he can't do without. Kate's in her room, sleeping I hope. She has flat worn us out today."

Lance turned from the window. "You might as well know. Because the body was underground, it hadn't been disturbed. She had a crushed skull."

Loralee sobbed, breaking the sudden silence.

Lance stopped for a moment before going on. "Since the police look first at the nearest and dearest, I guess I'm the number-one suspect."

"Don't say that!" Monica blurted. She looked ready to cry. "You would never have hurt Tara, no matter how badly she behaved. You just went ahead and put up with her."

"That's probably what will nail me. They'll claim I finally got tired of her." Looking worn down, Lance ran a hand over the lower part of his face.

"All of this is supposition," Brad said. "They'll need proof." It made him sick, though. He knew what Lance would be put through. He'd been there himself.

"It isn't that simple, and you know it," Lance said. "Look at what happened to you."

"That was different," Brad protested, trying to offer comfort. He hoped he wasn't just giving false hope. "They arrested me a few hours after Kelly was killed. It's been three years. There's nothing to tie you to Tara's death."

"I hope you're right." Lance sat down and braced his elbows on the chair arm.

"Who would have known about that cistern?" Stephanie asked.

"Practically anyone, I guess." Lance said. "Half the county has hunted out there."

Loralee roused enough to take part in the discussion. "Would a casual trespasser know about it, though?"

Monica frowned. "The people who hunted out there were locals who knew my family and are familiar with the property. We've never kept it posted for no trespassing."

Brad stretched his legs out in front of him, staring at his boots. That certainly opened it up, but even with every able-bodied man in the area acquainted with Tara Harrington and knowing the location of that cistern, Lance was still the obvious choice. Most murders were committed by someone connected to the victim. Rob and his team would be taking a close look at Tara's husband.

19

The minute Stephanie opened the door to the barn and stepped inside she knew something was wrong. Boxes had been rearranged, stacks of sheet music moved. She stood motionless, looking around. From what she could see, nothing had been damaged.

Without realizing it she must have begun to identify with the collection, becoming emotionally involved. This was a violation of her space. She didn't know what they were looking for, but maybe she'd do a little searching on her own. She could ignore the boxes she had already sorted and packed, having found nothing relevant there, so that only left a good half of the barn's contents to go through. *Sure, Stephanie, a piece of cake.*

She hung her jacket over a chair and dug in, looking for anything that could possibly have any connection with Marty or Tara. Letters, documents, anything.

Three hours later, dirty and exhausted, she sat down on a stack of magazines to rest. If there was anything here that could throw any light on their double murder, she hadn't found it.

The magazines shifted with her body weight, and she hit the floor. Her elbow slammed against something hard. Stephanie sat in a frustrated heap, rubbing her bruises. She was tired of Harrington Lodge and murder and bones and police investigations. If she did what she wanted to do, she'd just give up and go home. Rob would probably let her leave if she asked him. What made her think she could contribute anything to solving this case, anyway?

She got to her feet, looking at the jumbled mess she had created. A wooden box had been concealed behind the stack of magazines. Carved oak, about two feet long, maybe a foot and a half high, secured by a hasp and lock.

Stephanie stared at it, one hand gripping the key she wore around her neck. A key that just might fit that lock. Marty's box? The one mentioned in the will? She carried it over under the light. She'd been looking for this box with no luck up to now. Maybe the intruder had done her a favor, making her mad enough to really search.

An exquisite carving of a duck coming in for a landing decorated the lid. Stephanie took the key from the chain, hands clumsy with excitement, and inserted it in the lock. It fit. One turn and she could raise the lid and see inside, but the box didn't belong to her. Marty had left it to Monica. She slowly withdrew the key. She'd have to carry it back to the lodge, but first she'd call Brad and have him assemble everyone in the library.

Her phone call completed, she locked the door and started up the path. The box was heavier than it looked, and she was tired by the time she reached the lobby. She chose the elevator over the stairs. Brad waited in the open doorway of the library. He stepped aside and let her enter.

She set the box down on the desk and handed the key to Monica. "I think this is what Marty left to you."

Monica ran her hand over the carved top. "I feel like I'm opening Pandora's box."

Stephanie shook her head. "Marty wouldn't have left you anything that would hurt you. He loved you."

Monica nodded. She turned the key and lifted the lid. Stephanie held her breath, wondering what they would find.

Monica reached inside and riffled through paper. "Why, it's songs, a lot of them. It must be half full."

She lifted song after song, reading the titles aloud: "Searching," "Love Found Me," "Brighten My Night." Her eyes brimmed with tears. "I can't wait to try these. I've been so afraid I couldn't find new material, but with Marty's songs and my own theater, I can sing as long as my voice holds out."

Monica dipped deeper into the box to bring up more song sheets. "Look!"

A gold chain dangled from her hand, a flash of ruby fire, a glitter of diamonds.

Stephanie gasped. Tara's pendant? In the box that Marty had left to Monica? How did her father get that pendant? The one that Tara always wore.

Lance took the necklace, his face like a mask. The others were silent, watching. He rubbed his thumb over the ruby. His expression changed, becoming pensive. Was he thinking of the woman who loved the necklace so much she wore it every day?

He looked up to meet their eyes. "Rob will want this. It's evidence of some sort, I guess. Stephanie, you're an outsider, never knew Tara. I want you to come watch me put it in the safe."

He slipped the necklace into his pocket and motioned for Stephanie to follow him. They descended the flight of stairs and walked the hallway to his office. He spun the dial on the short, squat safe and swung open the door.

"I'm going to put it here, and I want you to see what I'm doing."

"How many other people know the combination?"

"Only Brad, as far as I know. However, that doesn't mean much, we've had the thing for years. Mom bought it second-hand and we've never kept anything very valuable in it. This is a first."

He closed the safe door, spun the dial, and then tried the handle. "We have a more modern model downstairs, but too many people know the combination to that one. I'd rather have the necklace up here. I'll call Rob, and he can pick it up."

Stephanie waited until he stood before speaking. "I'm sorry about Tara. Coming on top of Marty's death, it must seem like you're under siege."

"It's been rough, but it's not over. We're all under suspicion until the person who killed your father and my wife is caught."

"You still think the same person killed them both?"

"Don't you?"

"Marty had the necklace maybe he killed Tara." It broke her apart inside to say this, but it had to be said.

He leaned one hip against the edge of the desk. "I don't know why he had the necklace, but they were too much alike for me to think he killed her. She couldn't hurt him, because he wouldn't have cared what she thought or did, and he'd have known better than to take her games seriously."

"Why would anyone kill her?"

He took so long to answer that she had time to wish she had kept quiet. "I can think of quite a few reasons someone might want to. Tara was trouble."

"Then why did you stay with her?"

"Because of my daughter. Tara fought dirty. She threatened to accuse me of having an affair with Loralee. I couldn't risk losing custody of Kate, but I would have had to take the chance someday."

"Did she have any basis for her claim?"

"No, of course not." His expression suggested she should have known that without asking. "I like Loralee, but she was always so quiet she just sort of blended into the background. Tara was flamboyant. She totally eclipsed everyone else."

"Loralee seems pretty spectacular to me. She doesn't make the most of her looks, but she really is beautiful."

"Yeah, I guess so." He shrugged. "I've not paid much attention. She's just always been there."

"Judging from Tara's picture, they looked alike."

He shook his head. "Not really. They looked like those before and after pictures. Loralee was always kind of prim, while Tara . . ." He stopped to think. "They didn't look so much alike when you saw them together. Tara sort of glittered. She was always moving, always talking and waving her hands around. She liked bright colors and lots of jewelry. Expensive jewelry. She was beautiful and exciting . . . and dangerous."

He moved over to the window, staring out at the lighted grounds surrounding the lodge. "She was already working her poison on Kate when I wasn't around. For three years, I've dreaded the thought that she might come back. I'm glad she's dead."

He stood so close to her their shoulders touched. His large, capable hands hung by his side. Those hands could throttle a small woman. Or stab an enemy to death. She turned away from the window, away from the man beside her, conscious of the deserted office.

"Ready to go?" he asked.

The rising bubble of terror in her chest subsided. This was just Lance, not a monster who could kill two people and pretend he didn't know anything about it. But as they descended the stairs to the main level, she kept hearing his voice, tough as sun-dried rawhide, uncompromising, unforgiving: "I'm glad she's dead."

Stephanie quickened her steps, anxious to join the others. When she reached the doorway to the office, she paused. Monica and Loralee were huddled over a song sheet, working out the melody. Brad had left the room.

Clyde, his back to the others, was digging through the box of songs. He looked up and saw Stephanie, and a dark red flush stained his cheeks.

Monica turned to greet them, and Clyde dropped the songs

and stepped away from the desk. His face twisted into something resembling hatred, then his features smoothed, and he was as polished and urbane as ever. Stephanie gripped the door frame, feeling she had just encountered something very dangerous.

* * *

The telephone rang as Stephanie was laying out jeans and a sweater, and she knew before she answered it would be Brad. He had scheduled a trip to town for fertilizer, and she had promised to ride along.

"You ready to go?" His voice came over the line with a familiar informality.

"Give me fifteen minutes."

"Not a second more. If you're not ready by then, I'll find some other beautiful woman to go with me."

She hung up the phone, smiling to think that Brad had referred to her as beautiful. She met her time limit with two minutes to spare.

Brad looked at his watch. "You just made it, girl. One minute more, and I would have left you behind." His smile said he was glad to see her.

She grinned. "What about breakfast?"

"A McDonald's special coming up, if that's all right with you."

"Sounds great. I haven't had fast food since I came here. Not that I'm disparaging Chef Mackey's cooking, you understand. A few more weeks of his gourmet meals and I'll have to buy a new wardrobe."

Driving to Eureka Springs was pure delight. Bits of gardens

were tucked into the most unexpected places. Lilacs waved purple branches in the fresh spring breeze. A pool of creeping phlox wreathed a concrete birdbath. "Oh, look over there," Stephanie exclaimed for probably the twentieth time, pointing to yet another gorgeous floral picture.

"Do you want me to watch the road or look at the pretty flowers?" Brad asked.

"If you can do only one, then by all means, watch the road. I can do both at the same time."

"Then why didn't you wave at Rob when we passed him?"

She looked at him, crestfallen. "You're kidding, right? We passed the sheriff's car and I didn't even see it?"

"You were exclaiming over a bed of phlox, if I remember right."

"You win. You watch the road. I'll watch the flowers. How much farther to McDonald's?"

"Just a few minutes more. Why? You hungry?"

"I'm always hungry."

"Yeah, I noticed." He maneuvered around a slow-moving car from Arizona. "The guy who gets you is going to pay out a bundle for groceries."

"He'll be so overwhelmed by his good fortune he'll be happy to pay my food bills," she bragged.

He laughed and pulled into the McDonald's parking lot. As Brad chowed down on a sausage biscuit and Stephanie indulged in an Egg McMuffin, they discussed what little they knew about the case. They had a lot of bits and pieces but no idea where they all fit.

Brad drank the last of his coffee. "Amazing what we don't know, right? I always thought when people were involved in a murder case they knew everything the cops knew. We don't know anything."

"Maybe we know more than we think we do," Stephanie said.

"You could be right," Brad agreed. "I'm going to write down everything on index cards and see if I can make something fit. You did find that box for Monica. That's something."

Stephanie looked down at the table, not wanting to say the obvious. "We also found Tara's pendant. Why do you think Marty had it?"

Brad lifted his hands in a who-knows? gesture. "I wouldn't even try to guess. We'll probably never find out, since they're both dead."

"Do you think he killed her?"

"Is that what you're worried about?"

She nodded.

"Well, don't. You're not responsible for what Marty did. Whatever he's done, he paid for it. Besides, you're borrowing trouble. There might be a legitimate reason for him to have that necklace."

She raised her eyebrows. "Such as?"

He shook his head, wearing a pained expression. "How would I know? I'm trying to make you feel better."

It wasn't working. Stephanie hesitated. She didn't want Brad to think she was blaming Clyde again, but she needed to let him know. "Someone has been searching the barn."

"How can you tell in all of that mess?"

"Because I work over there. I understand the mess. Something else. I've seen Clyde acting like he's looking for something. He pops up all over the place, going through desk drawers and digging through that box of songs."

Brad put his fork down and looked at her. "Clyde?"

She nodded. "Here's something else. Whatever Clyde or whoever is looking for, it wasn't in that box. I hardly think he'd be interested in song sheets."

Brad pursed his lips, looking thoughtful. "You need to quit working over there until we solve this case."

"We've been over that. I'm not hiding in my room. If someone wants to get at me, they will. There's nothing I can do to stop them."

She knew from his expression he agreed with her. It was sweet of him to want to protect her, but no one could stop a determined killer. There were too many ways to commit murder. You couldn't protect yourself from them all. Just the same, although she wouldn't admit it except to herself, she was scared. The way things were going, it was like sitting on a powder keg, knowing it was going to blow but not sure when.

At the farm store they bought fertilizer. Brad added two bags of sunflower seed, one gray-striped for cardinals and one of black oil seeds for the smaller birds. Filling the bird feeders was Kate's job, and she loved doing it.

Stephanie wandered over to the plant wagon to drool over containers of impatiens and petunias. Someday she wanted time to plant and care for flowers. She was planning a cottage garden when Brad joined her.

"You want any of these?"

"I want them all, but I don't have a place to plant them."

"What about your home in Independence? Do you have flowers there?"

"A few. I never had time to take care of plants. Maybe someday."

She turned away from the tempting blooms and climbed into the cab of the pickup. When they were on the highway, driving toward home, Brad said, "I guess you'll go back to Independence when this is over."

"I guess so." She didn't want to think about that. "I can't make plans until Marty's collection is catalogued." When he didn't answer, she added, "I found a picture of my parents in a box of photographs. They looked so happy, and they made each other so miserable."

"Marriage doesn't have to be that way."

"I know that. My aunt is happily married, but I think the happy ones are the exception. Look at my parents, and Lance and Tara. For that matter, look at Marty and Monica. Can you tell me any of those unions were happy?"

"I suppose they were happy for a while, but you're right, they didn't stay happy. But you have to be realistic. Can you tell me that any of those people worked at making their marriage a success?"

"I guess I want a guarantee before I take the plunge."

"There are no guarantees. That's what makes it fun. How's that for a slogan? Put a little fun in your life—get married."

"It isn't the getting married that scares me," she admitted. "It's the living together afterward."

"That can be fun too. It has its ups and downs, but the making up is terrific."

"So I hear, but I think I'll pass."

Sometimes she wanted Brad so badly she ached, but something held her back. She recalled the echo of muffled sobs in the night, her mother's distracted manner on holidays, the way her mother spent one day a year alone. That day, Stephanie had learned later, was the date of her wedding anniversary. No man was worth that kind of misery.

* * *

Brad didn't say any more. No matter how hard he tried, he couldn't break through the wall she'd built around her heart. Why was he surprised? God hadn't broken through that wall either. Today had been fun, a taste of what life with Stephanie could be like without a murder hanging over them. He glanced over at her. She was staring out the window, looking thoughtful and more relaxed than he'd seen her since she had come to the lodge.

He knew he was playing with fire where she was concerned. If he surrendered to preach, *a big if*, the way things stood, he couldn't stand before a congregation and talk about being obedient to God's Word while refusing to obey the commandment to not be unequally yoked with an unbeliever. Unless something happened to change Stephanie, they had no future together. That was his head talking. His heart wasn't listening.

He was still praying that God would change her and somehow fit her into his life. He felt more at peace with the idea, but whether that peace came from God or from wishful thinking, he wasn't sure. Although he knew how stubborn she could be, he couldn't help believing that God's plan for his future included Stephanie. He couldn't imagine life without her. God wouldn't expect him to give up everything, would He?

He knew the answer. He just didn't want to admit it.

The gates of Harrington Lodge loomed ahead. They rode the rest of the way in silence. Brad parked the car and got out. "I need to talk to Lance, so I'll go up with you."

They stopped at the library door. A piano had been brought upstairs, and Mac was seated at the keyboard. Monica beckoned to them. "Listen to these songs. Have you ever heard anything more beautiful?" She motioned for Mac to play again. Loralee stepped up to stand beside her, sharing the sheet music.

I was searching for light out of darkness,

Blinded but yearning to see.

How could I know

That while I was lost,

My Savior was searching for me?

Loralee's rich contralto blended in harmony as if they had been singing together for years instead of just a few days. Mac contributed a fine baritone. Stephanie let the lyrics drift through her mind, wishing she could have known the Marty who had written this song about a sinner saved by grace.

"It's the best he ever wrote," Stephanie said with enthusiasm. "So different from the others."

"You're a judge of that?" Clyde asked. "I shouldn't think you would be an expert on Marty's writing. You saw so little of him."

"I have all the songs he wrote and all of Monica's recordings. As beautiful as they are, this one is better."

Monica smiled. "Then you must have it as a gift from me. We're going to record it first."

Clyde looked at his watch. "You'd better hurry if we're going to make that three o'clock appointment to look at locations for your theater. You can talk about songs later."

"It will only me take a moment to change clothes." Monica scurried away.

Clyde leaned his elbow on the piano and spoke to Stephanie. "No offense intended, but I would like to see Monica try her luck with another composer. Marty was a good enough songwriter, but we have some great new talents coming along, and I think we could do better."

"We?"

"I'm going to be her new manager. As I say, Marty was good enough at his job but I have plans for the future. I'm going to make Monica twice the star she has been in the past. I'm not sure we'll use those gospel songs. I'm looking for something more contemporary. Gospel would have a limited appeal. I want to draw a different kind of crowd. With my business judgment and her voice, we'll be unbeatable."

Stephanie's chin tilted of its own accord. How dare he put her father down this way. "Marty was good enough at his job to make her one of the top female vocalists for fifteen years. You'll have your work cut out for you trying to beat that record."

He shrugged, but Monica came out of her room just then, putting an end to the conversation. The idea of Clyde and Monica as a team was impossible to consider, after all her years with Marty. Stephanie realized it was none of her business, but she couldn't help thinking that Marty's wife hadn't lost any time replacing him.

After they left, Loralee and Heather met in Stephanie's suite for tea. Stephanie had bought a hot pot and tea bags in Eureka, and now she handed out cups and sugar cubes. Sometimes she liked a cup of tea in her room without the bother of going downstairs.

Stephanie dunked an orange-spice tea bag in her cup. "I hope Monica finds a place for her theater."

Loralee chose lemon-mint. "She will. Clyde will see to that."

"Is Clyde trying to get something going with our stepmamma?" Heather asked. She dropped a tea bag into a cup and added hot water. "I'm not sure I'd like him for a stepdaddy."

"He and Monica go back a long way," Stephanie said. "He's a cousin, I think."

"A very distant cousin," Loralee said. "But he knows how to capitalize on the relationship."

"Loralee, have you figured out who Tara was seeing before she disappeared?" Heather asked.

"I don't have any idea. We used to laugh about her men, but I could never discover the identity of the last one. The only thing she said was that he was going to help with her career."

"What career?" Heather demanded. "The only thing I've heard she did was chase men. That's not a career—it's an obsession."

Loralee examined the turquoise ring she wore, a simple, rather cheap little thing. "Monica doesn't like to admit it, but Tara had a lovely voice. I think she might have been as good as or better than Monica if she had just gotten the breaks."

"If someone was backing her in a singing career, he evidently didn't get it off the ground. He must not have known much about the music business," Heather said thoughtfully.

"Or he was lying to her." Stephanie put her tea bag in a saucer to drain. "Or she wasn't as good as she thought."

"Wonder who bought her that necklace," Heather mused.

Loralee got up, moving as gracefully as a butterfly. "I don't want to talk about it anymore." She walked out, leaving the others staring after her.

"There goes one troubled female," Heather said. "That Tara sure did a number on her."

A scream cut across her words. Heather jumped up from the lounge and bolted toward the door. Stephanie followed closely.

"No! No! Stop it!" It was Loralee's voice.

Heather slid to a stop in the doorway of Tara's room, and Stephanie slammed into her. When they had untangled themselves, they stared at Mac, who was holding a struggling Loralee. Hotel employees were removing Tara's clothes from the large walk-in closet and packing them into cartons. One of the waiters was taking down the gold satin drapes. The bed had already been stripped, the bedding neatly folded and stacked.

"Stop it!" Stephanie exclaimed, shoving past Heather. "Why are you doing this?"

"Lance's orders," Mac said, wincing as Loralee's nails raked his arm. "Ow! Cut that out. Listen to me. Tara's dead. Let her go." His voice changed, becoming a rough growl. "I hated her. I hated the way she treated you, and I hate this room. Let them tear it apart."

Loralee's eyes flamed with anger. She struggled to break away. "Don't!" Tears rolled down her cheeks; her voice broke. "Stop it! Get out of here."

"Lance ordered this?" Stephanie demanded, stepping out of the way of a burly waiter carrying a box toward the door. "How could he be so cruel?"

"I was supposed to tell her," Mac confessed. "We had a problem with a customer and I didn't get here in time."

Loralee collapsed in his arms sobbing.

"Go on, take her away from here," Stephanie ordered Mac. "I'll stay and see that nothing is thrown away. She can pick out what she wants to keep later."

Mac led Loralee from the room, his big hands gentle. Heather, who had been silent, was now ready to do battle. "What are you going to do with this stuff?"

Lance spoke from behind them. "They're taking it to the storeroom. When Loralee and Kate feel they're ready to go through it, they can choose what they want to keep. As long as Tara's things are here, Loralee will never be able to accept her death. I should have done this long ago."

"You could have done it in a less brutal way." Heather stood facing him, feet apart, hands on her hips.

He rubbed his chin in a weary gesture. "I thought it would be better to just do it. She'd never have agreed if she knew what I was planning. Where is she?"

"She's with Mac," Stephanie said.

"He'll take care of her. He's been in love with her for a long time. Rob wants to see that necklace, Stephanie. I told him I wanted you to be there when I open the safe."

"That's not necessary."

"Just the same, I want you there. You saw me put it away, and I want you there when I take it out." His voice warned her that her opposition would be useless.

Rob was waiting when they walked into the office. "Let's get that safe open. I have work to do."

Lance carefully turned the knob. There was a click, and the heavy door swung wide. He turned to stare at Stephanie, and she knew what was coming. The compartment that had held the necklace was empty.

Rob took one look at their faces and nodded. "Gone, huh? Well, that's not surprising. There's something else I have to tell you. We can't get a match on the dental records. I don't know who we found the other day, but it wasn't Tara.

20

The next day, Clyde arrived at the lodge and joined the family where they were hiding out in the library. Facing the curious stare of guests and fending off reporters was becoming an ordeal. Clyde was underfoot so much that Stephanie took his presence for granted. If Monica and Lance were tired of having him there all the time, they were too well mannered to say so.

The DNA report was the main topic of conversation. The skeleton was of a small female, young, no previously broken bones, but the teeth didn't match Tara's dental records.

"So who do they think she was?" Clyde asked. "Someone must have turned up missing about that time."

"If they know, they aren't telling me," Lance said. "Rob did say they were checking out missing persons reported around the time Tara disappeared, and they had a couple of prospects, but he didn't give me any names."

"Will you stop talking about it?" Loralee caught her breath on a sob. Stress had dulled her beauty. She looked positively haggard. "I can't stand this. Don't you understand? If that body is someone else, then where's Tara? What happened to her? Why doesn't she come home?"

Stephanie thought about Tara's necklace. Lance claimed she would never have left it behind. The chain was broken, one link pulled loose and distorted as if it had been ripped from her neck. Which brought Stephanie back to her main question. Why did Marty have the necklace? And where was Tara? Did they have another body buried somewhere at the lodge?

Lance patted Loralee's shoulder. "Get a hold of yourself. We have the police looking for her now. According to Rob, they've already had a couple of possible sightings."

"But who put the woman in the cistern?" Clyde asked. "Did Tara kill *her*?"

Monica nudged him with her foot, but the damage had been done. Loralee gasped. Her eyes closed, and her body sagged. Lance caught her before she hit the floor. He carried her to her suite while the other women followed. Once there, he placed her on the bed and left while Monica took over, moving efficiently, bathing Loralee's face with cold water, rubbing her hands. Heather hovered nearby, her head bowed, lips moving in silent prayer.

Stephanie tried not to get in the way.

Loralee whimpered, sounding very young and helpless. Her eyelids fluttered, and just for an instant Stephanie met her eyes, and it was like looking into the depths of hell. She realized for the first time what the past three years had been like for Loralee: the uncertainty and pain she had lived with because of Tara's disappearance, the horror of the discovery of the bones, and now the fear that Tara was somehow involved with the body in the cistern. Lance had been right to hire a detective. They had to find Tara. It was the only way they could save Loralee.

Monica finally aroused Loralee and got her to take a sedative. Heather volunteered to sit with her, and with a sense of relief, Stephanie followed Monica to the library, where the others were waiting. The discussion turned to the missing necklace.

"Who else knew the combination," Monica asked.

"Just me," Brad said. "I guess we're the prime suspects, and no, I didn't steal the necklace. I don't know how much it was worth, but I don't want money that badly, and one tour of duty in the slammer is all I need. I'm concentrating on being a good boy."

"Lance, you said you bought the safe used. Who did you buy it from?" Stephanie asked.

"Rob asked me that, and I couldn't give him an answer. Mom, do you remember where we got that safe?"

"You got it from me," Clyde said. "I knew the combination once, but I've forgotten it by now."

"It's an old safe," Monica said. "Anyone who knows locks could probably get it open."

Lance looked at the wall clock and got to his feet. "Come on, Brad. I want to get that last acre planted today. We need to take advantage of the spring rains."

The two men left the room. Clyde started talking to Monica about the coming theater. Stephanie left them to it and went to her suite, where she changed into jeans and a tee shirt. The cool days of early spring were giving way to warmer weather. Clyde joined her as she was leaving the lodge by the back door.

"Do you have a minute? There's something I want to talk to you about."

He didn't seem to be in a hurry, because he walked in silence, kicking absently at stones in the path. His shoes were handmade of fine leather and shined but well-worn, probably part of his aristocratic image that although an Andrews could afford to buy the best, he didn't necessarily have to be a slave to fashion.

He stopped walking and motioned toward a rustic, handmade bench set under a low-branched dogwood tree. The white blossoms were packed so tightly that the emerging leaves were almost hidden.

"Let's sit here for a while. I don't want anyone else to hear what I say."

"That sounds ominous." Stephanie sat beside him, hoping this wouldn't take long.

"I wonder if you've given any thought to leaving and going back to Independence." He shifted slightly so that he could look directly at her, pinning her to the seat by his intensity.

"No," she stammered. "I have work to do here."

"You mean that collection? Monica will run out of money before she gets around to building a museum. I intend for her theater to be the biggest and most talked about place in Branson. I'm looking around now for better investors."

"Bigger than the Grand Palace? You do have ambitions."

His smile was a pure, self-satisfied smirk. "The Grand Palace will be a cheap imitation of the Monica Harrington Theater. I'm going to make her the brightest star in Branson. Then we'll tackle the rest of the world. I'm planning on an overseas tour in our future."

"I wish you luck. Is that what you wanted to talk to me about?"

"No." He patted her hand. "I've grown fond of you, Stephanie. Marty never realized what a wonderful daughter he had, but his loss has been our gain."

Stephanie smiled, not sure how to respond to this. She didn't really like Clyde, and she wasn't comfortable with this confidential talk. A blue-tailed lizard crept out from under a rock and crawled toward her.

"I've seen the relationship growing between you and Brad," he said, ignoring the way she stiffened. "It worries me. Perhaps you don't know his history."

"You mean about his wife?" Stephanie shifted away from him so abruptly that the lizard darted back to his hiding place. "I know all about it."

"I see. And you, of course, believe his version of the story."

"He was released from prison. They caught the real killer."

"So I've heard." He leaned back and stared absently at the flowers overhead. "A half-witted handyman who used to work for him. Some say the poor man was a convenient scapegoat for Brad's influential friends."

"Are you saying Brad killed his wife? I don't believe it." A niggling little doubt reared its poisonous head, and she promptly squelched it. Brad wouldn't hurt anyone.

"I don't believe it, either." He looked distressed at her reaction. "I was just repeating idle gossip. A contemptible thing to do, and I apologize."

Stephanie was close to tears. Was that what people said about Brad? No wonder he sounded bitter at times.

"I'm sure you've wondered who might have hated Marty enough to kill him." He straightened the crease on his trousers, not looking at her.

"Of course. It's the main topic of conversation when we get together."

"Ah, but one of us knows the truth." He waved his forefinger in her face. "The killer is only pretending to wonder."

"You know who the killer is?"

"Let's say I have my suspicions. But remember, I've known these people for years. If that wasn't Tara in the cistern, it's someone who got in the way and paid for it. And only one person had an excellent reason for wanting to be rid of both Marty and Tara. Mark my word, Stephanie, Tara's not coming back. She's dead."

Stephanie caught his sleeve. "Clyde, if you know anything, you need to tell Rob."

"Rob would want evidence, and I don't have any. I doubt if any exists, but I can assure you that it's all over. Nothing else will happen."

"You can't know that," she cried, sensing where this was leading. "Marty was killed because he knew what happened to Tara."

"Yes." He nodded his agreement, pleased that she was reaching what he apparently considered the proper conclusion. "That's exactly what happened. All her life Monica has refused to give up anything that once was hers. She would never have let Tara take her husband, so Tara had to die. When Marty confronted her, she had no choice. She killed him. Think, Stephanie. That door you heard closing led directly to her room. Who else would have dared use it?"

All of her original doubts about Monica resurfaced. "Why would she have shot Heather, and why hit me? What did she have to gain from disposing of us?"

"Heather was a mistake." His voice held a ring of truth. "She meant to shoot you. But you've apparently led a charmed life. Monica is a good shot. So was Tara. Loralee is frightened of guns."

"But that wasn't Tara's body in the cistern. She might still be alive."

"She's dead, I'm sure of that. Monica grew up in the hills, and I'd bet money that Tara's in one of these caves that riddle the Ozarks. It will be a miracle if she's ever discovered. Rob will never solve this case. He's been outsmarted." He smiled at her growing agitation.

Stephanie shook her head, denying what she was beginning to accept as the truth.

He gripped her hands. "Look at me, Stephanie. You know I'm right. It's the only solution that makes sense. Of course, I will deny we've had this conversation." His eyes misted with tears, and he smiled bravely. "You see, I've always loved her. I'm only telling you because it's time you forgot this obsession about Marty's killer. Leave the lodge. It's not a good place for you. You'll be safer someplace else, and Monica will have a chance to start over. I know what she did was wrong, but they drove her to it. I'll take care of her, and I'll see she never hurts anyone else again."

Stephanie didn't want to listen, but she couldn't help herself. The scenario he laid out made a crazy kind of sense. In spite of her efforts to hate Monica, there were times when she wished they could be friends. But if Clyde was right and she really was a murderer, she would have to pay for her actions. Stephanie couldn't just walk away while her father's killer went free.

"What about Heather? Is she in danger?"

"No, Heather's safe. Monica never had to share Marty with Heather. You're the one she hated. You see, Marty loved you as much as he loved anyone, and Monica never shared what was hers. She was the same as a little girl. People don't change. They just learn to hide what they really are."

Monica had said that Marty never talked about Heather, that Stephanie was the one. Stephanie moistened her lips, her throat suddenly dry. "All right," she muttered. "I'll think about leaving."

"You do that." He got to his feet, smiling down at her as if he hadn't just accused his cousin of murder. "If you need my help, I'll be there for you. I wish I'd been lucky enough to have a daughter like you."

Stephanie watched him walk back to the lodge, tall, distinguished, back straight, head high. The things he had said weighed heavily on her mind. Monica! Could she really have killed her daughter-in-law, whom she disliked? What about Marty, the husband who had let her down so many times? Her motives were as strong as or maybe stronger than anyone else's. But what about Clyde? Why had he been so determined to buy Monica's farm for three years, the same length of time Tara had been gone, and had changed his mind the week she had been found. And why was he so eager for Stephanie to go back to Independence.

Leave while you can. Some inner instinct prodded, but she knew she had to stay until she knew who had murdered her father.

* * *

Stephanie eluded Monica for the next three days. Eating with the family had become difficult, so she took a tray in her room. Monica came looking for her. At first Stephanie wanted to ignore her knock on the door, but as a guest at the lodge, she couldn't be rude. She opened the door and let her in.

"We need to talk, Stephanie. Have you been avoiding me?"

"Of course not."

"I think you have, and I believe you owe me an explanation. If I have hurt you in any way, I deserve a chance to apologize, don't you think?"

"You've not done anything." Stephanie felt guilty for suspecting her of killing two people. Looking at her now, her blue eyes troubled, those suspicions seemed impossible.

Monica pursed her lips, looking thoughtful. "I see. Somehow you've become convinced I'm behind our present reign of terror. Would you mind telling me how you reached that conclusion?"

Stephanie couldn't tell her what Clyde thought. Monica

needed him to help with her career, and she couldn't be the one to drive a wedge between them. She searched frantically for something to say.

"Let me guess. I didn't like my daughter-in-law, so I killed her. Marty found out about it, and so, of course, I killed him too. Have you given me a motive for hitting you or shooting Heather?"

This was so close to what Clyde had said it was scary. Stephanie tried to defuse the situation. "I'm sorry. I'm not really blaming you for anything. It's just that everything is so mixed up. I guess I suspect everyone. I just wanted to spend some time alone."

Monica relaxed a little. "All right. Let's forget it. I wanted to ask if you would help take charge of the museum display. You know more about the collection than anyone else. I'm having the plans drawn up next week."

"Clyde thought you wouldn't have enough money to build a museum."

"I wouldn't have if I built the kind of theater he wants." She shook her head in amazement. "You wouldn't believe all the far-out ideas he's come up with. I'm not made of money."

"I thought you were building something like the Grand Palace."

"Well, I'm not. Mine will be on a much more modest scale." She stood up, looking down at Stephanie. "Are you feeling all right? You didn't come down to eat."

The remains of her lunch were clearly visible, so there was no use pretending. "I got something from the kitchen."

"I see. Maybe you need to rest this afternoon."

"No. I'm going for a walk." She hadn't planned to do anything, but suddenly, getting out of the lodge seemed like a good idea.

"I'll leave you to it, then." Monica left without a backward glance, and Stephanie knew that she was hurt, but better that than angry at Clyde. He might have some wild ideas about building the theater, but Monica needed him. After this murder was solved and Stephanie left the lodge, their contact would probably be limited.

It took only a moment to change into walking shoes and stop by the kitchen to grab a bottle of water. She slipped out the back door and strolled toward the lake. Today would be a good time to walk all the way around. Loralee had said it was a five-mile hike. Just what she needed in her present mood.

The path was well marked and easy to follow. Stephanie passed a couple of fishermen and exchanged greetings. Frogs leaped into the water at the sound of her footsteps. A colony of lacy maidenhair ferns danced in the wind. Birds sang from the surrounding trees. About a stone's throw from the bank, stately geese floated past, their heads held high with elegant grace.

It should have been a peaceful setting, but for some reason she kept looking over her shoulder, expecting to see someone following her. She walked faster, dodging blackberry briers and overhanging branches until, embarrassed at her own foolishness, she sat down on a log to rest.

The water ran deep here, its murky depths a dark, dirty green. The hill behind her was a steep, boulder-strewn ledge with only a few scrawny saplings clinging precariously to narrow footholds. The geese had followed the path, and now they swam nearer, expecting a handout. The sun was warm on her back and she half dozed, letting tension drain away.

The geese warned her, swerving away from the shore as if fleeing hidden danger. A water snake darted past, creating vee-shaped ripples. When had the birds stopped singing? Stephanie got slowly to her feet with the sudden caution of a wild animal sensing a trap. She turned around to look behind her. No one was in sight, but she could feel eyes watching like a cold wind blowing over her.

A clatter of pebbles drew her attention. One of the huge boulders on the steep, sloping hill rocked gently, then broke away from its mooring to plunge directly at her. She wheeled to run. Her feet slipped on the muddy bank. Twisting, rolling, falling, she hit the water with a body-jarring splash. The weight of her clothing dragged her down into the icy depths. She flailed her arms in a desperate attempt to get out of the way of the stone juggernaut hurtling toward the spot where she had been sitting.

The rock missed her by inches. The waves lifted and hurled her toward the shelter of a grassy overhang. Protruding tree roots provided a handhold. A stealthy footstep caused her to freeze in place, waiting. A light, satisfied chuckle confirmed her fears. That rock hadn't fallen naturally.

When the boulder had come hurtling down the slope, she'd had a blurred impression of someone scrambling to get out of sight, but things had happened so fast she hadn't been sure. Now she knew. Someone had tried to kill her. Someone who waited on the bank, ready to finish the job if necessary.

Stephanie hung there, half submerged, jaws clenched to keep her teeth from chattering. After what seemed an eternity, she sensed she was alone. She waited, afraid to move, until the bone-chilling cold of wind and water drove her to shore. She was still two miles from the lodge. The breeze had picked up, and she shivered uncontrollably. She had to get to shelter.

Running, tripping, falling, and scrambling up to run again, she plunged down the path, afraid to go back the way she had come, afraid of what might be waiting ahead. Held in a vise of terror and cold, she ran blindly, desperately toward the protection of the lodge.

Tom Mackey rushed toward her as she burst through the back entrance into the heavenly warmth of his kitchen. "Stephanie! What happened?"

She held him off. "I fell in the lake. Don't worry, Tom. I'm all right, but I need a hot shower and dry clothing. Don't tell anyone, please. They'll just make a fuss."

Stephanie could tell he didn't believe her, but she didn't give him the chance to say anything more. She brushed past him, running toward the elevator.

She started peeling off her wet clothes as soon as she hit her room. With the shower turned as hot as she could stand it, she let the driving stream of water beat against her numb flesh until she was warm again. Later, wrapped in her robe and snuggled under a blanket, she tried to stay awake while she thought back over what had happened. Clyde had been wrong. It wasn't over. The shadow of death still hung over Harrington Lodge.

She needed to talk to Rob. Someone had tried to kill her. But no one knew she would be out walking. Her eyes jerked open. No one knew. Except Monica.

* * *

The next day Heather found Stephanie and suggested they take a walk. They wandered down to the lake. The cool days of spring were giving way to warmth as the sun gained in strength. Stephanie sat down on her favorite rock, staring out over the water. The events of the past few days had clarified her thinking. She couldn't deny her feelings for Brad any longer. She loved him. If he wanted a deeper relationship, she was ready.

Heather broke the silence. "I'm thinking of leaving the lodge."

Stephanie turned her head to face her. "Why?"

"I don't know. I just think it would be best."

Stephanie nodded. "Because that body in the cistern wasn't Tara?"

"Something like that."

"You're in love with Lance." It was obvious if you looked for the signs.

Heather wiped away tears. "He's not free, and I can't go against what I believe. It's best if I go away."

"I see." Stephanie thought of Brad. He wouldn't go against what he believed, either. She might be ready to make a commitment, but he wouldn't be. Not as long as she wasn't a Christian. Her dreams turned to dust before her eyes. There would be no relationship. Like Heather, it would be best if she left the lodge.

A wave of sorrow engulfed her. She hadn't realized how much she loved Brad until she was faced with the possibility that she couldn't have him. Above the tumult in her heart she heard two words. "Trust Me."

She raised her head, startled by the clarity of the voice, but only Heather was there. Again, the words came, but this time she realized they were internal, in her mind. "Trust Me." She didn't know where the words came from, and she didn't really care. Nothing mattered anymore if she couldn't have Brad.

* * *

Brad drove through the stand of young pines, stopping the pickup at the top of the slope. He could see the lodge below, cars in the parking lot, people going about their business. Stephanie was there.

He got out and slammed the door behind him. After a moment's hesitation, he set off walking, driven by inner turmoil. *I can't do what you want. Leave me alone.*

The answer didn't come by words, but it was there all the same. "I will never leave you alone. Come unto Me."

A copperhead snake lay across the trail. Brad stopped, watching as it slowly eased across the path and out of sight. A serpent, wily, seductive. An age-old temptation, as old as the Garden of Eden. You can eat the fruit. Why should God deny you anything?

Forbidden fruit.

Brad walked on, knowing he had reached a crossroad. Which fork would he take? Turn his back on his beliefs, on the call to preach, on the Savior who had died for him? For Stephanie?

He slumped down on an outcropping of limestone, chest heaving with exertion as if he had been running. He breathed deeply, fighting for control. The trees, the clouds, even the rocks seemed to be waiting.

A sob wracked his body. He'd struggled for so long. Now worn with the constant conflict, he was ready to give up. *I can't fight You anymore. I surrender. Take away everything that stands between You and me.*

He gave up Stephanie, gave up his own desires. Words welled up inside of him. "Not my will, but Thine be done." The prayer of Gethsemane. It would serve him now. "If You want me to preach, I'll try, but You have to help me."

"If you go, I'll go with you."

Brad sat there for a long time, opening his heart and mind to a deep welling of peace and strength. No, he wasn't alone. He walked back to the truck, feeling as if a heavy weight had been lifted from his heart. He was ready for whatever the future held.

* * *

Heather dropped by Stephanie's room to chat. "Guess what I heard Lance tell Monica."

"No idea."

"Brad has surrendered to preach."

Stephanie absorbed the blow, too stunned to say anything. Brad a preacher? Now he was really lost to her.

Heather chattered on for a few minutes before leaving. Stephanie walked to the barn, feeling she couldn't stay in the lodge any longer. She needed to be alone.

She hadn't been sleeping well lately. That inner voice had changed the message. The words weren't clear, just a nagging feeling of something drawing her to someone, or something. She wanted to yield to the summons, but she was afraid, sensing that if she surrendered she would be changed irrevocably. She wasn't ready for that.

Lance had provided long boxes to hold Monica's costumes, which Stephanie worked with, wrapping each garment carefully in acid-free tissue paper for protection and packing them flat. After sealing the boxes and stacking them out of the way, she decided to start on the piles of song sheets. Monica wanted a special display created for them.

An hour later, she stretched her back and shoulders, trying to relieve the strain from sitting in one place for too long. A sound at the door sent her whirling to face whoever was there.

Clyde entered and stared at the accumulation of music paraphernalia. "Good heavens! I never realized how much stuff he had. Is all of this important, or is it just junk?"

"Most of what I've found so far is good. I think Monica will be able to create an excellent museum of the music industry."

He shook his head in disbelief at the stacks of books, the boxes, and the musical instruments, all cataloged and carefully labeled, sealed cartons on one side, boxes to be worked on on the other. Stephanie was gradually getting things organized. It only looked messy.

"What are you doing now?" He leaned forward, the better to see.

She held up a clipping showing Monica and Marty with others gathered around a piano. "Sorting out clippings so Monica can put them in chronological order."

He twitched the picture out of her hand. "I believe this one was taken at the Rookwood Lounge. Tara liked to drop in when Monica and Marty performed locally. She always hoped Monica would ask her to sing, but of course that was out of the question."

"Because Tara couldn't sing well enough?"

"Tara could sing. Loralee was right about that, but Monica didn't share the stage with anyone. She could have given Tara a place in her show. Singing backup would have been a start, but she wouldn't even talk about it."

The bitter tinge to his voice surprised her. "That doesn't sound like Monica. I've read about how well loved she is by her fans and the people who work with her."

"Publicity propaganda. I could tell you stories about people who crossed her and were kicked off the show with no second chance. There was always bad blood between her and Tara. She never approved of Lance's choice of a wife."

Stephanie didn't know how to respond to this.

Clyde looked at his watch. "I'll run along and not bother you. You have a job ahead of you, one I wouldn't care for. I was just curious about what we had over here. It will take months to go through all this."

"Actually, two or three more weeks should be enough to pull it all together. The real decision as to what goes into the museum will be up to Monica."

"I doubt whether she'll have time to bother with the museum.

She'll be too busy getting a show together and making decisions about the theater. I can take quite a bit of the load there. I've several ideas I think she will like." He snapped a salute and left.

Sam, never one to miss an opportunity, sneaked in through the door before Clyde could close it. Stephanie thought about putting him back out, but he was company of a sort. Obviously if Clyde had anything to do with it, there would never be a museum.

The afternoon wore on, and Stephanie was amazed at the number of cartons she had opened, sorted, and sealed. A mouse ran across the floor, and Sam leaped after him in a frenzied pursuit. Stephanie screamed at him to stop, but he was too excited to listen. He bumped a stack of boxes, causing them to sway violently.

The top box tumbled, hitting the floor with a tinkling of shattered glass and a metallic jingle. An antique music box in the shape of a gazebo rolled out onto the floor. The sides were of white painted metal; one side was badly dented. Glass panels, decorated with red and blue daisies, formed the roof. Several of them were broken.

At the bottom of the box Stephanie found a dark-blue, leather-covered book. A diary. Something glittered in the corner. She dumped it out and gasped in surprise. Aunt Margaret's necklace! So this was where Marty had hidden it. He had probably stopped by on his way to the lodge and, not having the key to the box with him, had stashed it in this top box intending to come back later. He hadn't had a later.

Stephanie examined the necklace closely, and as far as she

could see, it was fine. A double row of gold roses, each centered with a diamond, hung from a delicate gold chain. She had forgotten how pretty it was. She would personally deliver it to Aunt Margaret and never borrow anything expensive again. Lesson learned.

She slipped the necklace into her pocket and opened the diary. The owner's name was written in a slanting script: Tara. Stephanie cleared a space on the desk by sweeping everything to the floor. A red ribbon marked the place where Tara had stopped writing.

"All these months wasted when I could have been putting a show together and hiring a band. He wants me to marry him. As if I would. At least as Monica's daughter-in-law I have access to the music business. I thought he could help me, but he can't. The sooner I break it off, the better. I'll tell him tonight."

Stephanie turned back a few pages, looking for a name, a clue, but all the entries were about Tara, her wants, her needs, her ambitions, laced with her success at attracting men, all more or less confirming the first impression of Lance's wife as a selfish, self-centered, destructive woman. One entry caught her eye.

"He's always talking about how much better job he would do for Monica if Marty were out of the way. I told Marty he'd better watch out. He just laughed."

So someone wanted Marty out of the way. And Tara planned to break up with the man she was having an affair with. Was that when he killed her? The door swung open, and Stephanie made a frantic movement to hide the diary, but it was too late.

"Monica wants everyone to come to the library. She has

something to announce." Clyde stopped, seeing what she held in her hand. "So, you found it."

He started toward her, accidentally stepping on Sam. The pup yelped and leaped to his feet, startling Clyde and throwing him off balance. Stephanie shoved the diary into her jacket pocket and dashed for the back door. Sam scrabbled after her.

Stephanie paused long enough to knock down stacks of boxes to block the path, knowing she was only buying a little time. The back door was in the far corner, almost hidden by a collection of carousel horses—probably a violation of the fire code and something she planned to bring up if she ever got out of there.

She scrambled over one horse and shoved another out of her way. A quick look behind her showed Clyde working his way though the last barrier of boxes. Stephanie dropped to her knees and crawled under the horses toward the back door. Sam, her brave protector, kept trying to climb into her arms. She shoved him aside and scrambled around a wooden lion. A carved black bear blocked her path.

Once around the bear, only two more horses stood between her and the door. Sam, thoroughly scared now, whimpered loudly. Stephanie felt like joining in. Clyde had reached the first horse and was coming fast.

"Stephanie, wait!" He called. "I want to talk to you."

Wait? Not likely. She shoved the white horse out of her way, dived under the black one, and reached the door, praying it was unlocked. The doorknob turned under her hand, and she plunged out into cold, fresh air.

Stephanie could hear Clyde pushing his way through the

clutter. Night had fallen, and she knew she might have a chance to escape if she could just get away from the barn. She ran toward the lodge, looking for the side path that led toward Brad's cabin.

"Stephanie, quick! This way!" Loralee was there, pulling her into the woods. "Hurry. He's coming."

They ran blindly, plunging through thickets, dodging around trees, until Loralee stopped, frozen in place. "Hush. I think we lost him. We're close to Brad's cabin. We can call the lodge from there."

Somehow, she had brought them out onto a path. They crept along, clutching each other, freezing at the slightest noise. Their fear must have infected Sam, because he walked when they walked, stopped when they stopped. Stephanie could feel him quivering against her ankles.

Light glowed in the cabin, and Loralee peered through the window, her body pressed against the side of the house as they huddled in the shadows. Reassured that it was safe, they eased across the porch and slipped inside.

Stephanie heard the click of the lock as she ran to the phone. "I'll call Brad."

"No, wait."

Stephanie turned, catching her breath at the sight of the gun in Loralee's hand.

"What are you doing? Point that thing somewhere else."

"Poor Stephanie." Loralee's eyes were bright with laughter, as if they were playing a game. "You found the diary, didn't you? I've poked into every corner of the lodge trying to find it before

Clyde did, and you got lucky." Her laughter trilled as sweet and as clear as birdsong.

"Loralee! He killed Tara. Put that gun down and let me phone the lodge."

Her mouth twisted in a gesture of distaste. "Don't call me Loralee. I'm tired of pretending to be that simpering little fool."

She had a wild, untamed look about her. She didn't look like Loralee. She looked like . . . Tara!

She laughed. "Ah. So you know. That's right. I'm Tara."

"But you can't be. If you're Tara, then where's Loralee?"

She didn't answer, and Stephanie stated the obvious. "You killed her?"

"I had to. It was self-defense. She attacked me." A log fell in the fireplace, but Tara didn't even flinch at the sound, she was so focused on what she was saying. "She was wild, screaming at me. She meant to kill me. I could see it in her eyes."

The gun in her hand was steady. Clyde had said that Loralee was afraid of guns. That, above everything else, convinced Stephanie that this was really Lance's wife. Cold sweat ran down her armpits.

"That's why you destroyed her pictures, isn't it?"

Tara's hand tightened around the gun. "I couldn't allow anyone to compare them to me. She wanted Clyde! Can you believe that? She actually remembered every single thing I'd ever done to her. That shows she was sick, doesn't it? She even said she had to kill me so she could live. Have you ever heard of anything so crazy?"

"I can't believe you got away with it."

"I'm a better actor than Monica thinks. You want to know how I did it? I pretended to be sick for a week, keeping to my room, and then I left."

"I'm surprised no one noticed anything, even if you did look so much alike."

Tara laughed. "You've never seen a picture of Loralee. You don't know how she looked."

"Lance and Monica knew."

Tara reached into her mouth and removed a wire contraption. Immediately her face settled into a different shape, thinner, cheekbones more prominent. "You heard Monica. I played in little theater. I know how to change the way I look. And I've been gone for two and a half years. They expected Loralee, and so they saw Loralee."

"You took a chance when you came back."

Tara's expression hardened into lines of anger. "Monica set a detective on me. Prissy little Loralee would have jumped at the chance to come back to the lodge. I didn't dare say no."

"Marty knew, didn't he?" Stephanie remembered what he'd said, that people didn't really change. For some reason he had been suspicious.

"Oh yes, he knew. He claimed we were too much alike, that I couldn't fool him."

"You didn't have to kill him."

"He was going to tell the truth. He actually said I had to pay for killing Loralee. I could have gone to prison. I tried to talk to him, but he wouldn't listen. He gave me a time limit to tell Rob or he would do it."

"How did he get your necklace?"

Her expression registered raw rage. "He jerked it off my neck. Said he needed it for evidence and I wouldn't need it where I was going. Imagine *me* in prison!"

This was what Marty wanted to make right? If only he had told her the entire truth, they could have ended their reign of terror before it had gone this far.

"He said you were coming to the lodge and you knew about me, but I didn't believe him. I grabbed the knife, just trying to scare him, but he tried to take it away from me, and I hit him with it. I had to kill him. You can see that. He made me do it."

"Why did you keep stabbing him? Fourteen times!" She was so lovely, so delicately made, that even now it was hard to believe she could do anything so monstrous.

"I couldn't stop. I hit him once, and the knife seemed to take over." Her lips parted slightly, showing the pink tip of her tongue. Her eyes shined like sapphires. She laughed. "Oh, Stephanie, if you could just see your face. You don't understand, do you? You never could."

She held out her hand. "I'll take that diary. You'll be found here with Clyde's gun beside you. I'll be so grief stricken they won't even consider me."

"But there's nothing in the diary that would cause problems for you."

"There is if you know where to find it. Rob's nobody's fool. I can't take a chance on you, either. I can blame Clyde for killing you. No one will ever suspect me."

"You meant to shoot me when you hit Heather by mistake,

didn't you?"

She laughed. "That was no mistake. I may not want Lance, but I'm not about to let someone else come in and take my place. Too bad she moved just as I pulled the trigger. I think little Heather will have a fatal accident sometime soon."

Stephanie sank down onto the chair in front of the telephone table, sitting sideways with one hand resting behind her, fingers curved around a glass ball paperweight. It wouldn't be much use against the gun, but it was all she had.

Sam scratched at the door, and Tara's lips parted on a quick breath. "That's enough talk. They'll come looking for you, and I want to be back at the lodge when they sound the alarm. Tough luck, Stephanie. You should have stayed in Independence."

Stephanie threw the paperweight, striking Tara in the shoulder. At the same time she leaped out of her chair and hurtled across the room, hitting the smaller woman with a full body slam. Tara grunted from the impact. They fell to the floor, scrambling for the gun.

Stephanie's height and weight gave her the advantage, but Tara's nails raked the side of her face from eyebrow to cheekbone. Stephanie screamed in pain, stunned into slackening her grip on the smaller woman, as Tara rammed the hard ring of the barrel of the revolver against her chest. Stephanie grabbed the gun shoving it aside. The room rocked with an explosion.

Tara cried out once and went limp.

The stench of cordite stung Stephanie's nostrils. Sam howled. Someone shouted her name, but she couldn't answer. The door rattled as something heavy slammed against it. She tried to get up off the floor, but her legs wouldn't hold her. The door banged back against the wall, and Brad plunged through the opening. Lance stumbled over Sam. Clyde was there, staring horrified at Tara's crumpled, bleeding body.

Brad scooped Stephanie up in his arms and carried her to the couch. He cupped her face with his hands, looking as scared as she felt. "Are you all right?"

She nodded, and his fingers traced the furrows dug by Tara's fingernails and came away stained with blood. Anger turned his face into a bronze mask. Sam jumped up beside them, snarling when Brad tried to make him get down.

"Let him alone. He's my bodyguard."

"Some bodyguard," Brad said. "He almost let you get killed." The pup licked Stephanie's hand, evidently considering himself the star of the evening.

A siren screamed, and Lance spoke for the first time. "That's Rob. We called him when Clyde sounded the alarm."

Clyde approached the couch. "I'm sorry, Stephanie. I almost got you killed because I didn't want anyone to know what a fool I'd been. I saw Loralee intercept you, and I knew something was wrong. There was no reason for her to help you hide from me."

"I thought you'd killed Tara." Except this *was* Tara. She had to tell them that.

"No. I had an affair with her. I'm sorry, Lance. It was a despicable thing to do. I can't believe it now, but at the time, I couldn't seem to help myself. I didn't intend to scare you, Stephanie. I just wanted the diary. I thought that if I could destroy it, no one would have to know."

Footsteps pounded across the porch, and Rob dashed through the door. He stopped, staring at the body. "Who shot her?"

"I guess I did," Stephanie admitted. "We were struggling for the gun, and it went off."

"I see. Well, maybe it's better this way." He put his hand on Lance's shoulder. "I wish I didn't have to tell you this, but the truth has to come out."

Stephanie knew what he was going to say, and suddenly she couldn't bear it. The Harrington family had been through enough. The reporters would have a field day. "Rob, don't."

He looked at her, realizing she knew the truth. "I have to, Steph. We got a new report on the DNA evidence. I can't hide it."

"What are you talking about, Rob?" Lance asked. "If there's something you have to say, get on with it."

"Son, I hate to tell you how we've all been fooled, but that body in the cistern was Loralee. This is Tara."

Lance dropped down into the rocking chair, his face muddy white under his tan. He clung to the chair arms, his shoulders hunched forward as if warding off a blow. They waited in silence, giving him time to come to grips with this new information. Brad's eyes questioned Stephanie, reading the truth in her expression. For once, Clyde had enough sense to keep quiet.

Lance looked up, his face white and strained. "I should have known. I even joked about how much she was like Tara, but she looked like Loralee, she acted like Loralee, she worked in the office and seemed satisfied to stay at the lodge. Tara hated the lodge."

"She fooled me too." Brad sounded dazed. "I can't believe it."

"She told me about it," Stephanie said. "She said people see what they expect to see. She studied makeup with the little theater. It wasn't any problem for her to change her looks, and of course she's been gone. She said you expected Loralee, so you saw Loralee."

Lance sighed. "I guess she killed them both. Is that what you haven't told me yet?"

Rob nodded. "I'll want to talk to you later, Stephanie, but why don't you go back to the lodge now. Brad can go with you. You've had a rough time."

He reached out to help her up, and Sam lunged forward, growling deep in his throat. Rob stumbled backward. "What's wrong with that mutt?"

"He's appointed himself my bodyguard."

The pup crawled into Stephanie's lap and licked her chin. She hugged him, grateful for his warm, wiggly little body drawing her attention away from the horror of the night. They'd been through a lot together.

"Maybe you need a bodyguard," Rob said.

"A keeper would be more like it." Brad held out his hand. "Come on. I'll take you back to the family quarters before we have Monica and Kate down here."

He held her hand all the way to the lodge.

21

A week passed, and Stephanie had unfinished business. She found Monica digging in the flower bed at the back of the lodge. The sunlight revealed the fine network of wrinkles on her face, which hadn't been visible when they first met.

Stephanie stopped at the edge of the flowers. "I need to talk to you."

Without a word, Monica got to her feet. Stephanie motioned toward a weathered bench. After they were seated, she hesitated, not sure how to start.

Finally, she sighed and began. "All my life I have resented you, believing it was your fault Marty left us. I know now that he would eventually have left anyway."

Monica shook her head, but Stephanie stopped her. "No, let me finish. I have to say this."

She looked away from the compassion in Monica's eyes. "I've tried to hate you, but you weren't what I expected." Tears blurred her sight, turning the bright flowers into a fluid wash of color. "You said once that you wanted to be my friend. I wasn't ready for that kind of relationship, but if you haven't changed your mind, I'd like to start over. Can we be friends?" Sobs choked her, forcing her to stop.

Monica reached for her. Their cheeks pressed together. Their tears mingled. "I'm so sorry for all the hurt I caused you." Monica sobbed. "When I almost had that breakdown, I came back to God and asked His forgiveness, but I realize now I haven't completed the process. I have to ask you too. Can you forgive me, Stephanie, for what I did to you and your mother?"

"I forgive. . ." The instant she said the words, a burden of anger and hurt vanished. She closed her eyes, accepting the surge of peace.

"Stephanie?"

She opened her eyes and smiled. "That's finished. Let's put it behind us."

"We can try. I'd like to think we can have a new beginning." Monica wiped her eyes. "I believe Marty would have been pleased, don't you?"

Marty had changed. After he had become a Christian, he had tried to make amends in his own way to the people he had hurt. Now, his wife and his two daughters were trying to create a family.

Stephanie laughed. "He'd have written a song about it." They walked back to the lodge, all restraint between them gone.

That afternoon, Stephanie worked in the barn. The reporters had gone away, the case was closed, and with both Loralee and Tara finally laid to rest, the shadow that had shrouded Harrington Lodge had dissipated.

The police had broken the code in Marty's notebook. He had written in detail of Tara's deception and his suspicion that she had killed Loralee. Heather and Lance spent more time together, walking along the lakeshore, taking Kate with them on day excursions. They hadn't made any announcement, but everyone knew they were making plans.

Brad hadn't made any special effort to talk to Stephanie since the night Tara died, but Stephanie often looked up from whatever she was doing to find him watching. She loved him. Maybe more than ever, but his commitment to preach was a barrier between them. The museum would soon be ready for occupancy, and Monica wanted her to move to Branson to work on the displays.

The barn door opened, and Mac stepped inside. Learning about Loralee's death had changed him. He was quieter, less prone to haunt the local bars. Monica kept him busy working with her on songs she wanted to record.

Stephanie moved a box from the only extra chair and smiled at Mac. "Hi. You doing okay?"

"I am now. I wanted to talk to you." He sat for a moment without speaking, and she waited, letting him work it out in his own mind. When he did speak, she was surprised. "Lance says Loralee tried to kill Tara?"

"That's what Tara claimed, but she wasn't very truthful. I guess we'll never know."

"I know." He let his glance slide away from her. His big hands clenching and unclenching. "I was the one who told her about Tara and Clyde. If I'd kept my mouth shut, three people would still be alive."

"You can't know that."

"I do know it. She went sort of wild, called me a liar. I shouldn't have told her, but I loved her, and she wouldn't look at me." He looked up, bewildered. "She wanted *Clyde*."

Stephanie didn't know what to say. Everything she could think of sounded wrong. She took a deep breath. "Mac, listen to me. Something would have set Loralee off. It would have happened eventually whether you said anything or not. Tara was the one who caused this tragedy. She's the one who mistreated her cousin until she rebelled."

The silence lengthened as she frantically searched for something more to say. Mac sighed. "I know you're right, but it seems like I was the match that lit the flame."

"You know, Mac, I blamed myself for Marty's death. He asked me to come with him, and I refused. If I'd been here, maybe Tara wouldn't have gone to his room that night. But it seems to me that Tara through her behavior set certain actions into motion that had to be carried through. It was beyond our control."

He still looked troubled. "I keep feeling I should have suspected something, but she really didn't look like Tara anymore."

"Let it go. You'll only hurt yourself by holding on to the past. Are you going to stay at the lodge?"

"No." He grinned, for the first time since he'd entered the barn. "Haven't you heard? I'm Monica's new manager. She fired Clyde. The way she put it was she couldn't afford him."

"What's Clyde going to do now?"

"Go on being an Andrews, I guess. It's the only thing he's ever been good at."

"That's pathetic."

"Don't waste your sympathy on him. He wouldn't have cared for the music business. It's low-down and dirty sometimes. You have to be a scrapper, willing to fight for what you get. Clyde couldn't get off his dignity long enough to get involved. Monica gave him a lifetime pass to her theater, and that sweetened the pot, a little."

He looked at his watch. "I gotta go. I have some phone calls to make this afternoon. I really stopped by to tell you the museum is going up fast. We'll soon be ready for you to start working on the displays."

He left, and Stephanie tried to get back to work, but she was restless. A pressure built slowly in her chest until her heart felt like it would burst. Tears stung her eyes. She knew what was wrong. She had felt His presence too many times. She seemed to stand at the edge of a dark precipice, unable to see a way to safety.

A golden light gleamed just out of reach. She yearned toward the light, but the weight of her sins held her back. She wasn't worthy of the light. A voice whispered, "Give them all to Me."

"I can't."

The darkness swirled around her, blotting out the light. "No!" she cried. "Don't leave me."

She fell to her knees, sobbing. "I'm sorry. I need You. Don't leave me."

The words came back, clear and strong. "I will never leave

you."

She let go of her fears, her doubts, her last remnant of self-will. The light fell softly around her, filling her heart, her soul, her mind. She understood now. God was real. She stayed on her knees, emotionally drained. At last, filled with a joy she'd never known before, she locked the door to the barn and walked down to the lake.

The waves lapped at her sneakers. She sat down on her favorite rock, watching minnows play in the shallows. She would miss this place.

Footsteps crunched over the rocky shoreline, but she didn't turn. He came to stand beside her. "When are you leaving?"

"In another week. Monica wants me to see to the museum."

"We'll miss you."

Stephanie knew that that was as far as he would go. If she wanted him, she would have to go to him. She kept her eyes on the far bank, afraid to face him. "When I leave, I'll take something new with me."

Silence.

"Like what?"

She took a deep breath, praying for guidance. "I'll take Jesus. He changed my life today."

Brad's hands grasped her shoulders, turning her to face him. She waited, seeing the hope in his eyes. "You're sure."

She nodded. "I'm very sure."

"You said once you were afraid of marriage. Do you still feel that way? It doesn't come with guarantees."

She grinned. "No, but I hear the making up can be terrific."

"When I get married it has to be forever."

"Forever would be about right." She pulled his head down and kissed him fully on the lips. His arms closed around her.

Stephanie tilted her head to look up at him. "Brad, will you marry me?"

His expression showed his surprise. "I always thought I'd be the one to do the asking."

"I don't want to take a chance on your getting away."

"In that case, the answer is yes."

"You know what you're getting—a hot-tempered redhead."

"You're getting an ex-jailbird turned preacher. I'll never be able to give you as much as Lance can give Heather."

"You can give me your love. That's all I want." She grinned up at him. "There's just one condition."

"Oh yeah?" He looked wary. "What is it?"

"I want to sell my house in Independence and buy Monica's farm. We'll build on the old house site. A new home for a new beginning."

"You sure you want to do this?" he asked. "You don't have bad memories of the farm?"

"I've wanted a house there from the first day I saw it. It's a good place to raise a family. We'll create our own memories, and we'll make it a happy place again."

"That's a great idea, particularly the part about raising a family. I can see them now, a passel of redheads, with their mother's temper and their father's sunny disposition. I think I can scrape up a few dollars to help with your plans. You save your money for a wedding gown."

"I can't wait to tell everyone. Heather will be so surprised."

"Not too surprised. She's the one who sent me after you." He kissed the top of her head. "Happy?"

"As long as I have you." Her old insecurities and resentments were a thing of the past.

Brad brushed his fingers along the ridge of her cheek. "I've been praying the last few weeks that God was working on you, and I believed that it was just a matter of time until you gave in. From the first I felt that He was drawing us together, that our love was part of His plan."

"We can't go wrong then."

Arms around each other, they walked toward the lodge. Stephanie thought of her parents and the mistakes they had made and knew that Monica had been right. Love wasn't always enough to make a good marriage. It also took commitment and respect and understanding. Stephanie still wasn't sure she could make the grade, but she was ready to try.

They stopped at the gate, just out of sight of the lodge. Brad put one finger under her chin, tilting her face up within kissing range. "You're awfully quiet. Having second thoughts?"

"Not a chance. I was thinking about what I want for a wedding present." She laughed at his surprised expression.

"What now, woman?" he asked. "You've got me. What else could you possibly want?"

"I was thinking Kate might give me Sam."

"What, no diamonds? No emeralds? No treasures?" he asked, his eyes twinkling with laughter.

"Like you said, I have you. Throw in Caesar and Sam, and I'll have enough treasures to do me for now."

"I can see you're going to make a thrifty wife. It sounds like I'm getting a bargain. Tell you what." All of a sudden, he was serious. "I'm going to do everything I can to make this marriage work."

"Me too," she promised.

They sealed their vow with a kiss.

About the Author

Except for a few years spent in Kansas City, Missouri, Barbara Warren has always lived on a farm in the beautiful Ozarks.

Her love for God's Word, and for writing, led her to write for the Christian market. Barbara writes mysteries, because the darker side of human nature, and the struggle between good and evil intrigues her.

She also publishes an on-line newsletter with a section for writing news and book reviews. The newsletter can be found at her website, www.barbarawarrenbluemountainedit.com where interested parties can sign up for a free membership. She is a member of several on-line writing groups, and enjoys hearing from her fans.